Praise for Ragnar

"A classic crime story . . . first-rate and highly recommended."
—Lee Child, author of the Jack Reacher thrillers

"A modern Icelandic take on an Agatha Christie–style mystery, as twisty as any slalom."
—Ian Rankin, author of the Inspector Rebus series

"This classically crafted whodunit holds up nicely, but Jónasson's true gift is for describing the daunting beauty of the fierce setting, lashed by blinding snowstorms that smother the village in 'a thick, white darkness' that is strangely comforting."
—*The New York Times Book Review*

"Jónasson skillfully alternates points of view and shifts of time . . . The action builds to a shattering climax."
—*Publishers Weekly* (boxed and starred review)

"A chiller of a thriller whose style and pace are influenced by Jónasson's admiration for Agatha Christie. It's good enough to share shelf space with the works of Yrsa Sigurdardóttir and Arnaldur Indridason, Iceland's crime novel royalty."
—*The Washington Post* (Best Mysteries and Thrillers to Read in January)

"Jónasson's whodunit puts a lively, sophisticated spin on the Agatha Christie model, taking it down intriguing dark alleys."
—*Kirkus Reviews*

"In this debut novel, Jónasson has taken the locked-room mystery and transformed it into a dark tale of isolation and intrigue that will keep readers guessing until the final page."

—*Library Journal Xpress*

"Jónasson spins an involving tale of small-town police work that vividly captures the snowy setting that so affects the rookie cop. Iceland noir at its moodiest." —*Booklist*

"Required reading." —*New York Post*

"What sets *Snowblind* apart is the deep melancholy pervading the characters. Most of them, including Ari, have suffered a tragic loss. That's bad for them, but along with the twenty-four-hour darkness closing in, it makes for the best sort of gloomy storytelling." —*Chicago Tribune*

"Perfectly capturing the pressures of rural life and the freezing, deadly Icelandic winter, *Snowblind* will keep readers on the edge of their seats—preferably snuggled beneath a warm blanket."

—*Shelf Awareness*

"A real find. I loved it. The turns of the plot are clever and unexpected, and Ari is a wonderful character to spend time with." —*Mystery Scene*

"*Snowblind* has the classic red herrings, plot twists, and surprises that characterize the best of Christie's work. Jónasson's latest is nicely done and simply begs for a sequel." —*BookPage*

"If a Golden Age crime novel was to emerge from a literary deep freeze, then you'd hope it would read like this."

—Craig Robertson, author of the Forever series

"Seductive . . . an old-fashioned murder mystery with a strong central character and the fascinating background of a small Icelandic town cut off by snow. Ragnar does claustrophobia beautifully."

—Ann Cleeves, author of the Vera Stanhope and the Shetland Island series

"A dazzling novel . . . Thór is a welcome addition to the pantheon of Scandinavian detectives. I can't wait until the sequel!"

—William Ryan, author of the Captain Alexei Korolev series

"Ragnar Jónasson writes with a chilling, poetic beauty—a must-read addition to the growing canon of Iceland noir."

—Peter James, author of the Roy Grace series

"A classic whodunit with a vividly drawn protagonist and an intriguing, claustrophobic setting, *Snowblind* dazzles like sunlight on snow, chills like ice, and confirms the growing influence of Scandinavian crime fiction." *—Richmond Times-Dispatch*

"A satisfying mystery where all the pieces, in the end, fall together." *—The Dallas Morning News*

"[Ragnar] definitely shows a knack for the whodunit business."

—Star Tribune (Minneapolis)

"Ragnar Jónasson is simply brilliant at planting a hook and using the magic of a dark Icelandic winter to reel in the story. *Snowblind* screams isolation and darkness in an exploration of the basic Icelandic nature, with all its attendant contrasts and extremes, amid a plot filled with twists, turns, and one surprise after another."
—Jeffrey Siger, author of the Chief Inspector
Andreas Kaldis mysteries

"A chilling, thrilling slice of Icelandic noir."
—Thomas Enger, author of the
Henning Juul series

"A stunning murder mystery set in the northernmost town in Iceland, written by one of the country's finest crime writers. Ragnar has Nordic noir down pat—a remote small-town mystery that is sure to please crime fiction aficionados."
—Yrsa Sigurdardóttir, author of the
Thora Gudmundsdóttir series

"*Snowblind* is a brilliantly crafted crime story that gradually unravels old secrets in a small Icelandic town . . . an excellent debut from a talented Icelandic author. I can't wait to read more."
—Sarah Ward, author of the Inspector
Francis Sadler series

"Is King Arnaldur Indridason looking to his laurels? There is a young pretender beavering away, his eye on the crown: Ragnar Jónasson."   —Barry Forshaw, author of *Nordic Noir:*
The Pocket Essential Guide to Scandinavian
Crime Fiction, Film & TV

"*Snowblind* is a beautifully written thriller, as tense as it is terrifying—Jónasson is a writer with a big future."

—Luca Veste, author of *The Dying Place*

"The descriptive prose Jónasson uses is gorgeous and even the actual crime scenes themselves are oddly beautiful sounding. There is a mature elegance to his writing style that really captivates the reader."

—*Novelgossip*

"A classic whodunit set in a stark place with a twisted ending."

—*Auntie M Writes*

"If you are a fan of Nordic noir that is an excellent example of the crime fiction genre, look no further. This series needs to go on your must-read list."

—*The Suspense Is Thrilling Me*

"It is surely only a matter of time before *Snowblind* and the rest of Ragnar's Dark Iceland series go on to take the Nordic noir genre by storm. The rest of the world has been patiently waiting for a new author to emerge from Iceland and join the ranks of Indridason and Sigurdardóttir and it appears that he is now here."

—Grant Nichol, *Volcanic Lilypad*

"A truly chilling debut, perfect for fans of Karin Fossum and Henning Mankell."

—Eva Dolan, author of *Long Way Home*

"An isolated community, subtle clueing, clever misdirection, and more than a few surprises combine to give a modern-day, Golden Age whodunit. Well done! I look forward to the next in the series."

—John Curran, author of *The Mass*

"*Snowblind* brings you the chill of a snowbound Icelandic fishing village cut off from the outside world, and the warmth of a really well-crafted and -translated murder mystery."
—Michael Ridpath, author of the
Power and Money thrillers

"The complex characters and absorbing plot make *Snowblind* memorable. Its setting—Siglufjördur, a small fishing village isolated in the depths of an Icelandic winter—makes it unforgettable. Let's hope that more of this Icelandic author's work will be translated."
—Sandra Balzo, author of the
Maggy Thorsen mysteries

"In Ari Thór Arason, Nordic noir has a new hero as compelling and interesting as the northern Icelandic setting."
—Nick Quantrill, author of the Joe Geraghty series

"Ragnar Jónasson brilliantly evokes the claustrophobia of small-town Iceland in this intriguing murder mystery. Let's hope this is the first of many translations by Quentin Bates."
—Zoë Sharp, author of the Charlie Fox thrillers

"Has all the skillful plotting of an old-fashioned whodunit although it feels bitingly contemporary in setting and tone."
—*Sunday Express* (UK)

"*Snowblind* is morally more equivocal than most traditional whodunits, and it offers alluring glimpses of darker, and infinitely more threatening, horizons."
—*The Independent* (UK)

"If the rest of the Dark Iceland series is as accomplished as *Snowblind*, Ragnar Jónasson's name is poised to become as common place as that of Stieg Larsson's." —*BOLO Books*

"*Snowblind* is one of the most beautifully written crime novels I have ever come across." —*Liz Loves Books*

"An intricately plotted crime novel, *Snowblind* is a remarkable debut. Ragnar Jónasson has delivered an intelligent whodunit that updates, stretches, and redefines the locked-room mystery format. A tense and thrilling book that paints a vivid portrait of a remote town in long-term decline, facing the chilling aftershocks of the global financial meltdown. The author's cool, clean prose constructs atmospheric word pictures that re-create the harshness of an Icelandic winter in the reader's mind. Destined to be an instant classic." —*EuroDrama*

"This has all the ingredients—a young policeman, a girlfriend left behind, murders both old and new for solving, together with the intertwining of relationships within a small community as it goes through a snowbound dark winter. An absorbing read and one I didn't put down." —*Thinking of You and Me*

"*Snowblind* was beautifully written; the landscape alone makes for good reading." —*Bibliophile Book Club*

"Jónasson has produced a tense and convincing thriller; he is a welcome addition to the roster of Scandi authors, and I really look forward to his next offering." —*Mystery People*

"*Snowblind* is a dark, claustrophobic read, and Jónasson evokes perfectly the twenty-four-hour darkness, the biting cold, the relentless snow, and fear of a killer on the loose in a village suddenly cut off by an avalanche. His crisp, bleak prose is an exemplary lesson in how to create atmosphere without producing overinflated books that would cause their own avalanche if dropped."
—*Crime Review*

"Ragnar Jónasson is a new name in the crime writing genre and I urge anyone who is a fan of Nordic crime noir to rush out and get yourself a copy of *Snowblind;* this you will want to add to your collection. It is really that good."
—*The Last Word Book Review*

"If Arnaldur is the King and Yrsa the Queen of Icelandic crime fiction, then Ragnar is surely the Crown Prince . . . more, please!"
—*Euro Crime*

"Jónasson's prose throughout this entire novel is captivating, and frequently borders on the poetic, constructing something that is both beautiful and uncomfortable for the reader. . . . A simply stunning piece of prose that will certainly put him in the thick of the crime genre in the United Kingdom."
—*Mad Hatter Reviews*

"Ragnar Jónasson is an outstanding new voice in Nordic noir."
—*Crime Thriller Girl*

"Dark Iceland? This man not only invented it, he rules it."
—*The Booktrail*

"*Snowblind* is a subtle, quiet mystery set in the most exquisite landscape—a slow burner that will suck you in and not let you go until you finish the final page."

—*Reading Room with a View*

"It is dark, it is gripping, and it is fascinating."

—*The Welsh Librarian*

"A damn good thriller." —*OMG That Book*

"*Snowblind*—a master class in scene setting and subtle tension building . . . Where Agatha Christie created a murder mystery with a small suspect pool on a fast moving train or within a large country house, Ragnar Jónasson creates the same feel in a whole town." —*Grab This Book*

"*Snowblind* is as atmospheric a murder mystery that you could find."

—*For Winter Nights*

"A delight." —*ELLE* (France)

SNOWBLIND

Also by Ragnar Jónasson

Nightblind

SNOWBLIND

RAGNAR JÓNASSON

TRANSLATED BY
QUENTIN BATES

MINOTAUR BOOKS
A THOMAS DUNNE BOOK
NEW YORK

A THOMAS DUNNE BOOK FOR MINOTAUR BOOKS.
An imprint of St. Martin's Press.

SNOWBLIND. Copyright © 2010, 2017 by Ragnar Jónasson. Translation copyright © 2015 by Quentin Bates. Maps copyright © 2015 by Ólafur Valsson. All rights reserved. Printed in the United States of America. For information, address St. Martin's Press, 175 Fifth Avenue, New York, N.Y. 10010.

www.thomasdunnebooks.com
www.stmartins.com

Designed by Steven Seighman

The Library of Congress has cataloged the hardcover edition as follows:

Names: Ragnar Jónasson, 1976– author.
Title: Snowblind : a thriller / Ragnar Jónasson.
Other titles: Snjóblinda. English
Description: First U.S. edition. | New York : Minotaur Books, 2017. | "First published in Iceland under the title Snjoblinda. Previously published in Great Britain by Orenda Books" — Verso title page.
Identifiers: LCCN 2016037564 | ISBN 9781250096074 (hardcover) | ISBN 9781250096081 (ebook)
Subjects: LCSH: Police—Fiction. | Violent crime—Fiction. | Iceland—Fiction. | BISAC: FICTION / Mystery & Detective / Police Procedural. | LCGFT: Detective and mystery fiction. | Thrillers (Fiction)
Classification: LCC PT7511.R285 S5613 2017 | DDC 839/.6934—dc23
LC record available at https://lccn.loc.gov/2016037564

ISBN 978-1-250-14468-3 (Minotaur Signature Edition)

Our books may be purchased in bulk for promotional, educational, or business use. Please contact your local bookseller or the Macmillan Corporate and Premium Sales Department at 1-800-221-7945, extension 5442, or by email at MacmillanSpecialMarkets@macmillan.com.

First published in Iceland in 2010 by Veröld under the title *Snjóblinda*

Previously published in Great Britain in 2015 by Orenda Books

First Minotaur Signature Edition: November 2017

10 9 8 7 6 5 4 3 2 1

For Kira, from Dad

AN INTRODUCTION FROM THE AUTHOR

Snowblind is set in the northernmost town in Iceland, Siglufjördur, close to the Arctic Circle and surrounded by high mountains and the sea. Siglufjördur is the town where my father grew up and where my grandparents lived. My family visited Siglufjördur every summer when I was growing up and we still have a house there, so I go there as often as I can. Siglufjördur is a place of rich history. It used to be the center of herring fisheries in Iceland in the mid-twentieth century, with a much larger population than today, and is now undergoing quite a rejuvenation through tourism. My late grandfather wrote a series of books about the history of Siglufjördur and so when I needed a setting for my series, back in 2010, it was really the obvious option, as it was a town I knew very well. Also, I felt it was a town fitting for a crime novel: it is very isolated, only accessible via a mountain tunnel, and with extreme darkness and snow in winter and very long and bright nights in the summertime. In

November, the sun disappears behind the mountains, and does not appear again until January. In June and July, however, the town enjoys an almost twenty-four-hour daylight. And needless to say, in real life it is a very peaceful town.

Snowblind is the first book in the Dark Iceland series, currently consisting of five books, set in and around Siglufjördur. The main character in the series, Ari Thór, is just embarking on a career in the police. He was orphaned as a boy, when his mother died in an accident and his father disappeared. When Ari Thór graduates from high school, he starts studying philosophy at university and subsequently theology, but gives up on both subjects, eventually graduating as a policeman. In Icelandic, Ari means "eagle" and Thor is the name of the famous god from Norse mythology. When I started writing about Ari Thór, I decided to introduce him to readers as quite a young man, in his early twenties. There were two reasons for this: First, I wanted to make him a few years younger than I was when I wrote the book, so I could put myself in his shoes in some ways. The second reason was linked to the Queen of crime, Agatha Christie. I was, and still am, a great admirer of Christie, and translated fourteen of her novels into Icelandic before I started writing my own books. In her autobiography, Christie mentioned that she made a mistake when she decided to make her famous detective Hercule Poirot a retired police officer in her first book, adding that her fictional detective "must really be well over a hundred" by the time she wrote her autobiography. This fact was at the back of my mind when I created Ari Thór, so I thought I'd better not make him too old at the outset in case I wanted to write a few books about him.

Going back to Christie, two of her best traits as a writer were her plotting and her sense of place, where the setting was often almost like a character in the story. This also applies to many writers of the Golden Age of crime, which I have read with great pleasure through the years, including also key American authors such as Ellery Queen and S. S. Van Dine. When writing *Snowblind*, and the Dark Iceland series, I felt it was important to honor these elements of the Golden Age, the twist in the tale and the importance of the setting. However, I also felt it would be vital to make the stories both Nordic and contemporary, providing some insight into life in the north; Iceland, this peaceful country, known for its magnificent landscape, but also a place where the forces of nature are always lurking in the background, in the form of fire and ice. I hope that the readers will enjoy this mixture of old and new influences, and feel that Siglufjördur may be a place worth visiting again.

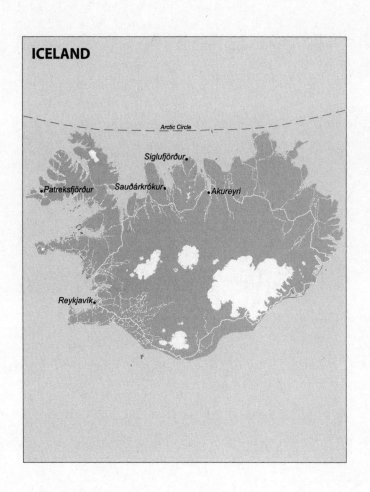

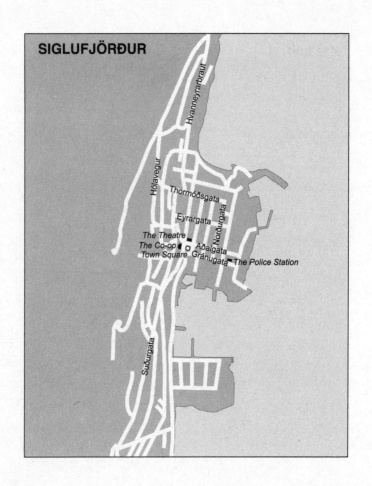

SIGLUFJÖRÐUR

Hvanneyrarbraut

Hólavegur

Thormóðsgata

Eyrargata

Norðurgata

The Theatre

The Co-op

Aðalgata

Town Square

Gránugata

The Police Station

Suðurgata

PRELUDE

SIGLUFJÖRDUR: WEDNESDAY, 14TH JANUARY 2009

The red stain was like a scream in the silence.

The snow-covered ground was so white that it had almost banished the winter night's darkness, elemental in its purity. It had been snowing since that morning, big, heavy flakes falling gracefully to earth. That evening there was a break in the snowfall and no more had fallen since.

Few people were about. Most people stayed indoors, happy to enjoy the weather from behind a window. It was possible that some of them had decided to stay at home after the death at the Dramatic Society. Tales travelled swiftly and the atmosphere was heavy with suspicion, in spite of the town's peaceful outward appearance. A bird flying over the town would not have noticed anything unusual, would not have sensed the tension in the air, the uncertainty and even the fear, not unless it had flown over the little back garden in the middle of the town.

The tall trees surrounding the garden were in their winter

finery, taking on shadowy shapes in the darkness that were reminiscent of clowns rather than trolls, decked in delicate white from the ground up, in spite of the snow weighing down some of their branches.

A comforting light shone from the warm houses and the street lights illuminated the main roads. This back garden was far from being hidden in gloom, even though it was late.

The ring of mountains protecting the town was almost entirely white that night and the highest peaks could just be glimpsed. It was as if they had failed in their duty these last few days, as if something unexplained, some threat, had stolen through the town; something that had remained more or less unseen, until that night.

She lay in the middle of the garden, like a snow angel.

From a distance she appeared peaceful.

Her arms splayed from her sides. She wore a faded pair of jeans and was naked from the waist up, her long hair around her like a coronet in the snow; snow that shouldn't be that shade of red.

A pool of blood had formed around her.

Her skin seemed to be paling alarmingly fast, taking on the colour of marble, as if in response to the striking crimson that surrounded her.

Her lips were blue. Her shallow breath came fast.

She seemed to be looking up into the dark heavens.

Then her eyes snapped shut.

1

REYKJAVÍK: SPRING 2008

It wasn't far off midnight, but it was still light. The days were growing longer and longer. It was the time of year when each new day, brighter than the day before, brought with it the hope of something better, and things were looking bright for Ari Thór Arason. His girlfriend, Kristín, had finally moved into his little flat on Öldugata, although this wasn't much more than a formality. She had been staying there most nights anyway, except those just before an exam, when she liked to read in the peace and quiet of her parents' house, often far into the night.

Kristín came into the bedroom from the shower, a towel around her waist.

'God, I'm tired. Sometimes I wonder why I went for medicine.'

Ari Thór looked round from the little desk in the bedroom.

'You'll be a fantastic doctor.'

She lay on the bed, stretching out on top of the duvet, her blonde hair spread like a halo on the white of the bedclothes.

Like an angel, Ari Thór thought, admiring her as she stretched out her arms and then ran them gently down her torso.

Like a snow angel.

'Thanks, my love. And you'll be a brilliant cop,' she said. 'But I still think you should have finished your theology degree,' she couldn't help adding.

He knew that well enough and didn't need to hear it from her. First it had been philosophy, until he had given up on it, and then theology. He had packed that in as well, and found himself enrolling in the police college. Roots were something he had never been able to put down properly, always seeking something that suited his temperament, something with a little excitement to it. He reckoned he had probably applied for theology as a challenge to some god he was convinced didn't exist; some god who had snatched away any chance he had of growing up normally when he was thirteen, when his mother died and his father had disappeared without a trace. It wasn't until he had met Kristín and – only two years earlier – been able to puzzle out the mystery of his father's disappearance that Ari Thór began to achieve a little peace of mind. This was when the idea of the police college had first crossed his mind, with the expectation that he'd make a better cop than a clergyman. The police college had left him in fine physical shape, and the weight-lifting, running and swimming had made him broader across the shoulders than he had ever been before. He had certainly never been this fit when he was poring over theology texts night and day.

'Yeah, I know,' he replied, a little stung. 'I haven't forgotten the theology. I'm just taking a break from it.'

'You ought to make an effort and finish it, while it's still fresh in your mind. It's so hard to start again if you leave it too long,' she said, and Ari Thór knew she wasn't speaking from experience. She had always finished everything she set out to do, flying through one exam after another. Nothing seemed capable of stopping her and she had just finished the fifth of the six years of her medical degree. He wasn't envious – just proud. Sooner or later they would need to move abroad so that she could specialise, something that had never been discussed, but of which he was all too keenly aware.

She put a pillow behind her head and looked at him. 'Isn't it awkward having the desk in the bedroom? And isn't this flat way too small?'

'Small? No, I love it. I'd hate to move out of the centre of town.'

She lay back, her head sinking into the pillow. 'Anyway, there's no hurry.'

'There's plenty of space for the two of us.' Ari Thór stood up. 'We'll just have to be cosy.'

He removed the towel and lay carefully on top of her, kissing her long and deep. She returned the kiss, wrapped her arms around his shoulders and pulled him close.

2

How the hell could they have forgotten the rice?

She was livid as she picked up the phone to call the little side-street Indian place that was five minutes from their sprawling detached house. With its two stylish, brick-built storeys, orange roof and large garage capped by a sunlit patio on its roof, it was a dream home for a big family. They were still happy here, even though the children had all flown the nest and retirement wasn't far away.

She tried to calm down as she waited for the phone to be answered. She had been looking forward to sitting down in front of the television to watch a Friday-night sitcom over a piping-hot chicken curry with rice. She was home alone, her husband away on business and probably now on his way to the night flight that would bring him home the following morning.

The infuriating thing was that the Indian place didn't do deliveries, so she could see herself having to go out again while the rest of her dinner cooled. Bloody mess. At least it was warm enough outside that walking wouldn't be any great hardship.

When someone finally answered, she came straight to the point.

'Who has a curry without rice?' she complained, her voice rising out of all proportion to the apparent offence.

When the waiter apologised and then hesitantly offered to prepare a replacement immediately, she slammed down the phone and, fighting back her anger, set off into the darkness.

|||||||||||||||

It look her longer than usual to find the keys in her handbag when she returned ten minutes later, the rice in a bag, ready for a relaxed evening with something good to eat. It wasn't until the key was turning in the lock that she sensed a presence, something that wasn't right. But then it was too late.

3

REYKJAVÍK: SUMMER 2008

Ari Thór came in from the rain. Coming home to the flat in Öldugata had always given him a warm feeling, but this past summer that feeling had never been warmer.

'Hi, is that you?' Kristín called from the desk in the bedroom, where she sat over her textbooks when she wasn't on duty at the National Hospital.

He felt that the flat had taken on a new life when she moved in. The white walls, which had been neutral before, suddenly became bright. There was an aura about Kristín, even when she sat silently over a book at the desk, an energy that Ari Thór found captivating. Occasionally he had the feeling that he had lost control of his own life. He was twenty-four and the future was no longer a blank sheet. He never said anything to her; feelings weren't the easiest thing for him to talk about.

He looked into the bedroom. She sat there with a book.

Why did she have to sit over these books all summer?

The sunshine didn't seem to have tempted her.

'Walking to work and back is enough for me. That'll do for time outdoors,' she teased, when he nicely tried to persuade her to walk downtown whenever he had a sunny day off. That summer he was in training with the police force at Keflavík airport, while his final term at the police college approached.

He sometimes wondered what had prompted him, only a year ago, to give up on theology – although perhaps only temporarily – and test his talents elsewhere. He had never been one for spending a lot of time over textbooks. He needed to have some activity, a little variety. There was something about police work that fascinated him: the excitement and the drama. It certainly wasn't the money. He had been accepted by the police college even though the term had been about to start.

He found he relished police work, enjoying the responsibility and the buzz of adrenaline.

Now his training was almost over; just one term to go and then he'd be qualified. It still wasn't clear what the next step would be once he graduated. He had applied for several posts with the police, had been turned down a few times and still had no offers.

'It's me. What's new?' he called to Kristín, hanging up his damp coat. He went in to where she was absorbed in a book and planted a kiss on the back of her neck.

'Hi.' Her voice was warm, but she didn't put the book aside.

'How's it going?'

She closed the book, having carefully marked her place, and turned to him. 'Not bad. You went to the gym?'

'Yes, and feel better for it.'

His mobile phone began to ring.

He went out into the hall, took his phone from his coat pocket.

'Ari Thór?' said a booming voice. 'Ari Thór Arason?'

'That's me,' he answered, slightly suspiciously as he hadn't recognised the caller's number.

'My name's Tómas. I'm with the police in Siglufjördur.' The tone was slightly friendlier now.

Ari Thór moved into the kitchen to be able to speak without being overheard. Siglufjördur was one post which he had applied for without telling Kristín. This was a place he didn't know much about, only that one could hardly travel farther north in Iceland; a place probably closer to the Arctic Circle than to Reykjavík.

'I'd like to offer you a job,' said the man calling himself Tómas.

Ari was slightly taken aback. He had never seriously considered Siglufjördur as an option. 'Well . . .'

'I need your answer now, lots of kids lining up for this one, people with more experience than you. I like your background – philosophy and theology. Just what you need to become a good copper in a small village.'

'I'll take it,' Ari Thór replied, almost to his own surprise. 'Thanks, this means a lot to me.'

'Don't mention it. We'll start you off with two years,' Tómas said. 'A two-year sentence!' he boomed, laughter echoing down the line. 'And then I'm sure you'll be able to stay on if you want. When can you start?'

'Well, I have some exams this winter, so . . .'

'You can do the final ones from here, I think. How about November, mid-November perhaps? Perfect time to get to know the town. The sun will be about to leave until January, and the ski slopes will be opening. We have great slopes here. Then perhaps you can take Christmas off.'

Ari Thór thought of saying that he didn't really ski, but instead only said thanks again. He had a feeling that he would get along well with this loud but friendly man.

|||||||||||||

When he went back into the bedroom, Kristín was again deep in her book.

'I have a job,' he said abruptly.

Kristín looked up. 'What? Really?' She closed the book and turned quickly towards him, this time forgetting to mark her place. 'That's brilliant!'

There was pure happiness in her voice. Kristín was always softly spoken, as if nothing ever took her by surprise, but Ari Thór was starting to learn how to read her expressions. Those deep-blue eyes that contrasted so powerfully with the short blonde hair could have a mesmerising effect to begin with, but underneath there was someone naturally determined and assertive; someone who knew exactly what she wanted.

'I know, it's unbelievable. I hadn't expected anything so soon. Loads of us are graduating in December and there aren't many jobs to be had.'

'So where is this job? Here in town? A relief post?'

'No, it's a two-year contract . . . at least.'

'In town?' Kristín repeated, and he could see from her expression that she suspected it might not be.

'Well, actually, no.' He hesitated before continuing. 'It's up north. In Siglufjördur.'

She was silent and each passing second felt like an hour.

'Siglufjördur?' Her voice had lifted and the tone gave a clear message.

'Yes, it's a great opportunity,' he said mildly, almost pleadingly, hoping that she would see his side, that it was important to him.

'And you said yes? Without even thinking to ask me?' Her eyes narrowed. Her voice was bitter, verging on anger.

'Well . . .' He hesitated. 'Sometimes you just have to grab an opportunity. If I hadn't made a decision on the spot, then they would have taken someone else.' He was silent for a moment. 'They picked me,' he added, almost apologetically.

Ari Thór had given up on philosophy and then he had given up on theology. He had lost his parents far too young and had been alone in a hard world since childhood. Then Kristín had picked him. That had given him just the same feeling he was experiencing now.

They picked me.

This would be his first real job, and one that would carry responsibility. He had made an effort to do well at the police college. So why couldn't Kristín just be happy for him?

'You don't decide to move to Siglufjördur just like that, without talking it over with me, dammit. Tell them you need to think it over,' she said, her voice cold.

'Please, I don't want to risk this. They want me there in the middle of November, I'll take the last couple of exams there, and be back for a break at Christmas. Why don't you see if you can come as well?'

'I have to work here as well as studying; you know that perfectly well, Ari Thór. Sometimes I just don't understand you.' She stood up. 'This is bloody ridiculous. I thought we were partners, doing all this together.' She turned aside to hide her tears. 'I'm going for a walk.'

She left with rapid steps, out of the bedroom and into the passage.

Ari Thór remained rooted to the spot, dumbstruck that he had completely lost control of the situation.

He was about to call out to her when he heard the front door slam shut.

4

SIGLUFJÖRDUR: NOVEMBER 2008

Ugla the owl perched on a stump.

Ágúst had always recited the old rhyme when they sat in the attic window at her parents' house in Patreksfjördur, overlooking over the road.

The memory brought a smile to her lips. Only recently had she found herself able to smile again when she thought of him. Four years had passed since she had moved – alone – to Siglufjördur.

It was also four years since she had last seen Patreksfjördur.

Her parents came to see her regularly and had been here as recently as October, staying with her for two weeks before travelling back west. Now she was alone again.

She had made some good friends here, but none were especially close and she never talked about the past. As far as they knew, she was just someone who had moved from the Westfjords.

She was aware that the town boys spread gossip about her that was pure fabrication. Not that it mattered now that she had grown a thick skin. As if she cared what the Siglufjördur boys said about her. There was only one boy for whom she had even the slightest care.

That was Ágúst, the handsomest boy in Patreksfjördur – as far as she was concerned, at least.

They had been friends from the age of seven, and their relationship developed into something deeper in their teens. They had been virtually inseparable ever since.

Ugla and Ágúst, names that were inextricably linked – in Patreksfjördur, anyway. But not here in Siglufjördur, where nobody knew anything about them.

That's the way she wanted it and she decided that she quite liked being this mysterious young woman from the west, the one about whom tales were spun. Although, perhaps it wasn't entirely true that she didn't care about what was whispered about her. One story in particular was hurtful. Somehow word had got around that she was an easy lay and she failed to understand how that piece of gossip had found its way into circulation.

Immediately after the incident that had changed everything, she had made the decision to leave the Westfjords behind her. To begin with her parents had been completely against it. She hadn't finished her studies; she was in her penultimate year at Ísafjördur College.

Ugla managed to get through the spring exams, and then she had applied for jobs in other parts of the country. Soon she had an offer from the fish processing plant in Siglufjördur. Like most people in Patreksfjördur, she had worked in the fish as a youngster and knew that, although her ambitions lay elsewhere, this was work she was used to. After working in the factory for a few months she had been told there might be a part-time position in the office. Having applied, and got the job, she had been able to reduce her hours on the factory floor and was now spending half her time doing clerical duties. She hoped that this miserable recession that now seemed about to blight Iceland wouldn't affect her too much. She needed the work and the last thing she wanted to do was to lose her job and have to go back to Patreksfjördur to live with her parents.

The personnel manager at the fish plant had told her about a short-term lease on a small basement flat – a good place to lay her head while she decided how long she would be staying in Siglufjördur. She was escorted round the flat by Hrólfur, a spry gentleman who looked about eighty, although she later discovered that he was approaching ninety.

Before long she was told that old Hrólfur was Hrólfur Kristjánsson, the well-known writer. She remembered his book, *North of the Hills*, from her school days. The class was asked to read a book written in 1941 – probably some unbearably dreary, bucolic love story, she had thought. But she had been wrong. She read *North of the Hills* in a single evening, and was, even now, swept away by its beauty. As a whole, the class hadn't been particularly enamoured of the book, any more than any of the other books on the reading list, but there was something about it that Ugla found captivating, undoubtedly the same something that had made the book sell by the truckload during the forties – at home in Iceland and all over the world.

It was a mild, clear day in the spring of 2004 when she found herself facing the author himself. There was a warmth to this slightly stooped man, who had clearly been exceptionally tall and imposing in his younger years. His voice was strong, but somehow paternal, although he had no children of his own. He was lean, his grey hair receding, and had about him an authority of the kind that comes with being accustomed to respect.

He lived in a magnificent house on Hólavegur, with a view out over the fjord. The house had been well maintained and next to it was a large garage containing his elderly red Mercedes. As far as Ugla could make out, the basement flat had been rented out now and again, mostly to working people newly arrived in the town, or to the occasional artist in search of peace and quiet amid the encircling mountains. But Hrólfur had apparently never been inclined to allow just anyone to stay there, making sure he met every potential tenant in person; he had been known to turn people down on the spot if he didn't like the look of them.

'Working in the fish, you said?' he had asked, his powerful voice husky and with a force that made it carry throughout the flat. He looked her up and down, his eyes sharp and enquiring, with both joy and despair behind them.

'To start with,' she replied softly, speaking to the basement flat's floor rather than to him.

'What? Speak up, young lady,' he said impatiently.

She raised her voice. 'Yes, to start with,' she repeated.

'And your parents know about this? You look pretty damn young.' He peered at her and his lip twisted oddly, as if he was trying to smile, but at the same time hold it back.

'Yes, of course. But I can make decisions for myself.' She was speaking clearly now, more assertively.

'Good. I like people who make their own decisions in life. And you drink coffee?' His voice was slightly friendlier now.

'Yes,' she lied, deciding that acquiring a coffee habit would be no more of a challenge than anything else.

It was obvious that he liked her. He accepted her as a tenant for the basement flat and she soon settled into a routine with Hrólfur, sitting together to share a pot of coffee once a week. There was no obligation to do this, and it certainly wasn't a burden. It became a genuine pleasure to talk over the past with him: his time abroad until the outbreak of the Second World War had brought him home to Iceland; the years of the herring boom; his travels in later years overseas and the conferences in which he had taken part as a well-known author.

In turn, Hrólfur prised her out of her shell and she came to enjoy life a little more.

She rarely spoke about the past and never mentioned Ágúst. They talked mostly about books and music. She had studied piano since childhood, at home in Patreksfjördur. He encouraged her to play for him every time she visited. At the end of one such performance, a small piece by Debussy, Hrólfur said, rather surprisingly: 'Why don't you advertise for students?'

'Students? I'm not a qualified teacher.' She felt slightly embarrassed.

'You play well enough. Really well actually. I'm sure you could teach the basics?'

She felt the support and belief in his voice. What had begun as an acquaintance had gradually developed into valued friendship.

'You can use my piano,' he added.

'I'll think it over,' she replied, self-consciously.

One day when she felt that life was being good to her, she placed an ad in the Co-op window, a quickly written A4 sheet:

"Piano lessons. Price negotiable", along with her name and phone number written on five strips at the bottom that anyone interested could tear off for future reference. This initiative had delighted Hrólfur, although there had been no enquiries yet.

They didn't discuss only music; she had admitted to having an interest in the theatre while she had been living in Patreksfjör-dur and at college in Ísafjördur, where she had taken part in ama-teur dramatics. The subject arose on a June evening when she and Hrólfur sat and talked over coffee and pastries by the win-dow. The water of the fjord was as still as a mirror and the town sparkled, although the sun was dipping below the mountains, its light illuminating only the peaks on the eastern side of the fjord.

'You know, I'm the chairman of the Dramatic Society,' he said casually but with purpose.

'A Dramatic Society? Here in Siglufjördur?' She could not disguise her surprise.

'Don't be fooled by appearances. This town used to be big, and still is, despite the dwindling population. Of course we have a Dramatic Society.' He smiled. She had become used to his slightly crooked smile, knowing that there was real warmth behind it.

'It isn't a large society, though. One production a year at most. I was thinking, perhaps I should mention your name to the director.'

'Oh, please don't. I wouldn't be any good.'

Her rejection wasn't entirely convincing, and she knew that he would probably do it anyway. He eventually did, and the fol-lowing autumn she found herself cast in a comedy.

She could hardly believe how easy it was to lose herself on stage.

As she looked into the footlights, it was like stepping into another world. The audience no longer mattered, they could be one, two or fifty, they all merged into one in the glare of lights. When she was on the stage she was no longer in either the Westfjords or Siglufjördur, as she concentrated on recalling the text of the play, and playing emotions that were not her own to the audience. Such was the intensity of her concentration that she even forgot for a moment to think of Ágúst.

She found the applause at the end of the play exhilarating, as if she was floating over the stage. She made a habit of sitting quietly after each performance to bring herself down to earth, and then the gloom would return once again; the memories of Ágúst. But with each performance it somehow became more bearable and every time it would take a little longer for the sorrow to return.

It was as if the stage had become her way out of the darkness.

Getting to know the old man was a source of great happiness to her, and she was also very aware that she would never have approached the Dramatic Society on her own.

That made it all the more difficult to tell him about her decision to move away from his basement flat. She had been offered a larger, fully furnished flat to rent in the centre of the town, on Nordurgata; what made her mind up was the fact that it included a piano. She was determined to move there, and it was time to find herself somewhere more permanent in the town to call her own. The basement flat, cosy though it was, was never going to be a long-term prospect. The Nordurgata flat was a step

in the right direction. Not only was it more spacious and convenient, but it came with a small garden.

Ugla was still single. Of course there were a few men in the
town whom she found attractive, but something held her back.
Maybe it was the memory of Ágúst, at least to start with, or
maybe she simply wasn't ready to decide yet if Siglufjördur was
the place she wanted to make her home. She wasn't ready to put
down roots, not right away.

Her contact with Hrólfur continued after she moved and she
walked up the steep hill from her apartment in the town centre
to his house on Hólavegur every Wednesday afternoon for coffee with him, just as if she were still living downstairs. They
chatted about this and that, his past and his travels, and her future. A fine old man, she thought frequently, always hoping that
he had many years in front of him.

Now her life had taken yet another turn. Úlfur, the Dramatic Society's director, had recently offered her a leading role
in a new play. Rehearsals were about to start, with the play to
open soon after Christmas.

Playing the lead? The butterflies began fluttering in her stomach. It was only an amateur society, but all the same, a lead is
still a lead.

It was a good part. The play had been written by someone
local and with a bit of luck, it might even be shown further
afield, maybe in neighbouring Akureyri, the north coast's largest
town, or even in Reykjavík.

It was November and she had settled well into her new apartment, proud to be standing on her own two feet, and in particular looking forward to her role in the play. It was snowing; she

looked out of the window at the beautiful, pearl-white snow, which gave her such a deep sense of tranquillity.

She opened the door to the back garden to take a deep breath of chill night air, but the sharp north wind forced her to close it quickly, and suddenly she found herself thinking about Ágúst.

Why did this have to happen to her? Why did he have to die so suddenly? Why did she have to experience such tragic loss at such a young age? It wasn't fair.

She closed her eyes and thought of the window seat at home in Patreksfjördur, reciting in her mind the old nursery rhyme.

Ugla the owl, perched on a stump.

Who's next?

One, two,

And it was you.

5

Her initial reaction wasn't fear, but anger that she hadn't realised something was wrong, that someone was standing there behind her in the dark. Then the fear overwhelmed her.

He shoved her hard against the door, a hand coming from behind to cover her mouth, turning the key in the lock with the other. The door opened and as he pushed her through the doorway she almost lost her balance; his hand still clamped hard over her mouth. The shock was so paralysing that she wasn't sure she had the strength to yell, call for help, even if he did relax his grip. He closed the door carefully and the next few seconds were a blur, as if she was in another world and she had lost the strength to resist.

Unable to turn around, she still hadn't had a chance to see him.

He stopped suddenly and for what felt like an entire lifetime, nothing happened. She sensed that it was up to her to do something. He was holding her with his right hand, not the left, and she tried to work out what her chances might be. She could take him by *surprise with a punch or a kick, get free of him and run, scream for help . . .*

But then it was too late. She had hesitated too long by thinking through the options, giving him time to act first, to unsheath the sharp hunting knife.

6

SIGLUFJÖRDUR: NOVEMBER 2008

Unless visitors wanted to travel by sea or drive over the mountain pass, which was completely inaccessible during the winter, or unless they knew someone with an aircraft who could land at the small Siglufjördur airfield, which no longer had scheduled flights to or from the town, the narrow, old tunnel provided the only access to Siglufjördur.

Ari Thór had decided that he had no need of a car in such a small place, so the little yellow Toyota had been left behind for Kristín to use. She had been too busy with work and her studies to drive him to his new job in Siglufjördur, in spite of his best efforts to persuade her that a trip north would be a good opportunity for some peace and quiet together.

Kristín remained unhappy with his decision to move. She didn't say much, but every time Siglufjördur was mentioned, a cold silence ensued and the subject was dropped. Both of them were occupied with their studies, and Kristín was working at the hospital alongside her usual lectures. Ari Thór was irritated that she hadn't found the time to go with him, particularly because they would be apart for a month up to Christmas. He tried to avoid thinking about it, but his mind repeatedly returned to the same thing as he wondered just how high up her list of priorities he was. At the top? Or was he in second place behind medicine? Or maybe in third place behind her studies and work?

She had hugged him tenderly and given him a farewell kiss.

'Good luck, my love,' she said, with warmth in her voice.

There was a new barrier between them, a thin and invisible line that he could sense and maybe she too knew was there.

Tómas, the police sergeant in charge at the Siglufjördur station, arrived to pick him up at the airport in the northerly town of Saudárkrókur, about sixty miles to the south of Siglufjördur, the closest airport with scheduled commercial flights.

'Nice to meet you in person,' said Tómas, and his voice boomed even louder than Ari Thór had remembered from their initial phone call. Tómas appeared to be in his fifties, with a warm face bordered by white hair – or what was left of it; the top of his head was clear of even a stray tendril.

'Likewise.' Ari Thór was tired after the turbulent morning flight.

'Usually it's an hour and a half or so from here to Siglufjördur, but the roads are terrible right now so it might take a little longer – if we get there at all!' said Tómas, laughing at his own gallows humour. Ari Thór said nothing, wondering quite how to take the man.

Tómas didn't talk much on the way, apparently concentrating on the road, although he had most certainly driven this route often enough before.

'You're from the north?' Ari Thór asked.

'Born and bred, and not going anywhere,' Tómas replied.

'How do strangers get on there?'

'Well . . . just fine, most of the time. You'll have to prove yourself. There are people who will welcome you and others who won't. Most of the townspeople know about you and they're looking forward to seeing you.' He paused for a moment. 'Old Eiríkur's retiring now and you're his replacement. He moved north in 1964 if I remember right, and he's been here ever since. But he's still an out-of-towner as far as we're concerned!'

Tómas laughed, but Ari Thór didn't.

Was this the right decision? Moving to a small rural community where he might never fit in?

The last few kilometres of road before they reached the mountain tunnel were unlike anything Ari Thór had ever seen before. The road snaked around the mountainside with precious little room for the car. On the right were the snow-white mountains, magnificent and formidable, while on the other side was a terrifying, sheer drop down into the broad storm-blown expanse of Skagafjördur. One mistake or a patch of ice, and there would be no tomorrow. Maybe it was as well that Kristín hadn't come with him. He would certainly have been worried about her driving back that way alone.

Thoughts of Kristín brought his doubts surging back. *Why hadn't she taken a few days off to be with him? Was that too much to ask?*

He relaxed as the tunnel entrance finally approached. They had made it all the way in one piece. But his relief was short-lived. He had expected a broad, well-lit, modern tunnel, but what lay in front of him looked forbidding. It was a narrow single track. Ari Thór later learned that it had been carved through the mountainside more than forty years ago when there were only a few tunnels in Iceland. It didn't help that water dripped here and there from the unseen rock ceiling above. Ari Thór suddenly felt himself struck by a feeling he had never experienced before – an overwhelming claustrophobia.

He shut his eyes and tried to shake it off.

He didn't want to begin his acquaintance with Siglufjördur like this. He planned to spend two years here, maybe more. He had driven through tunnels many times without any discomfort. Maybe it was the thought of this isolated fjord that was affecting him like this, rather than the tunnel itself?

He opened his eyes and as he did so a corner was turned and the tunnel's mouth appeared ahead of them, leading to the open air. His heartbeat slowed and he had calmed down by the time Tómas said, 'Welcome to Siglufjördur.'

The fjord greeted them with the oppressive grey of an overcast day. Cloud and squalls hid the ring of mountains, preventing it from showing off its full magnificence. The roofs of the town's houses were rendered dull by the gloom and a light covering of snow lay over its gardens.

Odd stalks of grass stuck their heads defiantly out of the snow, refusing to accept that winter had arrived, while the mountains towered overwhelmingly high above them.

'You think it's going to be a heavy winter?' Ari Thór asked, as if he needed to reassure himself that there were brighter prospects ahead. Maybe this was just a particularly drab day?

Tómas laughed at the newcomer's question and answered in his deep bass voice, 'Every winter is a heavy winter in Siglufjördur, my friend.'

There weren't many people to be seen and there was little traffic. It was approaching midday; Ari Thór expected there to be more activity during the lunch hour.

'Very quiet here,' he said to break the silence. 'I suppose the financial crash is going to affect you up here just the same as the rest of us?'

'Crash? There's nothing like that here. The crash belongs in Reykjavík and it won't stretch up north. We're too far away,' Tómas said as they drove into the square in the centre of town. 'We missed out on the boom years up here in Siglufjördur, so the crash doesn't worry us either.'

'Same here,' Ari Thór said. 'There weren't many boom years for students.'

'If there's a recession here, it comes from the sea,' Tómas continued. 'This place hummed with activity in the old days, before the herring disappeared. There aren't that many people here these days, something like twelve or thirteen hundred.'

'Not many speeding tickets here, I suppose? There don't seem to be many cars.'

'Listen here,' Tómas said solemnly, his voice becoming grave. 'This job isn't about handing out tickets. Quite the opposite. This is a small community and we're more than the local coppers. It's more about handing out as few tickets as you can! You'll find out soon enough that we work very differently from down south. It's a tight-knit community. Don't worry, you'll learn.'

Tómas drove along the main street, Adalgata, which was dotted with small restaurants, shops and some venerable houses that looked as if they still had occupants.

'Your place is down there a little way to the left, on Eyrargata,' Tómas said, pointing the way without taking his eyes off the road. 'I'll take you past the station first, so you can get a sense of what's where.'

He took a turn to the right, and then right again, into Gránargata, which ran parallel to Adalgata, and slowed down.

'You want to take a look, or do you want to go home first?' he asked amiably.

Home?

That discomfort again, claustrophobia and homesickness. Would he really be able to see this strange place with its impressive fjord as home? His thoughts flashed back to what Kristín would be doing right now, in Reykjavík. *Home.*

'I suppose I'd best make myself at home,' he said, suppressing a gulp.

Moments later Tómas parked the car in Eyrargata outside a house that stood in a tight knot of other imposing houses dating back a generation or more.

'I hope this'll suit you, at least to start with. The town bought this place a few years ago and it hasn't been looked after as well as it might have been, although it's mostly the outside that needs some attention. It should be comfortable enough. It's been up for sale for ages. It's far too big for you, but maybe your girlfriend will move north as well at some point. It's perfect for a big family,' Tómas said with a grin.

Ari Thór tried to smile back.

'You don't get a car but, believe me, in a place like this you won't need one,' Tómas added. 'When you need to go down south one of us will run you over to Saudárkrókur Airport, or we can find someone going that way.'

Ari Thór stepped back and looked at the house more carefully. It had last been painted in a pale red colour that had started to come off in flakes. There were two storeys, the upper level built into the eaves. The roof was a vivid red, mostly hidden under a blanket of snow. The dwelling had been built on a low-slung basement and two windows could be seen on the bottom level. A large shovel had been propped by the door to the basement.

'You'll need that,' said Tómas, his laughter dark but good-natured. 'It'll be useful when we get some real snow and you have to shovel your way out. You're no use to us if you're snowed in!'

The discomfort grew inside Ari Thór and his heart beat faster.

They made their way up the steps to the front door, where Ari Thór hesitated.

'What are you waiting for, young man?' Tómas asked. 'Open the door – we'll catch our death out here.'

'I don't have the keys,' Ari Thór said awkwardly.

'Keys?' Tómas asked, grasping the handle, opening the door and stepping inside. 'Nobody locks their doors. There's no point, nothing ever happens around here.'

But he fished a bunch of keys from his pocket and handed them to Ari Thór. 'I thought you'd like to have a set of keys anyway, just to be sure.' He smiled. 'See you later.'

Ari Thór was alone. He shut the door. In the kitchen he looked out of the window that gave him a view of the houses across the street and hopefully a view of the mountains on a good day.

Tómas's words echoed in his mind.

'Nothing ever happens around here.'

What have I got myself into?

What the hell have I got myself into?

31

7

She had seen hunting knives before. Her husband had several. But nothing could have prepared her for this moment. She stiffened, and then felt the strength draining from her limbs. Darkness spread before her eyes. He lost his grip, or let her drop, and she fell to the floor.

Then she saw him for the first time. He was dressed all in black – a shabby leather jacket, dark jeans and trainers, and a balaclava hiding everything but his eyes, nose and mouth. She was positive that it was a man, had been since she first sensed his presence, and the strength in his hands told her that he had to be young. She knew right away that she would never recognise him again, even if she did manage to escape with her life.

She heard him hiss, telling her to keep quiet, otherwise she'd feel the knife and he wouldn't hesitate to use it. She had to believe him. For the first time she was aware of her own mortality, and the thought that these could be her last few moments of life brought a cold sweat to her forehead. Questions darted back and forth across her mind. *What comes next? A black eternity, or heaven? She lay on the floor, every part of her wracked with pain from the fall, watching him standing there in the middle of the living room floor, dressed for action, the weapon in his hand.*

For the first time in years she found herself praying.

8

SIGLUFJÖRDUR: DECEMBER 2008

The ceiling was low in the room in which Ari Thór had chosen to sleep. This wasn't the largest room upstairs; for some reason he had chosen the smaller room with the single bed over the double in the larger bedroom. It was as if he was emphasising to himself that this was a solo venture.

He had shifted the bed around so that it gave him a view straight out of the skylight when he went to sleep and when he woke up, although there was rarely anything to be seen, other than pitch darkness.

The alarm clock buzzed for the fourth time. Ari Thór stretched for the button that would give him a precious extra ten minutes of dreams. He dropped back into sleep each time, and each time there was a new dream, different from the last. It was like watching a series of short films, in which he was all at once the writer, director and leading man.

It was getting on for ten o'clock and he had a shift that started at midday. The first couple of weeks had flashed past. The persistent feeling of discomfort had weakened; he had kept it at bay by concentrating on revising for his final exams and working long hours, taking every extra shift that was offered. The claustrophobia normally made an appearance towards evening when he lay alone in bed, gazing out of the skylight into the darkness. All the same, he preferred to look out through the glass, rather than at a bare ceiling.

Sometimes the days with bad weather were overwhelming, especially when it snowed heavily. He hadn't even got round to organising an Internet connection, as much by intention as for any other reason. He could check his email at work and appreciated being able to come home in the evening – yes, home, almost a new concept – and find himself in peace and quiet with little contact with the world outside. He could cook himself something delicious to eat. In one week, Ari Thór had almost become a regular customer of the local fishmonger, whose delightful shop by the town square always seemed to be filled with fresh fish. Ari Thór had tried the familiar haddock, which his mother had always cooked on Mondays, and the more savoury halibut. But his favourite so far had been freshly caught trout. He seasoned it ever sparingly, wrapped it in foil and baked it in the oven, just long enough for it to fall off the bone without losing any of its flavour.

After his meal he would immerse himself in his textbooks and other books he'd chosen for pleasure. That first week he had gone to the library during his coffee break, borrowing a handful of books that he had always meant to read but had never had the time to; it was these that he picked up when the textbooks became heavy going.

He had also borrowed a few classical music CDs, listening to these when he wasn't reading or working, sometimes simply sitting in the darkness in the living room, thinking about Kristín, his late parents, how alone he felt. One evening he had spent listening to the radio, a live broadcast of a concert by the Icelandic Symphony Orchestra – a name which never failed to conjure up memories of his mother, who had died in a road accident when he was a child. She had been a violinist in the orchestra.

He tried to avoid watching television as much as possible; occasionally catching the news. As far as he could make out, Reykjavík was descending into chaos after the crash of the big banks, with impassioned anti-government protests that seemed to become louder by the day.

After every shift he made a point of choosing a roundabout route home, passing along the shore, where he would stand for a while. There was something about being by the sea that was calming, helping him feel at ease in this distant and isolated town. Watching the often turbulent waves he was almost able to imagine that he was standing by the shore in Reykjavík. The sea had also been within walking distance from his flat on Öldugata. And at night, thinking of the sea helped him avoid the suffocating feeling of claustrophobia that he would sometimes feel engulfing him.

He liked his work well enough. The police station occasionally seemed to be more of a canteen than a workplace, almost a social centre. There were regular visitors who stopped off for a coffee – some of them several times a week – to chat about this and that; the crash, the protests and the government were the main subjects for debate, and then there was the weather. There had been a noticeable increase in traffic in the police station's coffee corner during the first few days after his arrival, as everyone wanted the opportunity to take a look at the new boy from down south.

One day, over coffee at the station, Tómas had mentioned that Ari Thór had qualified with a degree in theology.

'No, that's not quite right,' Ari Thór was quick to correct him.

'But you studied theology, didn't you?'

'Yes.' Ari Thór hesitated. 'But I never qualified. Took a break to go to the police college instead.'

Hearing himself say the word "break" took him by surprise. Deep inside he knew that he would probably never finish the theology degree.

'Well! That's quite something!' said Hlynur, a colleague who had worked alongside Tómas for several years.

Ari Thór knew that Hlynur was in his mid-thirties, but he looked older. His hair was starting to thin and he wondered if Hlynur was in good enough physical shape to meet the police force's fitness standards. He also came across as distant, as if to discourage anyone from getting too close to him.

'A priest in the making among us!' Hlynur went on.

Ari Thór forced himself to smile, although he was far from amused.

'Are you going to solve the cases we mortals can't handle?' Hlynur asked. 'With a little help from upstairs?'

He and Tómas laughed.

'The Reverend Ari,' Hlynur said. 'The Reverend Ari Thór solves the mystery!'

After that the most unlikely people took to calling him "the priest" or "the Reverend Ari Thór". He played along with it, even though he had never liked nicknames, least of all a nickname created on the basis of studies that he had started only half-heartedly, and then given up.

That first day at work he had tried to call Kristín, but she hadn't answered. He sent her an email describing the trip to the north, providing details about Tómas and the house. He left out anything about how he felt; he didn't mention that this isolated place had greeted him with gloom and darkness, that he was still unhappy with her reaction to his getting a job there, or his disappointment that she hadn't seen fit to take some time off to go with him – or at least spend a weekend together there. Maybe she didn't want to make things too easy for him? Or maybe she was hoping he'd be back in Reykjavík in a few weeks, having given up on the snow and isolation of the north.

Ari Thór had read her reply the following day. She wrote about work and her studies, mentioning as well that her father had lost his job at the bank where he had been for years, one among many who had been let go. He knew that she would be feeling distraught over this, and that her mother worked at an architect's practice where the financial crash would doubtless also make itself felt soon enough. Kristín didn't seem inclined to discuss anything in detail. It was a short message, lacking in any kind of emotion. As was his to her.

The next day he was able to reach her on the phone. He was just home from a long shift and not as ready as he would have liked to discuss what was troubling him. They talked for a while about superficial things, but nothing in any real depth. Kristín had always been calm and quiet, and was rarely inclined to let minor, everyday things upset her. So he wasn't able to decide if he was the only one unwilling to delve into things that affected them both.

As the weeks went on, they talked every day, but Ari Thór still avoided bringing up his disappointment that she wasn't supportive enough of his new job, and Kristín seemed to avoid the subject as well, probably still annoyed that he had left Reykjavík. Still, it didn't seem fair, he thought. She had her parents and her friends in Reykjavík. He was all alone in a new place and would certainly have appreciated some reassurance. But instead of tackling these issues, they kept their conversations short – friendly but trivial.

But now he needed to call her. It was already mid-December, he had been in Siglufjördur for over a month, and Christmas was approaching. He was going to have to let her know about Tómas's decision to assign him shifts over the holiday period, and it wasn't a conversation he was looking forward to. Tómas had actually phrased it as a request, but, realistically, Ari Thór couldn't say no: he was in no position to refuse and he wanted to prove himself.

He started the day with cereal, ice-cold milk and yesterday's newspaper. He had started to get used to seeing the papers late, as the morning editions didn't reach this far-flung fjord until at least midday. Not that it mattered. The rhythm of life was different here, time passed more slowly and there was less bustling hurry than in the city. The papers would be here when they were here.

He called Kristín and had to wait a moment before she answered.

'Hi, I'm at work, couldn't get to the phone right away. How are things?'

'Not bad,' he said and hesitated as he stared out of the kitchen window. There was a thick layer of snow over the town. This was no place for cars other than heavy 4×4s. What you needed here was a good pair of boots, or skis. 'Any snow where you are? It's coming down nonstop up here.'

'No, none at all here. Just cold and there's no wind, but it's icy underfoot. It looks like it'll be a snow-free Christmas in Reykjavík. You'll miss out on all that Christmas snow up north.'

Ari Thór was silent for a moment as he carefully thought about the words he was going to use.

Kristín continued, 'I've spoken to Mum and Dad and we'll have Christmas dinner with them like last year, so we can get away with not buying a Christmas tree, unless you feel like having one at home . . .'

'Listen . . . There's something I need to tell you.'

'Oh?'

'Yes. Tómas had a word with me yesterday, and I have to work a few shifts over Christmas . . .'

There was a silence.

'A few?' Her voice was sharp. 'Just what does that mean?'

'Well. Christmas Eve, Christmas Day, and a couple more days before New Year.'

The continued silence became deafening.

'So when are you coming south?'

'It's probably best if I come at the beginning of January when I can get a week off.'

'Next year? You're joking? You're not coming for Christmas?' Her tone was icy, but Kristín didn't raise her voice. 'We decided we were going to discuss everything at Christmas, sort out plans for next year. So I'm not going to see you until January? Or maybe even February?'

'I'll try and come in January. I'm the new man here so it's not as if I can throw my weight about. I ought to be thankful that I've at least got a real career opportunity here.' He was slightly annoyed, but tried to hide it, not wishing to add to the tension.

'Opportunity? You need to take the blinkers off, Ari Thór . . . Is this an opportunity to . . . to build a relationship, or start a family? There are five hundred kilometres between us. Five hundred, Ari Thór.'

Roughly four hundred, not five hundred, he silently told himself, realising that this wasn't the time to correct her.

'I can't do anything about it. The others have both been here longer than I have and they both have families . . .' he said, regretting the words the moment he had said them.

'So what? Don't you have a family in Reykjavík? What about me? And what about my parents?'

'I didn't mean it like that.'

Silence again.

'I have to go.' Her voice was lower, with a hint of a sob in it. 'I have to go. I'm being paged. We'll talk later.'

9

She had no idea what his intentions were.

A terrible foreboding overtook her, thoughts that she dared not think through to their conclusion. Was this a straightforward burglary, or something far worse?

The idea of ignoring his warning and just screaming, screaming with every ounce of energy in her flashed through her mind, but there were few people about to hear her and there were big gardens separating the houses.

She was a prisoner of her own prosperity, here in this spacious detached house in a quiet neighbourhood, where people paid to cut themselves off from the world's problems.

He was silent, looking around. She didn't dare speak, and hardly dared look at him. He looked over the living room, saying nothing, and the silence weighed heavily; the silence and the uncertainty.

What the hell; why couldn't he speak? Anything so that she didn't have to lie still among her thoughts.

Her mind turned to her two children, who had long since flown the nest, both with families of their own. They weren't likely to appear just when she needed them, rarely visiting their parents other than in the holidays or at Christmas.

No, she was alone with this unknown man.

He stood still and seemed to be reckoning the size of the living room. It was a wonderful room, as beautifully put together as anything in a property magazine, with two watercolours on the walls, both country landscapes, as well as the stylish coffee table and the newish sofa, the old wooden bureau inherited from her husband's family and, finally, the armchair, a ridiculously expensive designer piece in leather, to which she was deeply attached. She took a shocked breath as he dropped into the chair, stroking the armrest with the point of his knife, and looked over at her. He said something, one word in a hoarse voice, almost a whisper, as if he didn't want his voice to identify him later. That was promising, as was the fact that he had decided to cover his face. Maybe he was going to let her live.

She struggled to hear what he said.

'Sorry?' she almost whispered, terrified.

'I said, where's the jewellery?'

Just some bloody thief, she decided, with relief.

She stood up, but felt faint, trying to maintain her balance as she pointed along the corridor to the stairs. Some of her jewellery was in the bedroom upstairs, although her husband had put the most expensive pieces away in a safe in the little study downstairs, along with documents and other valuables. She took a slight comfort in the fact that she didn't know the combination needed to open it.

He was holding the knife almost carelessly, but still as if he knew just how to use it; as if this wasn't the first time he had used it. She made her way up the stairs with him following behind her. She quickly showed him the jewellery in the bedroom, carelessly deciding that there was no point in dragging this out, hoping that he would take what he'd come for, and then leave her alive.

He tipped the contents of the jewellery box on the bed and went through it, rifling through her memories: her engagement ring, birthday presents, wedding gifts. She thought of her husband; what if this man didn't let her go? What if . . . ?

She thought of the future, the golden years they had planned to spend travelling and exploring the rest of the world.

Was this bastard of a criminal going to take all that away?

10

SIGLUFJÖRDUR: SUNDAY, 14TH DECEMBER 2008

Two whole years. It was hard to believe. As if it had been only yesterday, Ari Thór remembered going downtown to buy Kristín a Christmas present for the first time. These memories skittered into his mind as he stood by Ugla's house, the church bells resounding along the fjord. The bells echoed through the town, making it difficult to tell from which direction the sound came. Ari Thór instinctively turned to face the mountains; the ringing seemed to tumble down from the hills rather than from the church. He had a sudden vision, not of mountains, but of a tranquil evening by the lake in Reykjavík, just two years ago.

With the end-of-term exams approaching, he had given up on the theology textbooks for the evening and left Kristín at home with the revision books from which she could only ever be reluctantly parted. He had walked down to the city centre, where he bought two books at a shop that stayed open well into the evening before strolling down to the lake that was such a landmark in the centre of Reykjavík. That day the weather had been unseasonably still, spiced with a chill that seeped under the collar of his jacket. Although the sky was heavy with clouds, it was still somehow bright, with Christmas lights illuminating every corner of the city. He had stood by the lake with his back to the Parliament building and the City Hall to his right. There had been few people about and he looked out over the houses as if he were detached from himself, purely an observer taking in a handsome view, a film sequence rolling from left to right. It was nine in the evening and there was a vista of dignified houses, their windows decorated with advent candles, Christmas trees with shimmering lights and the cathedral bells ringing. It was as if the peace of the city had proved itself stronger than the Christmas rush. The ducks on the lake called, answering the bells. He had stood stock still, breathing in the spirit of the moment, with time passing more slowly than he could ever have imagined.

The bells continued to peal, but this time they were the bells of Siglufjördur. Ari Thór stopped in his tracks, enveloped by his memories. Ugla laid a hand on his shoulder; it was as light as a feather, but it still made him start. He immediately – wishfully – thought of Kristín, even though he knew that it wasn't her.

He looked around and smiled.

There she stood, Ugla the piano teacher, in dark jeans and a bright white T-shirt, in her early twenties, tall and slim. There was a warm aura about her, despite the chill air, but also a hint of sadness in her eyes. The glow of the streetlights gleamed on her long, fair hair and she returned his smile.

'Aren't you coming in? You'll freeze to death out here.'

Ari Thór had seen her advertisement in the Co-op window a

couple of weeks ago. He had always wanted to play the piano, but never had the time or inclination to do anything about it. He had pulled off one of the strips with her name and phone number, and now he was here for his second lesson.

He was dressed for the cold and could see the goose pimples on Ugla's arms as she stood in her short-sleeved top on the steps.

A contraction of the muscles under the skin, he recalled Kristín telling him, providing a medical explanation for the phenomenon, when he had come out with the old cliché that he got goose pimples every time he saw her.

'Thanks,' he said, hanging his coat on a hook in the lobby and closing the door behind him. 'Of course I haven't been able to practise since the last lesson, as I don't have anything to practise on. I'm probably your worst-ever student.'

'Don't worry about it. You're the best and the worst. Let's just say right away you're the best as you're my only student. I'm still wondering why I bothered to place the ad to begin with, but I suppose old Hrólfur sparked my interest.'

'Hrólfur? The writer?' Ari Thór asked. He had heard of the old master who lived in the town.

'That's him. He's a wonderful old character. You ought to meet him; get him to sign a book for you. You never know – might be your last chance! Not that he isn't sprightly for his age, and he's as sharp as a knife.'

'I'd like a chance to meet him, although I've never read any of his books.'

'You have to read *North of the Hills*. It's a real masterpiece. It's his only novel and it's brilliant. After that he wrote short stories and poetry.'

'I didn't know that . . .'

'I'll lend you the book,' Ugla said, interrupting him. 'He signed it for me, so you had better not spill anything on it.' She gave him a warm smile. 'What would you like to drink? Coffee?'

'Do you have tea?'

Ari Thór had drunk so much coffee during his university years that even the smell brought back uncomfortable memories of late-night sessions, edgy with caffeine and stress. He was trying to wean himself onto tea instead.

'Sure. Take a seat and I'll bring you some.'

He sank into a deep, red armchair, letting his hands lie on the armrests and taking in the living room. During their first lesson, Ugla told him that she had rented the flat furnished, which included the old piano. Certainly nobody would have imagined that a young woman would have decorated a living room like this. It was like a step back in time, with a beautiful wooden floor, mostly hidden by an oddly patterned brown-and-white carpet. There were two narrow bookcases, dark brown and workmanlike. The landlord had clearly taken the books away – there were just a few paperbacks on the shelves, a mixture of whodunits and romantic novels, and one beautifully bound copy of *North of the Hills* by Hrólfur Kristjánsson. On the long wall behind the sofa hung a print of a well-known painting and opposite it stood the piano, buried under a stack of music.

Ugla appeared from the kitchen with a steaming mug.

'I hope I'm not breaking any laws by teaching piano lessons without a permit,' she said, handing him the mug and two tea bags. 'I only have two kinds of tea,' she apologised.

'Thanks. If it happens to be illegal, then I'll turn a blind eye.' Ari Thór smiled and dipped a tea bag in the hot water. 'The police have better things to do than chase unlicensed teachers,' he said, and wondered if that was really the case. Those first few days in Siglufjördur had been an interesting experience, with regular patrols undertaken in the big jeep but not a lot to do. Hardly anyone ever broke a speed limit, at least not inside the town and certainly not on the snow-covered mountain roads with that sheer drop on the far side of the tunnel. It was more to do with the danger than the possibility of a fine. He had attended one road accident, a minor rear-end shunt, and had twice been asked to unlock cars. A few times he had ferried drunks home; it was clear that the police provided a range of services here.

'I'm going to get myself a coffee,' Ugla said. 'Then we can start the lesson.'

Each lesson was supposed to be forty-five minutes, but the previous week Ari Thór had spent an hour after the lesson chatting to Ugla.

Over the last few weeks he had felt every inch the newcomer to a strange place. Nobody approached him and yet everyone knew who he was – knew who everyone was in this cloistered town. Nobody spoke to him at the gym or the pool, although he often caught the locals giving him appraising glances, checking out this new addition to the town's police force.

On one occasion he had been about to issue a fine for using a mobile phone behind the wheel to a local.

'Who the hell are you? You're a police officer? I didn't know we had a new cop here,' said the driver scathingly.

Ari Thór knew perfectly well that the man knew better.

'How do I know you haven't just stolen a car and a uniform?' the driver had pressed on, his half-smile arrogant.

Ari Thór had smiled back.

'I'm not going to issue a fine this time around.' He was courteous, in spite of his frustration. 'Just don't do it again.' Next time he wouldn't be so understanding.

He knew that people were keeping an eye on him. He had once forgotten to indicate at a corner while on patrol in the car and when he next ran into Tómas, he was told that an unidentified passerby had complained.

'You didn't think this would be a walk in the park, did you? There aren't murders and the like here, but it's still no kindergarten,' Tómas warned.

It made him feel very alone. He felt like a stranger who had come to Siglufjördur for a weekend, and then found his stay extended day by day; like a traveller who had forgotten to buy a return ticket.

He could chat to Tómas and Hlynur about everyday things over a coffee at the police station, but this was superficial stuff about politics and sport.

He saw right away that Ugla was different. She was warm and welcoming, gave freely of her time and could listen attentively when it was needed.

Ugla returned with her coffee and didn't seem to be in any hurry to start the lesson.

'Are you enjoying Siglufjördur so far?' she asked, half-smiling.

'Well, it's OK,' he said, rather hesitant.

'I know. It's difficult to begin with, it's such a small community. People talk about you behind your back. I've been there . . .' Her voice was comforting, soothing. 'Coming here from Patreksfjördur was a help, as I knew just what these small places are like

– although no two are the same. Living here is very different to being in the Westfjords, but I can't put my finger on exactly how. I suppose every town has its own charm,' she explained with a wry smile, as if she were trying to help him feel better.

There was something captivating about Ugla, something about her that invited trust.

'I heard you are studying to be a priest,' she said.

'Not really. I gave up on that a while ago.'

'You should finish it.'

Ari had no intention to be drawn into that discussion so he tried to steer the conversation elsewhere.

'How about you? University?'

'Yes,' she answered quickly. 'Eventually. I need to finish college first . . . I left Patreksfjördur in a bit of a hurry.' Her words faded away.

Ari Thór sensed that there was something about her time in Patreksfjördur that she wasn't sharing.

After a brief but slightly uncomfortable silence she continued: 'Maybe I can go to university in Akureyri, or in Reykjavik, although I don't think I'd like living in such a big city.'

'It isn't so big, you'd like it there. I have a flat in downtown Reykjavik, close to the harbour.'

He was surprised to find that he was already talking to her as if she were an old friend, but for some reason he didn't mention Kristín, and the fact that they had been living together in the flat in Reykjavik. For some reason he didn't want to bring up the fact that he had a girlfriend. And to be fair, Ugla hadn't asked him directly, so he hadn't lied.

'So it must be quite a change,' she said. 'Although, you're still close to a harbour, just a different one.'

There was still something about her that he couldn't fathom. Of course, she was far from her family, but there was a deeper sadness about her than just that. Each smile was accompanied by a flash of darkness behind her eyes.

'And the mountains, you know . . .' He smiled.

'It's like they're closing in on you, right?'

'Exactly,' he agreed. But then changed the subject to something less uncomfortable. 'Will you be here over Christmas?'

'Yes, my parents are coming to spend Christmas here. Christmas dinner isn't my strong point so I'll get my mother to cook something special.' Judging by her voice she was looking forward to this.

'It's not my strong point either,' Ari Thór said with a little false modesty. 'But I'll still try and come up with something celebratory.' He sipped his still-hot tea. 'I have a shift on Christmas Eve. I'll be on my own, so I'll take my dinner and a couple of good books with me.'

'That sounds miserable.'

Ari Thór liked her honesty. 'You're right. But I don't have a lot of choice.'

'Will your parents come up north for Christmas?'

It was an innocent enough question. He hadn't made a habit of introducing himself as a man whose parents had died, but he wasn't going to let her question upset him.

'No . . . I lost my parents a long time ago,' he said, looking into her eyes and then immediately dropping his gaze, as she looked awkwardly into her coffee cup.

'I'm sorry,' she said with sincerity in her voice. 'I'm truly sorry, I had no idea.'

'It's all right,' he said. 'You get used to it.'

'Really?' Ugla asked in surprise.

Ari Thór shrugged.

'You really get used to it?' she asked.

'Yes . . . Yes, I think I can say so,' he replied. 'But it takes time. It took a long time to get over it and it's not something that happens overnight. But it gets easier. You have to keep going, life goes on . . .'

Ugla sat silent.

'Why do you ask?' Ari Thór finally said.

She was silent for a while, staring into her mug as if it held the answer to every possible question.

Finally she looked up. 'I lost . . . lost my boyfriend a few years ago,' she said. 'That's why I moved here.'

Accustomed to being the one who had suffered loss – the one receiving the sympathy, Ari Thór didn't know how to respond.

'My condolences,' he said, not knowing what else to say, but recognising that his words were empty of meaning and he could just as well have given her a standard flower-shop sympathy card.

'Thank you.'

'How did he die?'

'Well . . . we were out on the town in Patreksfjördur. There's a small bar there and he . . .' *Ágúst*, she wanted to say, hesitating as if she couldn't say his name out loud. 'He got into an argument with someone from out of town, someone who was very drunk. He was punched, fell down and he never woke up . . . It was just that one blow,' she added.

Her expression was desolate, but Ari Thór had the feeling that telling him the story had been a relief for her.

'I'm sorry to hear it,' he said. 'Very sorry.'

'Thank you,' she murmured again.

She put aside the coffee mug and looked at the clock.

'I don't want to keep you here all evening,' she said, with a clearly artificial cheerfulness in her voice. 'Isn't it time we made a start?'

'Certainly. I need to go over what we did last week. It's not going to be pretty!'

He sat at the piano and placed his hands on the keyboard.

'No, that's not right,' Ugla corrected him, lifting his right hand and moving it. He flushed at her touch, feeling an agreeably warm energy from her.

'Thanks. That's better,' he said, and suddenly it was as if Kristín were a thousand miles away.

11

His voice louder this time, he asked again where the money was, loud enough to frighten but not loud enough to be heard outside in the street. Still wearing the coat she had put on to fetch the rice, she had handed him her purse the first time he asked.

The rice. Had she forgotten about that? She pushed the thought to the back of her mind, surprised that she could worry about takeaway rice at a moment like this.

He had taken a quick look in her purse, seen there was little cash, and demanded again where the damned money was hidden.

She shook her head and he asked about a safe.

Again she shook her head but her eyes probably gave her away. Like a cat with prey on his mind, he seemed to have found the scent.

He took a step closer, putting the knife to her throat.

'You get one chance. Make it count.' His voice terrified her.

He continued: 'If you tell me that there's no safe, I'll kill you right here, right now. I have zero tolerance for bullshit."

She answered him instantly, showed him the way down the stairs, along the passage leading from the hall and into the study. He switched on the light and the low-powered bulb illuminated the room, including the heavily built safe in front of them.

He looked at her.

She was quick to reply before he asked the question.

'I don't know the combination. You have to believe me!' she almost shouted. 'You have to wait for my husband to come home.'

He raised the knife and her heart pounded.

It was probably the phone that saved her life at that moment – or at least prolonged it.

12

SIGLUFJÖRDUR: CHRISTMAS EVE 2008

'Merry Christmas, my boy!' Tómas called cheerily, as he set off into the cold night. Ari Thór was going to reply when he heard the door shut and he decided there was little point in calling out Christmas greetings that only he would hear. He sat alone at the police station's computer. Red-and-white paper chains had been hung, and a plastic Christmas tree, adorned with cheap baubles, stood by the entrance; that was the full extent of Christmas at the police station.

Maybe that was enough; the place wasn't exactly going to be crowded over the holiday period. Ari Thór was the only one who would be there, with a shift from midday on Christmas Eve to midday on Christmas Day itself. It was going to be a lonely but well-paid shift and the overtime was welcome. He reminded himself that with the state of the country as it was, he could be thankful that he had work at all.

He had admitted to himself that it wasn't the Christmas

he had been expecting – the first one since he and Kristín had begun living together. At the same time he was struck by the thought that it was, perhaps, doubtful that they would be living together much longer *at all*. He had moved to the other side of the country and it didn't look likely that she would follow him. It wasn't much consolation that she was still living in his flat in Reykjavík. The flat wasn't any more his home at the moment than Siglufjördur was Kristín's.

He longed to send her an email or call her, but something held him back. She should be calling him. He was the one who was alone and abandoned in an isolated town, miles from anywhere, far from all his friends and surrounded by nothing but absurd paper chains.

Outside it snowed relentlessly and Ari Thór's attention alternated between the computer screen and the deepening snow. This was going to be a lonely shift. He went to stand on the pavement outside for a breath of fresh air – no question that it was fresher than Reykjavík air – and to shovel snow from the door. He had no intention of being snowed in, and, of course, he'd need to be able to get out if there were an emergency.

Ari Thór remembered Tómas's words.

Nothing ever happens here.

His work so far had been increasingly monotonous, with patrols and minor call-outs. The only serious incident that had landed on his desk was when a seaman had broken a leg on board ship and it had fallen to Ari Thór to take the crew's statements. He had done his conscientious best to write down their descriptions of the accident, but found himself struggling to fully understand what had happened. He suspected that the crew were going out of their way to use nautical terms that would confuse a youngster from down south with no experience on board a ship. But he refused to play along with them by asking for explanations.

He gazed out at the tranquil town.

The day before he had stopped off at the little bookshop and bought a newly released novel that was on his Christmas wish list, knowing that he wouldn't be able to rely on anyone but himself to purchase it. In fact, the wish list existed only in his head and even Kristín hadn't been able to guess what was on it when she had bought him a book last Christmas. His parents had always given him a book for Christmas. The Icelandic tradition of reading a new book on Christmas Eve, and into the early hours of the morning, had been important in his family's home. When his mother and father died and he was left an orphan at the tender age of thirteen he had gone to live with his grandmother. From then on he had made a point of buying himself a book at Christmas, something that he particularly wanted to read.

'You're welcome to go home around six for dinner if you feel like it, as long as you take the phone with you,' Tómas had told him before he left. But with nothing but silence and four walls waiting for him, it hadn't taken him long to decide that there was no point in going home to eat dinner alone. That morning he had cooked himself a traditional Icelandic Christmas dinner – smoked pork – wrapped it in foil and brought it with him, along with a couple of cans of Christmas ale, a large white candle, the new book, and a CD he had borrowed from the library.

He wouldn't be getting any Christmas presents this year, not even one from Kristín.

He tried to think of something else, but his thoughts kept straying back to Kristín, and he felt an inexplicable, burning resentment. But to be fair, he hadn't sent her a present either. He knew he had made a mistake in leaving her behind – taking the job without discussing it with her – but he felt too proud to admit it. They hadn't spoken since he told her he couldn't make it to Reykjavík for Christmas. He felt ashamed that he had let her down and he was afraid that she was still angry at him. Deep down, he hoped that she would take the first step, reach out to him, tell him that everything would be all right.

All day long he had waited for the post, hoping that she had sent him something. A small gift, a Christmas card. Finally something dropped through the letterbox, a single Christmas card. He impatiently ripped the envelope open, his heart in his mouth.

Hell.

It was a card from a childhood friend. Nothing from Kristín. He tried to shake off his disappointment and be happy that his old friend had thought of him.

Every now and again he picked up the phone to call Kristín, as if some voice were whispering in his ear to let the spirit of Christmas do its work, overlook their disagreements. But he was scared what her response might be. Better to avoid disappointment and not call.

IIIIIIIIIIII

Tómas adjusted his tie in front of the mirror. His eyes were tired and heavy.

He couldn't understand why his wife wanted to move away from Siglufjördur. He just couldn't get to the bottom of it. Was it something he had done?

They had been married for thirty years. She had started

dropping hints last autumn; she wanted to move, leave town, go south and enroll in university. He couldn't understand it, why she felt the need to go back to school at this point in her life. She said that he could join her in Reykjavík if he wanted to – not that that was really an option, as he couldn't bring himself to leave either Siglufjördur or the job. Hopefully she would change her mind, but it wasn't looking likely.

'Divorce? Is that what you're talking about?'

'No . . . I want you to come, too,' she said, her tone making it clear that he didn't have a deciding vote in this. 'I need a change.'

He didn't feel that he needed a change.

They still needed to discuss all this with the boy. Not that their son Tómas was a boy anymore, rather a grown man of fifteen and set on college in Akureyri next winter. The elder boy was long gone, leaving home over ten years ago, and rarely venturing back up north.

She would wait until the spring to make the move.

Change.

He could tell from the look on her face that she wouldn't be coming back. Then their son would be off to college and he'd be left on his own.

He tried to concentrate in front of the mirror; the tie was still too short.

Bloody tie, he thought.

She had given it to him last Christmas.

She's not coming back.

|||||||||||||

It was getting on for six that evening when the phone at the police station rang, making Ari Thór jump. The silence had been complete, with nothing but the hum of the computer and the ticking of the clock on the wall.

Claustrophobia had sneaked up on him, a feeling that had deepened as the snowfall around the station had become increasingly heavy. It was as if the weather gods were trying to construct a wall around the building that he would never be able to break through. He saw things around him grow dim and suddenly he found himself fighting for breath. But this time, the feeling quickly passed.

He wondered hopefully whether it was Kristín calling when he heard the phone's ring break the silence.

He looked at his mobile phone's blank screen and then he realised that it wasn't his phone ringing, but the one on his desk.

Nothing ever happens here.

Ari Thór hurried to answer.

'Police.'

There was no reply, although there was clearly someone on the line. He looked at the caller ID and saw that it was a mobile number.

'Hello?'

'. . . he . . .'

It was no more than a faint whisper, and difficult to guess if it was a man or a woman calling, young or old.

Ari Thór shivered and he wasn't sure if it was because of the call or the seeping chill of snow. The unremitting snow.

Would it ever stop snowing, he wondered?

'Hello?' he asked again, trying to deepen his voice and give it some authority.

'. . . I think he's going to hurt me . . .'

Ari Thór was now sure he could hear fear in the voice, fear

and despair. Or had he perhaps only transferred his own feelings of dread – his claustrophobia and loneliness – onto the caller?

'What did you say?' he asked, as the line went dead.

He tried to call back but there was no reply. He looked the number up in the police database. There was no registered user, so presumably it was a SIM card that had been bought in a kiosk somewhere, maybe even the kiosk in Siglufjördur. But the phone call could have come from anywhere in the country.

He had no idea what he should do, so he waited a moment and called the number again.

It rang, and this time there was a reply, the same whispering voice. 'I'm sorry . . . I shouldn't have . . . sorry . . .' And the line went dead again.

Perplexed, Ari Thór stared out into the darkness.

This bloody darkness.

'Just call if there's anything,' Tómas had said, conscience touching his voice; an awareness that it was unfair to leave the new recruit alone at the station over Christmas.

It was half-past five. A man who took life with equanimity and didn't let himself get stressed, certainly not at Christmas, Tómas probably didn't even have his suit on yet.

Hell, Ari Thór thought, and dialled Tómas's number.

'Hello?' On the other end of the line was the familiar, powerful but amiable bass voice.

'Tómas? It's Ari Thór here . . . Sorry to call you at such an awkward time . . .'

'Good evening.' Tómas sounded distracted and distinctly less cheerful than his usual self. 'Christmas doesn't start until we're ready and I'm not inclined to be hurried. We're still wrapping presents here. The worst of it is that the priest always starts his service at six on the dot, but it wouldn't be the first time that we showed up halfway through,' he said, with a laugh that seemed forced.

'I had a strange call, didn't know what to make of it, ' Ari Thór said. 'The caller, he or she, whispered something about being in danger, or that's what it sounded like. Then when I called back it seems it had been a mistake.'

'Don't worry about it,' Tómas said absently. He sounded tired. 'Every now and then we get these calls, someone playing a prank, normally youngsters. These kids.' He hesitated before saying more. 'So he, or she, pretty much admitted playing a prank when you called back?'

'Well, I suppose so.'

'Then don't worry about it. It's a nuisance being a cop at Christmas and there are people who just don't have any kind of a conscience. Well, Reverend, don't you have other things to think about? A sermon or something?'

The laughter was again forced and Ari Thór tried to smile to shake off the disquiet the whispering voice on the phone had left him with.

'I suppose so. Well, regards to the family.'

'I'll pass them on.'

'And Merry Christmas,' he added, but Tómas had already put down the phone.

Ari Thór picked up the book he had bought, in spite of the promise he'd made to himself to save it until after dinner. He was eking out his small pleasures to keep the boredom at bay. Only a few pages into the book, he realised that he hadn't taken anything in. Unable to concentrate, he stood up and opened the door, stepping out into the snow and looking up at the mountains. Man had beaten the mountains by tunnelling through them, and was doing his best to fend off the forces of nature with robust avalanche defences so big that they looked almost as if trolls rather than men had built them. But the darkness and the snow could never be defeated. Ari Thór lifted his face to the heavens and closed his eyes, letting featherweight snowflakes settle on his face, one at a time, offering them refuge.

There was a sound from inside, and this time there was no doubt that it was coming from his mobile and not the work phone. A text message.

Kristín!?

He wiped the snow from his face and a few steps on wet feet that almost had him slipping on the floor returned him to his desk. Old and made from pale wood, it was probably the most elegant piece of furniture in this otherwise cheerless police station. His phone lay on the desk, its flashing red light indicating that a message was waiting for him; this tiny light was more welcome than any Christmas illuminations.

Ari Thór forgot the earlier call, the whispering voice, the fear and the uncertainty, and snatched up the phone to see the message. And then there was disappointment. It wasn't from Kristín. It wasn't even a number he recognised.

He read it with great surprise.

'Merry Christmas! Enjoy your shift!' he read, and beneath it was a name, Ugla.

Had Ugla remembered to send him a Christmas message when Kristín hadn't?

He found his annoyance at Kristín's oversight – her intransigence – gradually give way to his delight at Ugla's message, and the thought of her brought a smile to his face. He imagined her: tall but not quite his height, and those delicate musician's fingers.

Ugla was probably at home with her parents, getting everything ready for Christmas, and she had still remembered him. He sent her a grateful reply, wishing her a happy Christmas, before sitting back down with his book, this time finding it easier to concentrate.

||||||||||||||

The church bells rang Christmas in, echoing through the town and up to the mountains, but no further, as if they were intended for the town's inhabitants only.

Ari Thór laid the book aside and removed the candle from his bag, setting it in the window and putting a match to its wick. Then he pushed the piles of paperwork aside to make room for his meal and poured a can of Christmas ale into a glass. His thoughts turned to his mother, who had always had a smoked rack of pork at Christmas, and always played the same music from an old record, before Christmas was rung in by the church bells relayed over the radio at the start of the nationwide broadcast of the Christmas Mass.

He took the CD from his bag and put it into the station's old but serviceable CD player. He turned up the volume before the music started, and knew precisely what he wanted to hear at this moment; the largo from Vivaldi's *Winter*.

And with that Christmas arrived.

13

The mobile phone in her coat pocket – why hadn't she tried to use it? Why hadn't she tried to call the police? She could have done it easily enough, punching in the three numbers by feel alone . . . Dammit. It was too late to think of that now, with her phone ringing and the piercing ringtone shrieking from her coat pocket.

He jumped, the razor-sharp blade that he had again rested against her neck nicking her. She put a hand to the wound and found that it was shallow.

He snatched the phone, looked at the screen and showed it to her. It was her husband, undoubtedly wanting to have a word before boarding his flight.

'Please, let me have the phone,' she whispered. 'It's my husband. He'll worry if I don't answer.'

All the same, she knew that wasn't the truth. He had taken care to call her mobile and not the house phone, thinking that she could be asleep with her mobile set to silent.

The black-clad man thought for a moment, as if trying to decide whether or not she was telling the truth, while the phone continued to shriek, each ring louder than the last.

Then he looked at her and deliberately dropped the phone into the pocket of his leather jacket.

'Give me the combination, now!'

'I don't have it!' She was pleading, her heart pounding. 'You have to believe me!'

14

SIGLUFJÖRDUR: THURSDAY, 8TH JANUARY 2009

Ugla stood up. She had been sitting on an old kitchen chair with a torn plastic seat. She stopped for a moment and looked deep into the eyes of the man standing in front of her. Karl. His thick, dark hair had not started to grey, even though he was a couple of years past forty. Ugla felt there was something odd about his expression, those eyes with a slight but permanent squint that seemed to be saying "come here" and "keep back" at the same time. She moved closer and he pulled her towards him, kissing her passionately.

Úlfur, the play's director, clapped and the sound echoed through the hall.

'Brilliant! I think we're almost ready for Saturday.'

It was getting late and the rehearsal had been in progress since five.

'We'll see,' said a deep but determined voice from the gallery, where Hrólfur, the chairman of the Dramatic Society, and the playwright, Pálmi, had been watching the rehearsal. 'We'll see about that,' Hrólfur repeated.

Ugla and Karl waited on the stage for further instructions from the director. Hrólfur's remark seemed to have taken the wind out of Úlfur's sails.

The rehearsal was taking place in the theatre on Adalgata. Old black-and-white posters advertising performances back to the Dramatic Society's early days in the fifties had been hung in the lobby.

A corridor led from the main entrance to the auditorium, where the stage was set. A staircase to the left of the stage led up to the gallery, and chairs had been arranged in the hall, ready for Saturday's opening night.

|||||||||||||

With a few quick steps, Karl strode down from the stage. Then he paused, waiting for the director to announce that the rehearsal was over. It wasn't worth risking offending him with the play about to open. It was obvious that Úlfur enjoyed being in charge, and this was his show. The only one who didn't respect his authority was the chairman of the Dramatic Society, old Hrólfur, who watched every rehearsal as keenly as a hawk, seated in the gallery. The few words he uttered were invariably negative.

Karl got a kick from being on stage, looking down on the audience – the ordinary people – with the lights upon him. On this stage, he was the undoubted star, absorbing the attention and the applause. The male lead role gave him even more time in the spotlight.

He fished his mobile phone from his pocket and keyed in a text message to Linda, who would be waiting for him at home. *Still at rehearsal, another hour to go. See you later.* He was taking a risk by lying. But he was a man who relished jeopardy.

It was six months since he and Linda had moved north to a rented flat on Thormódsgata, which Linda's salary as a nurse at the hospital paid for.

There was no reply from Linda, but Karl knew that she was on duty and unlikely to have time to respond. All the better, he reasoned. He could use the rehearsal as an excuse for not answering, even if she did call him. She wouldn't expect to hear back from him now. With a smile, he keyed in a second message, this time not to Linda.

'That's it for tonight, I suppose,' Úlfur said in the portentous voice lent by authority. 'See you all tomorrow – and be prepared for it to take all evening. It has to be perfect,' he said. 'Perfect,' he added for extra emphasis.

Karl quickly said his farewells and disappeared into the dark, winter night.

|||||||||||||

Pálmi came down from the gallery and met Úlfur, and they headed towards the exit of the auditorium together. They were both pensioners who had found new outlets for their energies in the Dramatic Society; Pálmi a former schoolteacher, and Úlfur with a diplomatic career behind him.

'Shall we sit down and go over everything one last time?' Úlfur suggested, peering up the steps, apparently waiting for Hrólfur to come down. 'Maybe Hrólfur will ask us in for a glass of wine and a good chat.' He smiled and dropped his voice. 'Or a glass of good wine and a chat.' He grinned again at his play on words.

'Unfortunately not on this occasion,' Pálmi said lugubriously. 'I have visitors who arrived from Denmark this morning.'

'Visitors?'

'Yes, an old lady called Rosa. She arrived with her son this morning and they're staying for a week. I can't think how I came to agree to it.'

'All right. Will you be entertaining them every day?'

'I don't know about that . . . She said I shouldn't go to any trouble. She just wants to relax and take it easy now that she's finally here.'

'A relative?'

'No, but she knew my father well in Denmark.' Pálmi regretted his use of words and emphasis. He hadn't meant to imply anything romantic or inappropriate, although that was how he suspected his words might be interpreted.

'Well? Do you mean . . . ?'

'To tell you the truth, I have no idea. It was all over between him and my mother by the time he moved to Copenhagen. I'm not inclined to ask too many questions, although I suppose I ought to grab the opportunity while I can – find out what the old boy was up to before he contracted TB there.' He paused for a moment.

'I've sometimes thought of asking Hrólfur,' he went on. 'You know he was studying in Copenhagen as well at the time? But even though they were good friends back here in Siglufjördur, it seems he didn't spend a lot of time with my father, not until close to the end, anyway.'

'Grab the chance with both hands – you may not get another. I hope the old lady doesn't find herself snowed in.'

'I'm certainly hoping that as well!'

Pálmi briefly placed a hand on Úlfur's shoulder and left.

‖‖‖‖‖‖‖‖‖‖

Leifur, the Dramatic Society's handyman, put the props away quickly, hurrying out to the Co-op and just reaching it as the shop was about to close. He was the only customer. He looked through the chiller cabinets without much interest. A sign for beef mince on special offer caught his eye; it looked more tempting than the sorry range of chicken drumsticks and flabby chicken breasts that surrounded it.

Leifur was in his mid-thirties and quite enjoyed his role at the Dramatic Society. There were just two days to go before the opening night. The theatre was a perfect way to smother memories and Leifur was particularly relieved that the first night would take place on a date when he would most definitely need a distraction. The fifteenth of January.

It was a date etched on his memory, just like another date – New Year's Eve more than twenty years ago.

He had been eleven years old. A child not much impressed by Christmas, but entranced by the idea of New Year's Eve – watching the fireworks and now old enough to help his father and elder brother set them off. He'd been looking forward to the day for weeks. His brother Árni, almost seventeen, was in charge that year and he'd saved up specially to buy more fireworks than usual. And then flu struck – his parents flatly refusing to let Leifur out of the house to take part, condemning him to watch the display through the window instead. It would be nothing like the excitement of seeing them live in the dark of a winter's night. Too old to shed tears, and filled with self-pity and frustration, he shut himself in his tiny bedroom at the back of the house, peeking out of the window as a few fireworks streaked past, but resolutely refusing to leave his room to look out the front where the festivities were taking place.

In the days that followed, Leifur's family mentioned more than once how well Árni had done, but Leifur refused to engage, still trying to convince himself that shutting himself away in his room was the right thing to have done. Of course, Árni saw through the pretence and tried to cheer him up, promising that they would see to the display together the following year. But this had been their final New Year's Eve together.

Leifur was a carpenter, according to his listing in the phonebook, although in truth the title was a mixture of wish and reality. He had always been clever with his hands and one way or another had expected to become a carpenter. When he was only ten, he and Árni had decided that they would one day run a big workshop of their own in Siglufjördur. It was an exciting prospect for a boy who knew no greater pleasure than spending his time in the garage with planks, a hammer and a saw, knowing that he had an older brother who would never break his word.

But like so much else, these fine intentions came to nothing.

After leaving school, Leifur had enrolled at the technical college and, after that and having returned to Siglufjördur, he set up a small workshop in his flat. The house was divided into two and Leifur had purchased the upstairs. It was about the right size for a single man and his faithful labrador. He fitted out one room as a workshop and took occasional jobs. His hourly rate was certainly fairly low, but there wasn't a great deal of demand either. Things were quieter here than in bigger places, and people chose to take the time to do things for themselves instead of employing a proper carpenter. But Leifur didn't give up, continuing to run the workshop in his spare time. His late brother would have wanted that.

When it came to a regular income, Leifur had to rely on the filling station where he had worked since leaving college and moving back to Siglufjördur. Settling elsewhere had never been an option, even though his prospects there would have been far brighter; he couldn't entertain the idea of leaving his parents and it had never even been discussed. It wasn't as if they had exerted any pressure on him to return, but he felt he couldn't let them down by leaving.

They didn't deserve to lose a second son.

The small flat in Thormódsgata was his home and he felt comfortable there. He enjoyed working with wood whenever there was an opportunity, and it was at these times that he felt happiest – in another world, a world of his own, where nothing could trouble him. The theatre was a godsend, providing him with plenty of opportunities to make the most of his talents, even though the work was voluntary. As far as he knew, nobody was paid to take part in the amateur productions, but there was a certain prestige attached to being a part of it.

Over the years, his fine handiwork had attracted increasing praise, and he was now tasked with building the sets for every production – given carte blanche within the limits set by Hrólfur and Úlfur, a colourful pair of characters who knew what they wanted. Leifur was never one for argument, preferring to let others have their way.

Alongside the carpentry, he had been given a chance to play a part in every performance in which he had been involved. In a small company everyone had to pull their weight and he was the understudy for the leading role, as well as having a few lines in other parts. He practised endlessly until he knew them inside out. Although Leifur suffered badly from stage fright, he was in his element in the Dramatic Society, even if his biggest part was always behind the scenes.

He started most days by walking the dog. When he finished at the filling station he would go to the swimming pool – not for a swim, but to use the gym there to lift some weights. He would often run into a few other regulars, though there weren't many who kept to a routine as strictly as he did. There were normally lads from the football team working out, younger than him, of course; and his downstairs neighbours, Karl – from the theatre group – and his wife Linda were frequent visitors. It was a good place to forget the rigours of the day, relax and gather his energy for another walk with the dog and some time in the workshop. He spent every evening in there, whether he had a job to work on or not; if nothing else, he would make something for his home, or to give away.

He felt at home in Siglufjördur. Except on the fifteenth of January. That date would never fade from his memory.

They say that time heals all wounds, but Leifur wasn't sure that he believed that. The sorrow was still there. He was still angry with someone: his brother's killer.

He, or maybe she, was probably living a good life right now, probably having moved on from it all. It may have been someone who hadn't even known Árni and didn't care what or whom that young man had left behind.

Árni would undoubtedly have wanted his family to carry on, absolving the reckless driver of any responsibility. That's just the way Árni was– an innocent teenager who had always been ready to forgive.

Leifur didn't forgive anything.

||||||||||||

Linda Christensen said she wasn't feeling well and went home early.

She was thankful that it had only snowed lightly the last few days. The cold was a burden, but the darkness was more difficult to cope with; she found it unnerving.

'I'm off now,' she called to the nurse in charge. Born in Iceland but having spent many years in Denmark, Linda spoke almost perfect Icelandic. The Danish accent had stayed with her for a year after moving back to Iceland, but now it had gone completely, although she still felt like an outsider – more Danish than Icelandic. Maybe that would change over time.

She put on her coat and set off home.

||||||||||||

The weather was unusually clear as Leifur strolled home.

It was bitterly cold but the walk was fairly short from the theatre to his home, passing a few colourful houses on the way. Some of them needed repair while others had been given a new lease of life by new owners. Leifur knew that to an extent some of the old houses in the centre of the town were being taken over by people from Reykjavík, who were using them as holiday homes. He wasn't sure whether that was positive or not, but at least it brought some vitality to the town.

As Leifur turned the corner into Thormódsgata, he saw his neighbour, Linda, outside the house. Her coat was clutched tightly around her and her face was pale, her eyes tired. She seemed surprised to see him.

'Hello,' she said and paused. 'Are you bunking off early from the rehearsal?'

The concern in her voice was clear, even though she did her best to hide it with a half-hearted smile.

'No way, Úlfur would never allow that,' Leifur answered, returning her smile. 'We all finished a quarter of an hour ago.'

He couldn't help noticing the confusion, anger and disappointment that flitted across her features, before she carefully rearranged them. Nodding her head, she took out her key and made her way into her flat.

SIGLUFJÖRDUR: FRIDAY, 9TH JANUARY 2009

Anna Einarsdóttir had missed the rehearsal the night before, as she did every Thursday, when she had an afternoon shift at the hospital. It didn't matter much as her part, unfortunately, wasn't a prominent one. It was convenient for the director to rehearse the scenes with Ugla and Karl on their own, every Thursday.

On Friday, Anna was at the theatre on the dot of four, as soon as her shift at the Co-op was finished. It wasn't far to go, just across the town square, and she had hurried through the rain. The weather had been clear and calm for most of the day, but not long before four it had begun to rain – hard.

In the lobby she carefully wiped her shoes on the big mat by the door. In the sales booth Nína Arnardóttir sat with her knitting on her lap, looking up to greet Anna warmly.

'Hi,' Anna answered. 'Have you been here long?' She asked the question even though she knew the answer already; when the Dramatic Society had an opening night in preparation, this became Nína's second home. She lived alone and seemed to relish the bustle and the tension, always the first to show up and the last to leave.

'I've been here since lunchtime. Someone has to make sure it's all ready for the stars when they make their entrance,' Nína said with a smile.

Looking around the lobby, with its old posters hanging on walls, some dating back to the war years, Anna felt transported to a long-gone era – a time she knew only from books and films. She was twenty-four, born and raised in Siglufjördur before moving south to Reykjavík to go to college and then straight onto university. During college she had been able to live with her mother's sister, but when she had started her history degree at the university, she had moved into a student flat at the first opportunity. Now that her studies were over, and with her BA behind her, she decided to keep an old promise to herself and take a year off to move back home before deciding on the next step to take in life. Work wasn't easy to come by in Siglufjördur and the only job on offer was in the Co-op, in addition to a few shifts at the hospital, which had the added advantage of giving her an opportunity to see her grandfather, who was a patient there.

A week into the New Year, she knew she would have to make decisions about the future. Not long after moving back north, she had heard that there would be a teaching position available at the primary school by the spring. It was a job that appealed to her, making it possible for her to stay in the town where she always felt most at home. Teaching jobs were hard to find in the south, with widespread cuts in the wake of the crash. She had long dreamt of being able to share the knowledge she had acquired in her studies, and teaching at a primary school would suit her perfectly. She had already let the head teacher know that she was interested, and it had obviously become common knowledge, with many expressing their delight at the idea that a young woman would be joining the school's staff. Nothing had been signed, but most people seemed to assume that the job was hers.

IIIIIIIIIIII

When Leifur came in, shaking the rain from his hair, he saw Anna gazing at the posters, in a world of her own. From his vantage point, Anna looked almost like a model, her long, dark hair and finely chiselled nose and lips striking in profile. She turned to him.

'Hi.' She smiled politely, barely acknowledging his presence.

Leifur returned the greeting, noticing how she changed once he could see her face. Suddenly she looked plain, all that glamour falling away as if it only existed in her profile. It was strange how a change in viewpoint could make this happen; she'd become a girl with two faces.

Maybe he ought to get to know her better. Not that being sociable was his strong point – and she was also a good few years younger than he was. He was sure she wouldn't be interested in spending time with him. But then he mentally kicked himself for succumbing to his characteristic negativity.

Looking out through the open door onto the street, Leifur saw a red Mercedes pull up outside as the chairman of the Dramatic Society arrived.

'We'd best try and make this miserable play work!' Hrólfur

said, as he stepped out of the car and appeared in the lobby, his voice louder than necessary.

'I think it will go very well,' Anna said politely.

'Oh you do, do you? It'll never be anything special, not with a script that's no better than average and a stage full of amateurs. But we could get away with it.'

He took off his overcoat and automatically handed it to Nína without a word.

'I recall being in Edinburgh, around '55, I think. I was there to read from my book and went to several productions as part of an arts festival. That was theatre, I can tell you, proper theatre. Sometimes I wonder why I bother with these part-timers.'

Nína hung up Hrólfur's overcoat, and turned as both Pálmi and Úlfur arrived. Pálmi furled his umbrella before coming inside, and Úlfur followed him, stamping the water from his boots, his face like thunder.

'Then maybe it's time for you to step aside,' Úlfur said in a low voice, but one that carried.

Hrólfur turned around and looked down at the stocky figure in front of him. With his round glasses and black felt hat, Úlfur looked old and tired.

Úlfur had always reminded Leifur of an old statesman slightly out of his league. He *almost* looked the part, *almost* knew how to behave, sought respect and admiration a little *too* much. Leifur always saw him as a slightly comic figure, and the arrogance of the old diplomat did nothing but enhance his comical features, in Leifur's view.

'Step aside?' said Hrólfur. 'Have you taken leave of your senses? I'm the only one who can keep all this together. I'll continue to sacrifice my time for this, and I have many years left. Have no fear of that, Úlfur.'

It was obvious that Úlfur had an angry retort ready; his cheeks flushed and his eyes narrowed as he snatched the felt hat from his head to reveal the bald pate beneath.

Hrólfur gave him no chance to reply, turning instead to Nína.

'Nína, my dear. Could you possibly find my overcoat for me? I left something in the pocket.'

She handed him his coat without a word.

Leifur watched as Hrólfur took a newspaper from his coat pocket, along with something that looked suspiciously like a small bottle, before handing the coat back to Nína and walking as fast as his old legs would allow into the auditorium. This wasn't the first time that Hrólfur had turned up to rehearsals with the little bottle. This time he was also driving, so there was every chance that he would ask Anna, who also lived on Hólavegur, to chauffeur him home that evening. Leifur had seen it all before.

Leifur gazed after the elderly gentleman as Karl and Ugla arrived at the theatre. Úlfur looked around. It was clear that he was upset, but trying his best to give the impression that nothing had happened, he clapped together his hands and forced a smile.

'Right, let's get to work, shall we?'

||||||||||||

From where she stood on the stage, Anna could see Ugla and Karl deep in conversation in the middle of the auditorium. She turned to watch Pálmi, who seemed unusually preoccupied. He was quick for an old man, she thought, but his age was evident in both his features and his movements. He was still a handsome man, in spite of his years, and she could well imagine that in his heyday he had been considered quite a catch. For some reason though, he had remained the perennial bachelor.

Now retired, he lived on his own in Siglufjördur and kept himself busy in the cold and the dark by writing.

Was this what Anna wanted for herself? Was she doing the right thing by applying for the job at the school? Putting down roots here? Would she be better off in Reykjavík? She wasn't entirely sure that she was making the right decision, but it was the most obvious and simplest option – easier than going back to Reykjavík, where she would have to stand on her own two feet. Here she could live in the basement of her parents' house for a few more years before finding herself a fairly cheap place to live. Partly she felt that maybe she lacked the drive some of her friends had. Living alone in Reykjavík had been fun in some ways, but she had found a life filled with responsibility harder than she had expected. She wanted to postpone all that for a while; and there was also the unspoken request from her parents not to leave.

She looked from Pálmi up to the gallery where Hrólfur and Úlfur were seated, rather imperiously taking in their view of everything beneath them. Ugla and Karl were on the stage, ready for the dress rehearsal, and Leifur was undoubtedly lurking somewhere behind the set. Anna always felt a twinge of irritation when she saw Ugla, who had stolen *her* lead role, an out-of-towner who should have just been grateful to be part of the company.

Anna was pretty sure how this had come about. The old man,

Hrólfur, had taken a shine to the girl who had rented his base-ment flat and they continued to meet for coffee long after Ugla had moved out. He was clearly holding a protective hand over her, and Anna had no doubt that this had made all the differ-ence when it had come to casting the roles. Of course, Úlfur was the director, in name at least, and supposedly the one to take the decisions, but Anna knew better.

The strong, decisive figure of Hrólfur was always there in the background. And everyone knew it.

16

He seemed as surprised as she was by the piercing ring from the other pocket of his jacket, as if he had forgotten that he had a mobile phone as well.

It gave her a chance to catch her breath, to compose herself and think. What would happen next? She couldn't give him the combination to the safe without calling her husband, and there wasn't much chance that he would allow her to do that. In fact, it was unlikely that she would be able to make any sense, even if he did let her make the call.

She was no use to him now. Maybe he would decide to wait for her husband and force him to open the safe. Maybe she was worth something: her life in exchange for the combination. But she couldn't be certain.

He answered his phone with a few sharp words. 'Yes . . . No . . . Not yet . . .'

He had already threatened to kill her once. Was he bluffing, or did he mean it? Again, she couldn't be sure.

He stepped out into the passage to continue his phone conversation. As she watched, he turned to his left, into the corridor leading to the guest bedroom and the door to the garden. To the right was the living room and the lobby, and the way out. It was an unexpected opportunity and required a quick decision.

The muttering of his voice was becoming fainter, telling her that he had gone a few steps farther along the passage, expecting her to stay where she was in the windowless cubbyhole of a study, like a trapped animal.

Her thoughts turned to her husband, probably boarding an aircraft on his way home. What would he want her to do? This was surely the only chance she would get. Take it – or wait and hope?

There was no telling what made up her mind; instinct took over.

She glanced quickly along the passage; he had his back to her. This was her chance. Run and attract his attention, or tiptoe silently?

She stepped into the passage. He still hadn't noticed her. She walked briskly away from him, but on silent feet. She didn't think he was coming after her.

Her heart hammered so loudly that she was certain that he would hear its beat.

She was round the corner and out of sight, with only a few paces to the front door. She knew the door was locked and would need both hands to open it, synchronised movements and firm hands.

Then she heard him. Throwing herself at the door handle, she fumbled for the locks, but her hands wouldn't do what they were supposed to. She knew she had only seconds before he would be upon her.

Choking back tears of frustration, she reached for the door.

And tried again.

17

SIGLUFJÖRDUR: FRIDAY, 9TH JANUARY 2009

Nothing ever happens here.

The lobby of the theatre was magnificent. The posters were witness to a past age and the air was heavy with the history of Siglufjördur, where the arts had flourished in good times and bad. There had been numerous performances by the Dramatic Society during the town's golden years, when the sea had been so full of herring that the salting yards had been busy night and day. The performances had continued after the herring had gone, when prosperity had become a word found only in dictionaries, although it was still a fact of life in the south. On the stage love had waxed and waned, people had lived and died, and even been murdered, all in front of packed houses.

It had rained without a break since the middle of the afternoon, when the skies had finally started to clear. Ari Thór didn't make a habit of going to the theatre, but still understood the excitement behind a good production. Tension in the air could sometimes be palpable, but never as overwhelming as it was that Friday evening in the Siglufjördur theatre. But this time there was no production taking place and the auditorium was empty. What he and Tómas – both of them on duty that night – could not avoid was the body. There was no doubt they were looking at a corpse; but Tómas still checked for a pulse.

The Dramatic Society had most certainly seen blood before, or at least, something that audiences saw as blood. This blood, though, which had seeped from the gash in the old man's head, looked starkly unrealistic, as if it didn't belong there, like ketchup in a bad B-movie.

'He must have fallen down the stairs,' Ari Thór said.

'That's obvious,' Tómas said brusquely. His usual cheerful nature had deserted him; it was clear for anyone to see that this was a serious incident and it would attract attention.

The town's most illustrious resident lay on the floor in front of them: Hrólfur Kristjánsson, who had once been Iceland's foremost author. Although his work had gone out of fashion in recent years – maybe even recent decades – there was still no doubt that his death would be front-page news.

Ari Thór and Tómas couldn't help but notice that Hrólfur had been drinking – the smell of alcohol was unmistakeable.

'Hell and damnation,' Tómas cursed under his breath. 'We can't have those damned journalists making more out of this than there is. Not a word to the press, you understand?' His voice was determined.

Ari Thór nodded, not certain quite how to react. Tómas was usually an amiable, paternal character and it had been many years since Ari Thór had had a real father to look up to. It was about ten years since he had lost his dad, and he had almost forgotten what paternal concern – or paternal discipline – felt like. He tried to maintain his equilibrium and looked around. Hrólfur lay on his back at the bottom of the stairs, his head on the floor by the lowest step.

'Looks like he's fallen backwards,' Ari Thór said. 'That could indicate he was pushed.'

'Don't talk nonsense,' Tómas barked. 'No damned nonsense, young man.'

Ari Thór was shaken.

'Concentrate on taking pictures.'

Ari Thór photographed the body and then went to the lobby, where Nína, who had called to report the body, was waiting. She seemed concerned, but not noticeably upset. Ari Thór was smarting after Tómas's robust rebuke, but he continued taking photographs. He had wanted to contribute something, show he could be useful. Eventually he turned to Nína.

'Was there a rehearsal for the play here?' he asked. 'Weren't you opening tomorrow?'

'Yes . . . there was a rehearsal.'

'Where is everyone, then?' he demanded.

'There is . . . there's a . . . dinner break. I just came back and found him . . . Hrólfur . . . lying there.'

Ari Thór put the compact digital camera in his pocket and headed back to the auditorium, stopping in the doorway as Tómas appeared. 'Shouldn't we call in . . . well, specialists?'

'Cops from Reykjavík, you mean? It's an easily explained accident. The old boy must have . . .' Tómas lowered his voice. 'He must have had a drop too much. Tired, anxious. It's an accident. We don't need a specialist team to work that out for us.'

Ari Thór saw that Nína had moved from the lobby, closer to

the auditorium, listening carefully to every word the police officers said. She looked aside, as if to hide the fact that she had been eavesdropping, put on a threadbare red coat, picked up a polka-dot umbrella from a hook and went into the auditorium to give the police officers a mournful look. 'Is there any reason I can't go home? I'm feeling faint. I've never seen a dead body before.'

'Is the ambulance on its way?' Tómas asked Ari Thór, and turned to Nína. 'I'm sorry. We'll need to speak to you before you leave. Why don't you sit down and try to take it easy?'

Her smile was tired and she sighed.

Ari Thór told Tómas that the ambulance was on its way. 'Can they remove the body?' he asked, nervous about making another faux pas in front of his boss.

'Yes, I expect so. You've taken pictures of everything, haven't you? There's nothing suspicious here. Was there anyone else here?' he asked, the question directed towards Nína.

Apparently miles away, she didn't answer.

Tómas coughed. 'Nína, was anyone else here when this happened?'

'What?' she stammered, looking wildly around her.

Tómas glared at her, his patience at a low ebb.

'Was there anyone else here?' he asked again, his booming voice echoing around the empty ticket hall.

'Yes . . .' She seemed to be thinking. 'No, I mean . . . I don't think so. I was down in the basement at dinner time. There's a cellar underneath the stage. The steps leading down to it are at the back. I was clearing up – we keep all the old costumes in the basement – and I had a lie-down on the old couch down there. I had already eaten, while they were rehearsing. There wasn't anybody here at dinner time apart from me and Hrólfur. He was on his own up in the gallery.'

'And you're sure there was nobody else here when you came in and found . . . found the body?' Tómas asked.

Ari Thór had done his best to confirm that Nína was the only person in the building when he and Tómas had arrived. He had checked the basement and the gallery, where he found only a few old chairs and a couple of tables. There had been an open newspaper on one table.

'Yes, I'm sure. I didn't hear anyone.'

'Do you know if he had been drinking?' Tómas asked.

'Yes, he brought a bottle with him, a small hip flask. That's why I think he didn't go anywhere during the dinner break. The weather is lousy and he was driving.'

Ari Thór was about to ask Nína a question, when Tómas jumped in ahead of him.

'That'll do. You can go home and relax. We'll have a word with you tomorrow if there are any more questions.'

'When are the others coming back from dinner?' Ari Thór asked.

'Úlfur gave everyone an hour's break. They'll be coming back soon, in another ten or fifteen minutes.'

The ambulance crew arrived before Tómas could say anything further. No words were needed and they set to work with quiet efficiency.

'Ari Thór, can you keep watch outside? There'll be people arriving and we don't need a crowd around us. We'll tell people there has been an accident, that Hrólfur slipped on the stairs and . . . lost his life.'

18

SIGLUFJÖRDUR: FRIDAY, 9TH JANUARY 2009

The door creaked as Leifur entered the auditorium through the back entrance. He saw Tómas look up quickly, as if taken by surprise.

Leifur mumbled a greeting and looked around. An ambulance crew were taking Hrólfur's body away on a stretcher.

'Have you been here the whole time?' Tómas asked.

'The whole time?' Leifur was taken aback. He ran a hand over his close-shorn scalp and the beard that had sprouted in the last few days. 'No, I've just come back from my dinner.'

Tómas waited.

Leifur knew what the next question was going to be before it was asked. 'There's a back door here, behind the stage. What happened?' he asked.

'There was an accident on the stairs,' Tómas said, his voice decisive. 'Hrólfur appears to have taken a tumble . . . he's dead.'

He's dead.

Those were words Leifur was never likely to forget, the words the priest had said to his parents when he arrived that evening, the fifteenth of January, twenty-three years ago. Leifur had been in the living room and probably wasn't supposed to have heard.

The family knew that Leifur's brother Árni was going out of town with a few friends, driving along the dangerous narrow road from Siglufjördur to a neighbouring town. They'd left in the early afternoon and were expected back that night. Leifur remembered that his mother had begged Árni not to go. Conditions were dreadful, with black ice on the roads and limited visibility. But Árni wouldn't listen, determined to use his brand-new driving licence. There was a knock at the door late that evening and Leifur recalled that his father had answered it. The priest, accompanied by the police, told Leifur's father that there had been an accident on the road, a car had rolled over. Árni's friend, who had been in the passenger seat, was in intensive care and was expected to make a recovery.

'But Árni is dead,' the priest had said.

Leifur returned from his thoughts and now looked at Tómas.

'Eh? What did you say? Hrólfur's . . . dead?' Leifur asked.

'Yes. It looks like an accident.'

'He had been drinking,' Leifur said. 'So . . .'

'It's all right, my boy. There's no doubt he'd had a drop. Were you out during dinner time?'

'I was,' Leifur said. 'Don't know what happened.'

'He just fell,' Tómas said sternly. 'You'd be best off going home. There won't be a rehearsal here this evening. We might be in touch later for details if necessary.'

Leifur nodded and left by the same door he had come through.

|||||||||||||

Ari Thór closed the doors to the theatre behind him and stood outside, as if he were on guard there. The air was damp after the rain and it sent a chill through him.

'What are the police doing here?' said a man as he approached the building. He didn't seem too worried though. A woman in her twenties walked with him. 'And an ambulance? Did something happen?'

'You're in the Dramatic Society?'

'Yes. I'm Karl. This is Anna.'

Ari Thór gave his name and the news.

'Dead? Really?' Karl said, shocked.

Ari Thór nodded. 'We need to investigate the scene,' he explained. 'It would be best if you were to go home. We'll be in touch later if we need to speak to you.'

Anna appeared to be taken aback. Karl put his arm around her shoulders, to her obvious surprise. Two older men joined the group.

'What the hell's going on here?' the shorter of the two demanded. 'And who might you be?'

'My name's Ari Thór. I'm a police officer,' he said, as if the uniform hadn't already made that clear.

'Of course. The Reverend. My name's Úlfur, I'm the director

at the Dramatic Society. What the hell is going on? Why's there an ambulance here?'

'There's been an accident.'

'Accident?'

'Hrólfur fell on the stairs.'

'The old fool's had a drop too much again.' Úlfur sounded more annoyed than shocked.

'He's dead,' Ari Thór said.

Úlfur looked dumbstruck.

The ambulance crew came through the doors with the stretcher.

'How terrible, the poor old man,' the second elderly man said.

'Your name?' asked Ari Thór.

'Pálmi,' he replied. 'I'm . . . I'm the writer. I wrote the play.' It was clear he couldn't hide his pride, in spite of the circumstances.

Úlfur was about to enter the building, but Ari Thór stopped him, barring his way with an outstretched arm.

'Considering what has happened, we're asking people to go home. We're investigating the scene.'

'Scene?' Úlfur stepped forward, batting away Ari Thór's arm. 'Is Tómas in there? Let me talk to him!' His fury was building with every word. 'You can't just close my theatre the day before opening night!'

Ari Thór thought quickly. There were two options: stand firm and risk a loud argument, or call Tómas. He had already been rebuked by Tómas, so it didn't take him long to decide to send the problem upstairs. Tómas clearly wanted to run things his own way.

'Wait a moment,' he said, trying to give the impression of

authority. He peered in through the door and called out for Tómas, who soon appeared in the doorway.

'Hello,' Tómas said to Úlfur and then looked at the other man. 'Good evening, Pálmi.' He nodded to Anna and Karl, who had taken a step back. 'Ari Thór has told you what happened?'

'This is a terrible shock,' Úlfur said gravely, calmed by Tómas's presence. 'Can't we talk inside?'

'I think we'll take off,' Karl said, still with his arm around Anna. Tómas nodded and they hurried away.

'Yes, come in,' Tómas said to Úlfur and Pálmi, 'but for heaven's sake don't go near the steps. We still need to examine them before we can say for certain what happened, although it looks straightforward enough to me.'

'Really? So what do you reckon happened?' Pálmi asked, as soon as he and Úlfur were inside the door. Ari Thór followed them in, trailing behind as Tómas took over.

'The poor old fellow fell down the stairs,' Tómas said with an air of finality.

'What's that you have there?' Ari Thór asked, his question directed at Pálmi, who was holding a shopping bag.

'The latest version of the script. A couple of copies.' He seemed surprised by the interest.

'Hrólfur and I made a few final changes earlier. Pálmi sorted them on the computer at his place and printed out new ones,' Úlfur explained. 'We're opening tomorrow night.'

'I don't think that's going to be possible,' Tómas replied firmly.

'We . . . we can't let Hrólfur's death ruin this for us!' Úlfur said passionately; but then immediately appeared to regret the outburst.

'That's no concern of mine,' Tómas said evenly, taking care to remain courteous. 'You might be able to have the hall back tomorrow, but it would be best if you postpone your opening night for a few days.'

Úlfur's expression swiftly darkened, his eyes bulging. 'That's impossible!' he exploded. Ari Thór had the feeling that this was a man who was used to getting his own way.

Glancing back and forth between the men, Ari Thór decided that this was a situation that Tómas could handle without his help. Hurrying outside, he positioned himself by the front entrance. He expected Ugla to arrive shortly – he was sure that she would have been at the rehearsal, and he felt a curious need to tell her what had happened personally. He didn't need to worry about what was going on inside, certain that Tómas, Úlfur and Pálmi would have no interest in his opinions. They'd undoubtedly known each other for years, and could argue and then go their separate ways with any differences settled. Ari Thór was conscious of being from out of town *and* wet behind the ears – the new copper who wasn't expected to stay long in Siglufjördur. He was only here to build up a little experience, while Tómas was here for the long haul.

'Hey, what are you doing here?' Ugla asked, shaking Ari Thór from his thoughts. He hadn't seen her coming.

He stopped and thought for a moment, unsure of himself, but not certain why. 'Something came up,' he said at last. 'An accident . . . an accident on the stairs.'

The darkness he had noticed before in her eyes suddenly reappeared. Her face asked the question.

'Old Hrólfur fell,' he said seriously.

'How is he?' she asked immediately, her face ashen.

'He's dead. The ambulance has just taken him away.'

Ugla stood still for a moment, wrapped in silence, and then a few tears began to creep down her cheeks. She stepped closer and put her arms around him. Ari Thór hesitated, and then held her in an embrace.

After a moment she relaxed her hold and dried her eyes.

'I can't believe it,' she said with a sob in her voice, struggling to contain her emotion. 'I just can't believe it.' She briskly wiped the tears away, and tried to smile. 'He was so sweet.' She paused for a moment, as if uncertain what to do.

'I think it's best if I go home. I can't let people see me like this,' she said at last and turned quickly away.

'Yes, of course,' said Ari Thór, after her, then stood in a confused daze as she disappeared into the darkness.

Úlfur appeared in the doorway; a truce with Tómas must have been reached. Pálmi was close behind him, his scowl thunderous. They said nothing to Ari Thór as they passed, and he slid back inside without looking in their direction.

'Back to the station?' he asked.

Tómas glanced at his watch.

'I'll finish the preliminary report. You can go home if you like. I'll see you tomorrow. I need to put in a few extra hours anyway,' Tómas said. He sounded oddly relieved to carry on.

Anyone would think he didn't want to go home to his family, thought Ari Thór, with some surprise, as he made his way out to the street and headed home.

19

SIGLUFJÖRDUR: SUNDAY, 11TH JANUARY 2009, EARLY HOURS

Ari Thór woke with a start, drenched with sweat and wondering where he was. Feeling like a prisoner in his own body, he struggled for breath. He sat up and peered around him, snatching short, sharp breaths and trying to drag them deep into his lungs. He glanced wildly around, sure that the walls were closing in on him; he longed to shout out loud, but knew that would be pointless. It was the same crushing feeling that had overwhelmed him at the police station on Christmas Eve. Pulling himself to his feet, he stared out of the window into the ink-black night. A glance at his watch, glowing faintly in the darkness, told him it was the middle of the night, and he could see that it had started to snow. He was in his bedroom in Siglufjördur, he remembered. Reaching for the window, he opened it and breathed in a deep lungful of fresh air, clean and ice cold, but he continued to shake, his thoughts tumbling around his head. He had to lose this feeling of being overpowered, out of control. He looked

over to his bed, the sheets tangled and damp. It was unlikely he
was going to get any more sleep. Maybe he needed to get out –
out of the house and into the night. As soon as the thought
entered his head, he dismissed it. That wouldn't be enough. No
peace of mind would be found standing in the street with his
eyes on the heavens, the snow filling his mind – knowing that
every flake that fell increased the likelihood of his being snowbound in this strange place. A prisoner.

The floorboards downstairs creaked.

Suddenly he understood why he had woken so abruptly.

There was someone in the house.

He wasn't alone.

His heart pumped a deafening beat. His fear confused him;
he knew he had to think fast, had to stop thinking about the
snow that had been stifling him a moment before. But he was
unable to move.

He shook his head, and crept as silently as he could into the
passage to the stairs, still aware of movement down below, faint
sounds that indicated that whoever was there was not keen to
attract attention.

Now more alert, Ari Thór swore silently.

Why the hell hadn't he locked the door?

I shouldn't have listened to Tómas.

He made his way down the stairs in as few steps as he could
manage, aware that loose boards in some of them would creak,
but unable to remember which ones they were.

He hesitated before going round the corner steps and down
into the hallway. He felt more secure a little higher up. He had
the advantage. He knew that the intruder was there – he could
take him by surprise. But equally, he wanted to stay on the

bend, remaining stock still. Trying to clear the haze from his mind.

In spite of all his training, he was still frightened.

He had no idea who he might meet, one person or several? A drunk looking for a night's shelter, a housebreaker, or someone who meant to do him harm?

He shivered at the thought of someone creeping about the house in the darkness.

Hell!

The lights were all off; only the glimmer from a street light outside, shining through the little window at the end of the passage, allowed him to see anything at all. The living-room door was shut, and as he knew the curtains were drawn, it had to be completely dark in there. The hallway led to the living room and from there Ari Thór could reach the kitchen, beyond which was a small office. The unwelcome guest might be in any of those rooms. Time to do or die.

He opened the living-room door as quietly as he could manage. As old as the house, the door was solid, its surface painted white and decorated with fretwork patterns. It must have been years since its hinges had last seen a drop of oil.

He looked into the blackness and listened intently, but not a sound was to be heard. He waited, his hand on the doorknob, patient, waiting and alert to any changes in the silence.

The rustling resumed, now clearly emanating from the next room. The door between the kitchen and the living room was closed, but he had no doubt there was someone there. He kept the living room door open behind him to make use of the faint light from the hallway and took a few cautious steps into the room, tiptoeing to avoid alerting his visitor.

He realised his mistake as soon as he was halfway across the room. The ancient floorboards were wildly uneven, the floor – in fact, the entire, century-old house – set on an angle. The living-room door started slowly to close, reducing what little light Ari Thór had to a faint glow. Without a doorstop to hold it in place, it would gather momentum as it swung back in its quest for equilibrium. He turned around, quickly but silently, trying vainly to reach the handle.

The crash as the door finally banged shut wasn't all that loud, but in the nighttime silence it was like the banging of a drum.

Hell.

He stood motionless in the middle of the room, hoping that the noise hadn't carried, but knowing that it had. The intruder reacted instantly, making no attempt to keep quiet now, and Ari Thór guessed that he would bolt for the front door, to exit by the most direct route.

I'll catch him, I have to catch him.

He heard the front door close with a bang just as he set off from the now pitch-dark living room. He tripped in the darkness, feeling searing pain jolt through his shoulder as he fell hard against the living room table, and was sure that before he passed out he heard an anguished cry somewhere outside.

20

SIGLUFJÖRDUR: SUNDAY, 11TH JANUARY 2009

Ugla sat at the piano and played an old tune, a light-hearted piece that dated back to the middle of the last century – a song she knew by heart and which Hrólfur had delighted in hearing. She played almost unconsciously as she waited for Ari Thór, who was late for his piano lesson.

It was still hard to believe that Hrólfur was dead. He had seemed so fit and healthy for his age . . . Damn it! Why couldn't he have been more careful on the stairs? They could have carried on meeting for coffee, continued deepening their friendship. Suddenly she stopped playing, and remembered the argument between Hrólfur and Úlfur at the theatre. Had it ended badly? Could Hrólfur have been pushed?

She had to admit that Hrólfur had been quite drunk that evening. She had always tried to avoid him when he had been drinking. Alcohol brought out his darker side. Hrólfur had quickly realised that she preferred not to meet him under those circumstances, never inviting her for coffee unless he was completely sober. Although he could be abrasive, inside he was as gentle as a lamb and Ugla would certainly miss him. Her thoughts suddenly turned to herself. Hrólfur had always been her guardian angel at the Dramatic Society and she was fully aware of that. So what now? Would things change? They could hardly take her leading part away now, but next time? Maybe the lead would go to Anna in the future?

Úlfur had sent everyone an email to confirm that the opening night would be postponed by two weeks. It had been a short, clear message that didn't waste any words or, for that matter, express any emotion about the situation.

Of course there was nothing to be done but wait for the new opening night. Ugla would have preferred to get on with it. She had prepared for the performance as if it were an exam all of that week, and she didn't know if she could bear to continue for another fortnight.

She glanced at the clock on the wall. She had been looking forward to Ari Thór's visit, and not just because he was her only student. She enjoyed his company and there was a calming air about him. She couldn't deny that he was a handsome man, elegant, even, but there was something else that attracted her to him, something invisible and intangible. Somehow he managed to smile with his eyes as well as his mouth. Was she attracted to him? The out-of-town girl with a crush on the out-of-town boy? No, hardly . . . but . . . she hadn't allowed her thoughts to wander in that direction before. She didn't even know if he already had a girlfriend down south. They had never talked about things like that, and he had never mentioned it. There was, at least, no ring on his finger. She had to admit that she had relished the strength and warmth of his embrace outside the theatre after hearing about Hrólfur's death.

A knock on the door brought her back to reality with a start. Half an hour late, but the fact that he was here brought a smile to her face. However, as she opened the door, her anticipation and welcoming smile were soon replaced by shock.

'Look at you! What happened?'

There was a large plaster on his forehead and an unmistakeable bruise showing under another plaster over his left eyebrow.

Ari Thór gave her a smile. 'I wish I could say that this is the result of tackling a criminal,' he said. 'Aren't you going to ask me in?'

'You're late, but come in,' she said warmly, smiling back at him.

'So what happened to you?' she asked when they were sitting down, touching his injured forehead gently. She was pleased to find he didn't flinch.

'I had a fall.'

She could sense there was more to it, so she sat quietly and waited.

'Someone broke in the night before last. Well, if you can call it breaking in when the doors aren't locked.'

'People don't lock their doors around here. It's the same in Patreksfjördur. Did you catch him?'

'No,' Ari Thór said, pointing at the plaster. 'I took a tumble in the dark and landed on the coffee table, which made me a bit giddy. It bled like nobody's business, so I had to get something to stop the bleeding and couldn't chase him, the bastard. I thought burglaries didn't happen here.'

'Perhaps it was someone from out of town?' she suggested.

'Maybe.'

'Stitches?'

'No. I closed it up with plasters and it looks like it'll be all right.'

'Are you sure it's nothing serious?'

'I hope not. A sore head, but I also hit my shoulder and that's more painful.'

'Any idea who it was?'

'I haven't a clue. I told Tómas and to tell the truth he didn't seem to take it all that seriously. He just said that the town has a couple of heavy drinkers who sometimes find themselves in the wrong house after a few too many. He told me not to worry about it and said I should just be grateful that whoever it was didn't decide to crawl into bed with me thinking he was tucking himself in with his wife!'

'But what does Tómas think . . . ?' she started, then paused before continuing. 'What does he think about Hrólfur?'

'Hrólfur?'

'Yes. Was it an accident?'

He hesitated before answering and she realised that it would be awkward for him to talk about a case still being investigated.

He replied with a question. 'It looks like it, don't you think?'

'I guess. But what do *you* think?'

'Tómas is sure. Completely sure. He wants to make as little of this as he can. He finds the whole thing very uncomfortable, a famous writer falls down the stairs, drunk . . .'

'But what do *you* think?' she repeated.

Ari Thór put his hand to his head, as if trying to assuage his headache. 'I haven't really thought about it.'

'I wondered if it had anything to do with that argument,' she said.

'Argument?'

'Hrólfur and Úlfur.'

'Really? I didn't know about that,' Ari Thór said. 'What were they arguing about?'

'Pretty much everything and nothing. It seemed to get worse as the afternoon went on. They were up in the gallery and were both in foul tempers. Hrólfur interfered more than usual and you could tell he had been drinking. It was really getting on Úlfur's nerves. In the end it turned into a shouting match. Úlfur said something like . . .' She paused before continuing. *'You'll shut up when you're dead.* That made everyone go quiet and Úlfur called a break in the rehearsal a few minutes later – dinner break – and then . . . well, Hrólfur was dead when we came back.'

'You think that . . . ?'

The seriousness of what she had told him was suddenly clear to her.

'No, of course not. Unless, well, unless it was unintentional, by accident,' she said and was silent for a moment. 'Úlfur was the last one to leave, I think. There was nobody in the auditorium or the lobby when Karl and I left. We walked together because he lives quite close by, in Thormódsgata. I remember that Anna had already gone and so had Pálmi, but Úlfur was still up there in the gallery with Hrólfur. He must have left right after me.'

'Yes,' said Ari Thór quietly, not quite meeting Ugla's eyes. 'He must have.'

21

SIGLUFJÖRDUR: MONDAY, 12TH JANUARY 2009

It wasn't yet seven o'clock on Monday morning and a deep layer of snow had fallen overnight on Town Hall Square.

Deep in thought, Úlfur Steinsson walked into the square, just as Pálmi entered from the other side, walking towards him. Pálmi was the taller of the two, thin, slightly stooped and tired, as if he bore a heavy burden on his shoulders.

Úlfur looked up before Pálmi. They nodded to each other, slowly, almost simultaneously and silently, as if a stray word at that time of the morning could wake the whole town from its slumbers. Úlfur thought of stopping, but wasn't really in the mood for a chat. Thankfully Pálmi didn't show any sign of stopping either, so they both went their separate ways.

He remembered Pálmi from way back, as a young man. Now Pálmi was in his seventies, and looking like the old man he was.

A year to go, Úlfur thought. *A year until I turn seventy, too.* He had to accept that his age was starting to make itself felt. He could see it every time he looked in the mirror and felt it in the heart of his being, every day. Even the slightest exertion now left him short of breath.

The air was perfectly still and there was no snow falling. Úlfur wore his usual black felt hat to cover his bald head. On the rare occasions that he ventured out when it was snowing hard, he'd leave the felt hat at home and wear a pair of thick ear muffs and a wool hat instead.

How on earth had he ended up back here, in Siglufjördur?

He knew the answer better than anyone. He knew that the responsibility for the decision to move home to Siglufjördur when he had retired was his, and his alone. But on the days when he regretted the decision most bitterly, he preferred to place the blame on his former wife.

Sonja was twelve years younger than he was, and a remarkably beautiful woman. In fact, she was so attractive that he had never understood what she saw in him, a forty-year-old man, working at the Icelandic Embassy in Sweden. By the time they'd met, he had been there for four years and had made a reputation for himself. He spent his weekends in nightclubs and was known for being a generous host – the exciting diplomat from Iceland with a real future ahead of him.

She had been only twenty-eight, and charmed him from the moment they met. From Stockholm, she had recently ended a long relationship with the father of her six-year-old son, with whom she shared custody. She wasn't overly maternal, and put off giving Úlfur an answer on whether or not they should have a child of their own.

The strange Icelander who had taken so long to get to grips

properly with Swedish, he had never been able to step into the role of father to her son, never been able to forge a proper relationship with the boy. Sometimes he wondered if he should have been more persuasive about their having children, but he had always been so busy with his career, gradually getting closer to the top.

And now he was alone, walking around the deserted streets of Siglufjördur and taking deep, reassuring breaths of the fresh, morning air. It had snowed heavily in the town, but it was a breathtaking sight all the same. He knew how dangerous the snow could be in these northerly parts; the blinding snowstorms, people sometimes having to dig themselves out of their houses after heavy snowfall, the threat of avalanches. Just now, though, everything was quiet. The calm before the storm, perhaps?

He lived on Sudurgata, a few minutes' walk from the theatre, in what had been his parents' house. His father was long dead, lost at twenty-six when Úlfur was only four years old. He had hazy recollections of his father and his memories were linked to the sea, the placid sea of a calm day. But the sea had been far from calm on the day of his father's last voyage. The boat was a big, well-founded vessel that had weathered plenty of storms. Úlfur's father and several of his old schoolmates had taken turns manning it for years, sailing close to the wind more than a few times, but always making it home. Until that winter's day and what people described as the worst of that winter's weather. Caught in the fierce conditions, the boat had finally limped into port, bruised and battered by the all-out fury of a winter northeasterly storm and two crew members short. The whole town mourned the men who hadn't made it back, and a boy of four wept for his father.

The idea of following in his father's footsteps had never even crossed Úlfur's mind. He avoided travelling by boat as much as possible, and was even repelled by working in anything to do with fish or fishing. Siglufjördur was no place for a young man who could not appreciate the silver of the sea, as they called the herring. He moved to Akureyri, the nearest large town, as soon as he was able, finished college and then went on to Reykjavík. But the fjord that had been home maintained a strong attraction, in spite of the sorrow that was tightly bound to it – and the presence of the dock that was the last piece of dry land his father had stood on.

Úlfur's mother had lived in Siglufjördur to her dying day, alone in the big house after Úlfur had left home; he often felt guilty about leaving her there. Sitting in the darkness, with only the light of his lamp over his college textbooks, there were times that his thoughts drifted towards his mother, alone by that mighty fjord where the forces of nature could be so cruel. She never complained, and she encouraged him to move on, to find his own way and make the most of his talents.

Talents? Had his talents been used to their fullest extent? He brooded over this during his long daily walks around the town – when he raked over the past. He was at an age at which it would be proper for him to sit down and write some kind of memoir, but who would have the slightest interest in reading about his life? It didn't occur to him to put words down on a page. Instead he used his long walks to reminisce and write his memoirs in his mind.

He hadn't allowed himself the luxury of being idle since moving north and had written several plays that he was pleased with. He found the theatre stimulating. He had directed several

productions and was now the Dramatic Society's regular director, a coup even if it was an amateur theatre group – and an
unpaid job. He had always been fascinated by the arts, although
he knew deep inside what he found so enchanting about this
position: he was in charge, gave instructions, was treated with
respect. He had been in positions of authority for so many years
in the diplomatic service that it had been a shock to lose it all
so suddenly – to become an ordinary pensioner living in a small
town in Iceland.

The Dramatic Society had given him a new platform, but
his ambitions went further than that.

He had sat over his latest play, night after night, polishing
and refining it. He dreamed of seeing it in production the following year, when it could mark his seventieth birthday, with
himself as both playwright and director. Until now the main
obstacle had been Hrólfur. Úlfur had shown Hrólfur a draft,
feeling rather proud, but Hrólfur had dismissed it after reading
only the first couple of pages.

'It's very poor, Úlfur,' he had said. 'You may have been a
good diplomat, but you'll never be a writer. Stick to what you're
good at.'

That had been that, and now they were staging Pálmi's play
instead.

But everything had changed, now that Hrólfur had died.

And who was Hrólfur to judge him? Yes, he had written a
good book. A very good one, Úlfur had to admit. But Hrólfur
had certainly been resting on his laurels for decades. He hadn't
written for years, but he made the most of his past fame, continuing to sell publication rights around the world and travelling
widely on the lecture circuit. He had lived in Reykjavík after

the war, but had moved to Siglufjördur as his star began to shine less brightly. To all intents and purposes, Hrólfur had retired early, which was probably a shrewd move on his part. Moving back to his home town, where he was well respected, where everyone knew him and where everyone had read his book, allowed him to reclaim some glory. He had continued to lecture and to attend literary festivals, sometimes in return for generous fees. There was no denying that the old man had been smart with his career, and he had probably been able to accumulate a small fortune.

Úlfur had to admit that in some ways he would miss the old man. Hrólfur had sometimes invited him and Pálmi over to his house for a drink, where the three of them had been able to chat into the night, like equals, all quarrels forgotten. Hrólfur had been quite a character, a cosmopolitan figure. There had been many memorable evenings when they had sat in the half dark, sipping red wine and discussing arts, culture or current affairs, listening to opera. Sometimes there had just been silence, apart from the music in the background. All three of them would fall silent when Jussi Björling sang *Una furtiva lagrima*, and it was agreed that talking over such artistry was little short of heresy. Normally they played recordings of old masters on vinyl records, and it was a surprise when Hrólfur acquired a CD player – he and technology were never the best of friends. Most of the time it sat, gathering dust, in the corner, its provenance a mystery. Úlfur had heard that it was the mysterious girl from Patreksfjördur, Ugla, who had convinced Hrólfur to buy the player and a handful of CDs. He had followed her advice, and Úlfur couldn't help but wonder what spell Ugla had cast over the old man. Hrólfur had become inordinately fond of this girl who had once rented his basement flat, and whom he continued to meet over coffee. The whole of Siglufjördur knew the story, and watched the unlikely pairing with interest.

Úlfur was certain that Hrólfur would never agree to his writing for the Dramatic Society. Hrólfur had been kinder to Pálmi, the old teacher. In fact, despite Pálmi's raw and less-than-promising first efforts, Hrólfur had continued to support him, giving him one opportunity after another. It had paid off. His work had improved – even Úlfur had to admit that. There was no doubt that the damned teacher had talent.

But that wasn't a problem any longer.

Úlfur had already decided that he would quietly offer to fund the performance of his play himself – surely that would be enough to convince the Dramatic Society to stage it to coincide with his seventieth year. He wasn't short of cash; his long diplomatic service saw to that. Despite his enjoyment of high living, he had invested shrewdly. The divorce had cost him dear, but there was plenty left of his savings.

The divorce. His suspicions that something was wrong had become too strong to ignore around the time of Sonja's fiftieth birthday. The age difference had never been a problem, until then. She was fifty and he was in his sixties, now an attaché at the Oslo embassy, a respected and highly placed diplomat, but with a few extra pounds around his middle and his hair long gone. Sonja had retained her youthful looks remarkably well. He knew what was coming the moment she mentioned to him – her voice sweet and unrepentant – that there was something they needed to discuss. She had met a younger man. In fact, quite a lot younger, a forty-five-year-old engineer from Oslo.

Although he had half-expected the news, it still came as a shock to hear the finality in her words. He didn't sleep for days, took sick leave for the first time in years, and lay at home in the dark trying to work out what had gone wrong.

He had seen some twenty good years with her, but had wanted more. He had known in his bones that it wouldn't last, but as the years went by, he held on to the slender hope that it would.

Eventually they divorced, and Sonja moved in with her Norwegian engineer. Úlfur stayed on his own, suddenly an old man, carrying out his duties through force of habit rather than embracing new opportunities, waiting quietly for retirement to roll around.

Two years later, his mother passed away in Siglufjördur. She had lived in the same big, old house where she'd raised her family far into her old age. Úlfur took three weeks leave and flew home to Iceland to arrange the funeral. He had been an only child, the last of his family. There was little chance that he would produce any heirs now.

The funeral had taken place in the Siglufjördur church on a balmy summer's day. His mother had been well liked and had many friends. Úlfur felt deep sadness at her passing, but he knew in his heart that she had waited patiently for over sixty years to meet his father on the other side. The ceremony was deeply moving. His mother's close friend from the church had sung, and Hrólfur had offered to read a poem, a beautiful poem from his famous book, *North of the Hills*.

An old schoolfriend ran a part-time estate agency business and offered to advertise the house for sale. 'An elegant building in the best part of town' the draft of the advert had read. 'Would make a magnificent summer residence.'

Úlfur asked for a little time to think it over and decided to stay in Siglufjördur for the remainder of his leave. Many years had passed since he had spent such a long time in his home town. He had tried to make the trip to see his mother once a year, normally at Christmas, Easter or during the summer, and generally with Sonja. Some years his mother had visited them, but stopped accepting invitations to travel to see them when her health began to fail.

He spent a couple of strange weeks in the old town. His feelings of loss were magnified while he stayed in the house, missing his mother and mourning his father, and feeling that he needed to stay there. There was something about this small town that had a strong attraction for him: the sea, the towering mountains, the old houses. He realised he had even missed the snow.

At least once every day he walked down to the dock and gazed out over the fjord, thinking of the father the sea had snatched away from him.

It was something of a revelation to realise that he had made his peace with the fjord and the sea.

It was time to come home.

|||||||||||||

The news was all over the front page of the Sunday newspaper that was on the table at the station's coffee corner. The paper hadn't reached Siglufjördur until Monday, but it provided written confirmation of what everyone already knew, that Hrólfur was dead.

Hrólfur Kristjánsson passes away.

There were no big headlines, just a restrained black-bordered feature at the bottom of the page.

The author Hrólfur Kristjánsson died in Siglufjördur on Friday evening at the age of ninety-one. He became a national figure in 1941, at the age of only twenty-four, when his novel North of the Hills *was published. The book is regarded as one of the finest examples of Icelandic literary fiction of the twentieth century and its unique style marked a new school of literature, a revolutionary, modern take on the classic romantic style of Icelandic nineteenth-century literature. The book's love poems, including the tragic* Verses for Linda, *written to the book's heroine, have long held a place of their own in the national psyche. Hrólfur Kristjánsson was born in Siglufjördur on the 10th of August, 1917 and graduated from college in Reykjavík in 1937 before taking up a university place in Copenhagen, where he studied first history and then literature.*

He returned to Iceland with the passenger ship Esja when it sailed in 1940 from Petsamo in Finland with two hundred and fifty-eight Icelandic citizens on board, shortly after the outbreak of the Second World War. He later settled in his home town of Siglufjördur and stayed there for the rest of his life. During his lifetime Hrólfur Kristjánsson received a great many plaudits for his work. His novel was published in the United States and widely in Europe, receiving highly favourable reviews and becoming a commercial success with the reading public in various countries. He published poetry and collections of short stories until he retired in 1974. The President of Iceland awarded him the Order of the Falcon in 1990. He was also awarded honorary doctorates in literature by universities in both Iceland and Copenhagen. He was unmarried and had no children.

Hrólfur Kristjánsson died in an accident on Friday during a rehearsal of the Siglufjördur Amateur Dramatic Society, of which he had been chairman for many years.

'He rang me up,' Tómas said.

Ari Thór looked up.

'Who?'

'He rang me up, the journalist. It didn't take them long to work it out. He asked if the old man had been drunk.'

Tómas scratched his head and raised one heavy eyebrow, giving him a strangely dramatic expression, while the other eyebrow remained practically still in its usual place.

'And what did you tell him?'

'He already knew. Someone must have told him. I said I had no comment to make. We'll let the old fellow rest in peace.'

'You're still sure it was an accident?'

'I am. Let's not be making mountains out of molehills.' Tómas's voice was firm.

'I heard there was an argument there on Friday.'

'What do you mean?' Tómas shot Ari Thór a suspicious look.

'Didn't you know? I heard that Úlfur and Hrólfur were going at it hammer and tongs.'

Tómas looked surprised. 'No, Úlfur didn't mention that,' he said, and looked thoughtful. 'It can't be anything unusual, just before a first night. You know what those artistic types are like

– too excitable, the lot of them. How do you know this, anyway?'

'Something I heard yesterday,' Ari Thór said, hoping he could get away without any further explanation. He preferred not to let Tómas think he had discussed police business with Ugla. 'Shouldn't we ask a few more questions?'

'Ask what? It was an accident. I have no intention of stirring up a hornets' nest,' Tómas said, his voice rising and his fist landing with a bang on the table.

That was clearly as far as things were likely to go.

'I'll go to the gym at the pool at lunchtime if that's all right with you,' Ari Thór said, and he saw that Tómas appeared to be relieved that he had dropped the subject.

'Fine. You do that.'

||||||||||||

CAUTION. NO RUNNING.
SHALLOW END. DEEP END.

Ari Thór read the lettering on the wall for the hundredth time as he went down the steps from the changing room to the pool. It was tempting to dive in and see how his shoulder would cope after his injury, but instead he went past the pool and outside into the fresh air where the hot tubs stood surrounded by a high wooden fence. It was bitterly cold outside, the air still, as if holding its own breath. The snow had held off, and the sunlight was almost impossibly bright, reflecting on the frost-dipped landscape. Ari Thór shivered and squinted as he made his way towards the tub.

Úlfur was there already, as Ari Thór had suspected.

Ari Thór had been to the pool several times before – usually during his lunch break, when his shift had been quiet. A dip in the hot tub relaxed his muscles, and he would slip quietly into the water and lose himself in his thoughts. In the past, Úlfur had frequently been in the tub around noon, but the two men had never spoken – their silence respectful and personal. That was about to change. It was certainly Tómas's right to decide whether or not to investigate the incident at the Dramatic Society, but he couldn't forbid Ari Thór from talking about it.

They were the only ones in the hot tub.

'I've never understood,' Ari Thór said, 'why there isn't an outdoor pool in a wonderful place like this, with a view out over the fjord. It's a real shame that the pool has a roof over it.'

'What?' Úlfur said with a start.

'Good morning. My name's Ari Thór. We met on Friday.'

Úlfur sniffed. 'Yes, well. I suppose we did,' he said. 'The Reverend, isn't it?' He added in a low voice.

'That's right,' Ari Thór said, letting the reference pass without comment. 'Don't you agree?'

'What? The pool?'

Ari Thór nodded.

'Actually, no. I well remember when it *was* an outdoor pool, back in the old days.' The look on Úlfur's face and his tired eyes said that he meant the good old days. 'It was no picnic in all that winter snow, believe me. It was a blessed relief when they finally built a roof over it.'

The ice had been broken and Ari Thór pressed home his advantage.

'I hear the opening night was postponed.'

'Yes, there was no other option. We had to put it off until after the funeral.'

'You knew Hrólfur well?'

'Fairly well. He was of a different generation, although the lines start to get blurred with age,' he said with a smile. 'We were both in the pension club.'

'Poor old fellow, falling on the steps like that.'

Úlfur nodded and looked skywards.

'It looks like snow,' he said.

'You must have been one of the last people to speak to him,' Ari Thór said, trying to make his words sound careless.

Úlfur appeared to take them that way and replied without thinking. 'More than likely . . . we had made some minor changes to the script during the rehearsal. You have to do that sometimes, even though it's irritating to alter things at the last minute. We were talking through some of the arrangements when the others had gone to dinner and, as usual, he came up with very apt observations. He was certainly alive and kicking,' he said, and then stopped himself. 'I'm sorry, that was a tasteless thing to say.'

'But you worked well together, didn't you?'

'We did, not bad,' he said and his gaze returned to the sky as if he was waiting for the first snowflakes of the day to fall.

A young woman came and joined them in the tub, without uttering a word to either Úlfur or Ari Thór.

Ari Thór wanted to ask about the drinking, to ask just how drunk Hrólfur had been, but this was exactly the kind of talk that could get him into trouble. There's little juicier than a good morsel of gossip in a society where not a great deal of note happens. The woman who had joined them was more likely a local, rather than a tourist – at this time of year, with the town shrouded in snow and darkness, and the roads dangerous to the point of being lethal, there were few visitors to the area. The forecast was also poor, or so Ari Thór had heard somewhere in passing. He had stopped taking notice of weather forecasts after moving north as there was a constant prospect of foul weather.

'He wasn't the easiest character?' pressed Ari Thór.

'Yes, well, sometimes. Sometimes,' Úlfur said and again looked up at the sky.

Ari Thór couldn't resist the temptation. 'I hear there was an argument between the two of you on Friday,' he said.

Úlfur wasn't fooled by Ari Thór's lighthearted tone.

'What the hell do you mean?' he demanded, and stood up as if to leave. The first soft snowflakes began to drift downwards. 'Is this some kind of damned interrogation?'

Ari Thór said nothing, smiled and looked towards the young woman to avoid Úlfur's eyes. Her expression remained un-changed, and it was clear that she hadn't come to the hot tub to involve herself in other people's arguments.

By the time he looked back, Úlfur was gone and the snow was descending – like a thick, white darkness. Ari Thór took a deep breath and tried to fend off the impending feeling of claus-trophobia.

22

SIGLUFJÖRDUR: MONDAY, 12TH JANUARY 2009

Pálmi Pálsson had been pleased that Úlfur had only greeted him with a nod when they met in the early morning on the Town Hall Square. Pálmi had continued across the square and down to the quay, his regular route for a morning walk. This was a habit that had developed since his retirement from teaching three years before, when the staff and pupils had held a reception on his final day to wish him on his way. That had been a Friday, the last day of the term, when spring had arrived practically everywhere in Iceland except in Siglufjördur, with its white-faced mountains. There was sufficient snow on their slopes to suggest that summer was still a long way off, but not enough to run down them on skis. Pálmi was still an enthusiastic skier, even at seventy-three.

Seventy-three. He could hardly believe it. His health was robust and friends and acquaintances commented constantly about his youthful looks. *You don't look a day over sixty, Pálmi.*

How on earth do you manage it? Of course, he knew that was a lie. His hair had gone grey, but that only served to make him look more distinguished. A glance in the mirror, however, told him he was far from young, the veins showing in a face that had become lean, his cheeks almost sunken. His mother had only reached sixty-seven before succumbing to a sudden stroke. In his younger years Pálmi had often feared that he'd go the same way, but he had long since got over that particular concern. He had already been teaching at the local primary for a good few years by the time his mother died, in 1983. She had lived in an old flat near the square and had steadfastly refused to move in with him, to the house he had bought on Hvanneyrarbraut, with its view over the fjord, where he still lived now. It was a location fairly close to the square and the theatre, but still pleasantly set – almost on the shore, with an unrestricted view of the sea.

These strong genes must have come from his father's side of the family, although his father's life had been a short one, cut off by tuberculosis at only twenty-four. Pálmi had always felt a strong connection to the father he did not remember. A few pictures of the two of them together remained, taken in 1936 and 1937, shortly before his father had left his family behind to seek his fortune in Denmark, back when Pálmi had been just a year old. He and his mother had been left behind in Siglufjördur, but Pálmi had never sensed any bitterness on his mother's part. *He needed his freedom,* he had heard her say once. His own warm feelings towards his long-departed father stemmed unconsciously from her positive attitude towards him, and she had loved his father, at least for a while.

It hadn't been easy for her, left behind with a small child in a remote coastal town in the north during some very hard years.

Like so many, his father had contracted tuberculosis in Denmark and died far too young, only a year after leaving Iceland.

Pálmi had been well liked at the primary school. He had been a conscientious teacher and spent his summers walking high in the hills and mountains. He had been abroad on only three occasions, each time on school trips with pupils. He had never experienced any strong urge to explore the wider world, something he imagined he had inherited along with his mother's genes. She had always been careful, had always lived within her means, painstakingly counting her pennies. Pálmi had been surprised after her death to find that her estate barely covered her funeral costs.

He had always been a loner. A good, well-regarded teacher, but he had struggled to establish friendships outside work. There had also been precious little romance in his life and now it was surely too late. Or was it? Maybe it was his own fault for hesitating, failing to leap when opportunity beckoned. He had been in love in his younger days, but let the chance slip away, not daring to gamble. If he thought back to those days it was with regret. However, he had a practical nature and trained himself not to look over his shoulder, as that generally brought too much pain.

Since retirement he had immersed himself in writing. He woke early every morning, long before the rest of the town had drawn its curtains, and made a habit of writing every day in his study with its view overlooking the fjord. After dinner, the evenings would find him back at his computer for another hour or more. Through the winter, with its early nightfall, he would light candles and arrange them in old jam jars in the window. Sitting in front of the computer, he would look out into the darkness, through the heat rising from the candles, to the sea and the point of land on the far side of the fjord.

His book was progressing well and he had already written three plays alongside his magnum opus. The plays came easily and made a lightweight counterbalance to his work on the novel. The first had been almost a farce, while the second had been a little more dramatic; the third, which he felt was the best, was a piece of real drama, with lighter moments neatly woven into the script. That was what people wanted, the chance to laugh and cry. The new play was the one that the Dramatic Society had intended to stage on Saturday.

He stood on the quay and looked landwards along the fjord.

His Danish visitors were still asleep, the old woman and her son. Why the hell did she have to come? She was staying in his basement – ninety years old and on a pilgrimage to Iceland with her son tagging along, asking to stay with Pálmi simply because she had known his late father during his time in Denmark.

'I want to take the opportunity to visit Siglufjördur. Your father always spoke so fondly of the place,' she had said over the phone in her clear Danish. After decades of teaching the language, Pálmi spoke Danish with ease. He had warned her that the weather could be unpredictable at this time of year, and that there was no guarantee that she would even be able to get to Siglufjördur, let alone leave it.

'All the same, I have to try. I so want to see the fjord with my own eyes before I die. I will be staying in Reykjavík at New Year because I want to see the fireworks,' she had said with almost childlike excitement. 'Could we visit you for a few days after New Year, if the weather is reasonable?'

How could he refuse?

A whole week to go. They were planning to travel back south next Monday. A whole week.

There was still no breath of wind, but Pálmi knew that in a place such as this the coming storm was inevitable.

23

SIGLUFJÖRDUR: TUESDAY, 13TH JANUARY 2009

The news spread like the first frost of winter.

Almost everyone heard that Úlfur had been interrogated in the hot tub at the swimming pool, and the tale grew with each retelling. By the time Ari Thór heard it from Tómas, it had been magnified beyond all recognition, although he had to admit that there was a kernel of truth to it. The core of the story was correct; he had certainly asked Úlfur about the sequence of events at the Dramatic Society.

It was clear that Tómas was angry with Ari Thór, and even Hlynur didn't try to take the opportunity to crack a joke, aware that there was no funny side to the riot act that was being read.

'The case is closed,' Tómas said, his voice determined. 'It was an accident and that's all there is to it. I thought I had made that crystal clear the other day.'

Ari Thór nodded.

'You step out of line one more time and you're through here.'

The atmosphere at the police station was almost viscous. There was no point opening a window, with the shingle-clattering wind, yet more snow falling and temperatures well below zero. Ari Thór hadn't slept well the last few nights. The break-in still preyed on his mind but, above all, he was terrified of waking up in the middle of the night, unable to breathe.

'People are frightened,' Hlynur said suddenly. 'That's my feeling.'

'What do you mean?' Tómas asked, turning to face him.

'Well, it seems people think we're investigating the ... the ... the Dramatic Society incident as a ...' Hlynur paused. 'As a murder investigation.'

You're not helping, Ari Thór thought.

He glared at Hlynur, with no visible effect. Hlynur was hardly on Ari Thór's side, even though they were both Tómas's subordinates. Ari Thór was the new boy, a new arrival and un-likely to stay for long.

'You think people are afraid?' Tómas said with a piercing look at Hlynur.

'That's the feeling I get, and one or two people have even mentioned it. There's something about a murder in a small com-munity that's disturbing, especially at a time like this – the middle of winter,' Hlynur said with a self-important look on his face. 'People's imaginations can run away with them.'

'Hell and damnation,' Tómas muttered.

Ari Thór nodded his head.

Hell and damnation.

He was on the point of making a royal mess of his opportu-nity. His first posting, and everything seemed to be going badly wrong.

Hell and damnation.

Wet behind the ears and only out of college for five minutes, this was the price of trusting instinct without having experience to back it up. He had allowed this young woman, Ugla, to arouse his suspicions about Úlfur and Hrólfur's death.

The weather brightened later in the day, and Ari Thór called at the little fish shop in the Town Hall Square on his way home, wading through the drifts of snow.

There were more people about than usual, relishing the opportunity to get out for a breath of fresh air, running their errands before the snow filled the streets again, making them impassable.

'Two haddock fillets,' ordered the man ahead of him.

Ari Thór recognised him right away: he had met him outside the theatre on the evening of Hrólfur's fatal accident; Karl, a member of the Dramatic Society. He had come across as a decent sort of character.

The man behind the counter passed him a package of haddock. Karl pulled a note from his pocket, dropping some change as he did so, but then ignoring it.

Ari Thór picked up the coin from the floor and tapped Karl's shoulder.

'Keep an eye on the pennies,' Ari Thór said, handing him the coin.

'Hello. Ari Thór, isn't it?'

'That's me. Hello again.' He wanted to use the opportunity to ask about that Friday evening, at the same time knowing that it would be better not to. He had learned from bitter experience that even the most innocent conversation could become a salacious and fast-travelling tale.

'How do you like Siglufjördur?' Karl asked.

'Fine, thanks.'

It was not, perhaps, an entirely truthful answer, but this was no time for baring his soul.

Karl's eyes half closed as he smiled. 'You get used to it.'

'Have you lived here long?'

'Born and bred here, but not long moved back. There's no better place to be.'

The word he had been searching for came to Ari Thór: reliable. There was a warmth to this man.

'I heard that you're treating Hrólfur's death as murder,' Karl said in a loud whisper. 'Was he murdered?'

'Can I help you?' The fishmonger said with a good-humoured glance at Ari Thór.

'No. It was just an accident,' he said to Karl.

Just an accident.

||||||||||||||||

Karl had never intended to move back home to Siglufjördur, and he had no particular affection for the place. But when the flat in Kópavogur had been sold from under their feet and the debt collectors still didn't stop hammering on their door, it seemed the obvious move for him and Linda. Brutal and ruthless, the collectors were after payments to clear his gambling debts, and weren't inclined to leave empty-handed. If there was nothing for them, the visits would usually end with blows.

There wasn't much that frightened Karl, but his pain threshold was low; so low as to be nonexistent. The decision to move north had been made one evening after an unexpected visit from just such a debt collector had ended badly. Karl knew he couldn't trust luck or his own strength, and was aware that the next time there would be two of them and they'd be more heavily armed. He suspected that they would be unlikely to follow him to Siglufjördur, but just to be certain, he didn't bother registering his new legal residence. The debt wasn't that high, half a million krónur or so; it had often been much greater than that.

He had promised Linda that he would stop gambling. Not surprisingly, she had completely lost it when she heard about the regular Wednesday poker night, only reluctantly calming down when he assured her that they played for nothing more than beer and Monopoly money. The beer, and booze in general, was never a problem. It was the gambling that was his Achilles' heel.

It was fun to meet old schoolmates, the few of them from his year left in the town. They met once a week, in the afternoon, at the house of a friend who had remained unmarried, and played poker. It was refreshing, a great way to relax, and no more than that.

Linda had no idea about the *other* poker club that met occasionally and played for real money, as often as not for serious amounts. Karl turned up whenever he had something to play with; sometimes he'd show up empty-handed in the hope of getting a place at the table. Sometimes someone would loan him enough to play – and sometimes not. He couldn't help but be drawn in; it was the same pull that had always been his downfall.

He and Linda had got to know one another fifteen years earlier in Denmark, where they had lived together for ten years before moving to Iceland. Her father was Danish, her mother

Icelandic and Linda herself had been brought up in Iceland until the age of twelve, when the family moved to Denmark. Karl had spent longer in Iceland and was seventeen when his parents decided to move from Siglufjördur to Denmark in the summer of 1983. They had lived in a dilapidated apartment on the outskirts of Copenhagen until Karl found his way to Århus, when he and Linda first met.

There hadn't been much common ground between Karl and his parents. They had been so conventional, so conservative and so adoring. He loathed their effusive, suffocating affection, and he moved out as soon as the offer of some cash-in-hand work in Århus came through. He snatched the opportunity gratefully and left his parents behind in their little Copenhagen flat.

Linda had been a stroke of luck for Karl. Her parents divorced acrimoniously and in the midst of the turmoil she found herself in Karl's arms. Unlike him, she had finished college and went on to train as a nurse. This had kept them afloat as she found work at hospitals in Denmark, Reykjavík and now Siglufjördur, while Karl had been out of work since they had moved north. There had been plenty of time that summer and autumn to refit a small fishing boat that had been earmarked for the primary school. An old acquaintance had told him the school was looking for a volunteer – someone clever with his hands – to take on the refurbishment, and Karl hadn't hesitated. He had always made an effort, whatever had been going on in his life, to do something either with or for children, and had frequently done voluntary work in Denmark. He didn't quite understand his compulsion to do things for children, except that he somehow wanted to help them maintain their innocence as long as possible. Strangely enough, it never occurred to him that he might have children of his own one day.

As well as his work on the boat, he took occasional manual work when it was offered. Every penny of that ended up on the card table.

He was like a car in low gear when he was away from the card table. It was only when he had cards in his hand that he felt fully alive, flush with high-octane petrol. He could feel the blood coursing through his veins and nothing else mattered, not Linda, and not even winning or losing. It was the rush, the heart-stopping recklessness that drew him back, over and over again, although losing produced a painful, guilty hangover the following day. What was worse was being left with a debt. This type of behaviour was so ingrained in his nature, in his lifestyle, that he no longer lost any sleep about debts. Instead, it had become a practical problem that needed to be solved before he could get back his place at the card table.

Sometimes he wondered what the future might have in store. Linda was anxious to move on, while he was satisfied with being in the town where he had grown up, where he had friends and acquaintances. He had even become a star of the local stage, damn it.

The place seemed empty as he opened the door of their flat on Thormódsgata. He peered into the living room; nobody there.

The living room was unusually colourful, with most of the furniture showing its age. There was a scruffy yellow sofa with a few embroidered cushions, a small coffee table, an old bookcase, a wall hung with little souvenir plates in every colour of the rainbow and a Danish landscape painting positioned over the sofa. A small television faced a tired old leather armchair; next to it stood a wooden table on which sat an old vase, something from the sixties that Linda had inherited from her family.

In the bedroom Karl switched on the light. Linda was asleep in the threadbare bed that probably dated back to the seventies. It had come with the flat when they agreed to rent it, along with the print of Jesus, who looked down from his place on the wall over the headboard. Two lamps flanked the bed, and they too were probably as old as the bed itself. The light woke Linda, and she stirred, rubbing her eyes.

'Up you get, sleepyhead. I bought haddock for dinner.'

24

SIGLUFJÖRDUR: WEDNESDAY, 14TH JANUARY 2009

The little boy had been allowed out after dinner to play in the snow, a fresh, delightful snowfall that created a wonderland where anything could happen. The flakes had stopped tumbling down around dinner time and his mother had finally let him go outside to play.

A small cat with a bell hung at her neck had stolen out into the evening calm and tempted him to follow her into the neighbouring garden, arching her back and purring as she led him along a frozen border into another garden. He knew where he could sneak through between the trees and still find his way home.

He revelled in the snow; it was in his blood. The darkness was comfortable and snug.

The sight of the angel, a beautiful snow angel, didn't frighten him.

He knew the woman. He had played often enough in her

garden that he even remembered her name. What he couldn't understand was why she was lying so still and why she wasn't wearing a jumper. In his eyes, the bloodred snow that formed a halo around her was beautiful, a vivid embellishment to the rest of the pearl-white garden.

He didn't want to disturb her and with one last glance at the wondrous sight, made his way home, stopping just once on the way to make a snowball.

||||||||||||||

Karl put down his glass of beer. Old habits born of experience ensured that he kept his cards close to his chest; nobody could be trusted. The six of spades and the seven of clubs in his hand, plus a four, an eight and a jack on the table meant he was in with a chance. The round table about which they sat was covered with a green cloth and a bowl of crisps had been placed at the edge. The tension was palpable.

His old schoolmates watched carefully, waiting for him to move. It wasn't a tough decision – playing only for Monopoly money. Hovering at the edge of his mind, and feeding his growing excitement were thoughts of the *real* game. This was child's play by comparison. Maybe next weekend? Except that he was flat broke and already owed his mate a few grand.

The phone rang just as he made the decision to stay in the game. He looked at the number but didn't recognise it. Seeing that it was a call from a local landline number, he answered it. Normally he avoided unfamiliar numbers, preferring not to find himself unwittingly engaged with debt collectors from down south.

'Karl?'

A woman's voice, a young woman's voice that he couldn't place.

'That's me.'

She introduced herself, an old school friend who lived not far from him and Linda.

'Listen, my Gunni, my little boy, was knocking about in your garden just now.' She hesitated, as if searching for the words to continue. 'I tried calling your home number, but there's no reply. He said he saw your Linda, out in the garden, naked.' She laughed awkwardly. 'These kids. They say such weird things . . . but it felt so strange. I just wanted to make sure everything was all right.'

'As far as I know,' Karl said. 'I'll check. Thanks for calling.'

He ended the call without another word, stood up and put his cards on the table.

'Sorry, guys. I have to shoot home. I'll be back.'

He took his jacket off the back of the chair, and went out into the cold. It had started to snow again, so violently he could hardly see.

||||||||||||

The ambulance was at the scene moments before the police jeep. Ari Thór and Tómas were on duty, disagreements about Hrólfur forgotten in the time it took to take the call from Karl on the emergency line. He now stood at the back door, in black jeans and a dark-blue sweater. His jacket lay in the snow and the paramedics crouched by the motionless body, feeling for a pulse. It looked like there would be no chance of identifying footprints, anything useful long obliterated by the fresh snowfall; and both the ambulance crew and Karl had trodden through the snow at the scene.

She lay in the snow, pale with blue lips and eyes closed. Ari Thór hadn't seen her before, Linda Christensen, Karl's wife. She looked disturbingly peaceful. Karl stood to one side and Ari Thór felt a surge of sympathy for this likeable man to whom he had chatted so easily only the day before in the fish shop.

Linda's arms were outstretched and there was a wide pool of blood in the snow, far too much blood. Ari Thór felt himself overwhelmed with anger, as he tried to control his breathing. It wasn't good to take things too personally and he knew he had to keep his distress, his rage under control and not let it cloud his judgement.

Who does this kind of thing? Who leaves someone to die in the snow and their own blood?

She was wearing jeans and nothing else. Bare feet, naked above the waist.

He was almost certain she had to be dead. There was a cut to her chest – it was a shallow one, but was startling on her pale torso – and a deeper cut to one arm. This one appeared more serious, and the cause of the crimson stain that had spread around her into the snow.

Defensive injuries?

Weapon?

Knife?

Ari Thór looked about and saw that Tómas also seemed to be searching for a weapon, but in the riddle of footprints and the still-falling snow, nothing could be seen.

'Should we call out a technical team from Reykjavík?'

Ari Thór had only been trained in the basics of crime-scene procedures, essentially just enough to know what not to do and how to avoid compromising evidence. But this was no usual crime scene. To begin with, efforts to save the young woman's life – if she were still alive – had to take precedence and the blizzard would make everything even more difficult.

'I don't think there's any point,' Tómas said, deep lines of concern etched on his face. 'But we need to call Hlynur out right away. He needs to go over the crime scene, both inside the flat, if that's where the attack took place, and out here. Take as many pictures as you can while there's still anything to be seen in the snow.'

Ari Thór nodded his agreement. It wouldn't take Hlynur long to arrive and it was unlikely he had left town in this weather; practically impossible, in fact.

They watched the ambulance crew, waiting for developments. Ari Thór pulled the camera from his pocket and took pictures.

Tómas moved closer to Ari Thór and spoke in the quietest voice he could, with every sound dampened by the thick snowfall, the conditions worsening by the minute.

'We have to ask Karl to come with us.'

'Ask?'

Or arrest him?

'Ask him politely. We need to get him to make a statement. I understand that they haven't always . . .' He paused. 'They haven't always agreed on everything.'

'Pulse!'

Ari Thór was startled and moved closer.

'We have a pulse!' a paramedic shouted.

The ambulance crew lifted Linda onto a stretcher. They had now covered her with a blanket, the narrow gash to her chest and the deeper one on her arm now hidden from view. The motionless body in the snow had at first looked artistic to Ari Thór, almost beautiful, but now reality had taken over, and he reminded himself that this was just a poor woman fighting for her life.

'She's alive?' Ari Thór asked in surprise.

'A very faint pulse, but yes. She's alive.'

25

SIGLUFJÖRDUR: WEDNESDAY, 14TH JANUARY 2009

'You'll have to come with us. We need you to make a statement.'

Tómas spoke in measured tones, struggling to keep any brusqueness out of his voice. Karl stood still as he watched Linda being lifted into the ambulance.

'Of course. I'm coming.'

'Can we have the key to your flat? We have to check for any signs of activity there.'

He nodded. 'It's not locked. There's nothing to see. I had a look just now to see if anyone was there.'

'Sit in the car.' Ari Thór ushered him to a seat.

The ambulance had gone, its lights lurid against the relentless snow. The garden behind the house on Thormódsgata no longer looked like a crime scene, washed clean by the flurries of snow that had now settled in a gleaming cold blanket. Linda had been taken away, Karl was in the car. Only traces of red could be seen. The garden was being transformed in front of Ari Thór's eyes; it could be any backyard in a quiet street of a small northern town.

Hlynur arrived a few minutes later.

'I'm going back to the station with Ari Thór,' Tómas said, his voice almost lost in the wind. 'Karl comes with us. I need you to investigate the scene as best you can. We need to locate the weapon. We don't have any details of her injuries – they were too busy keeping her alive – but my feeling is that it was a knife. Keep your eyes open. Take a look in the flat as well – see if there's anything that indicates a struggle.'

Ari Thór fought to keep his eyes open as the storm raged. The thick snowflakes no longer fell gently to earth but instead lashed anyone so unwary as to step outside in such weather. He sat next to Karl in the squad car's back seat. Tómas drove them in silence.

The police station provided a welcome refuge from the force of the blizzard with its safe, familiar environment. It wasn't until he was inside that Ari Thór realised how hard his heart had been pounding. He could clearly feel himself relaxing and felt the pain in his shoulder return.

They showed Karl into the office that was used as their rarely needed interview room. Ari Thór was finding it difficult to comprehend Karl's attitude. He seemed strangely placid, considering the circumstances. He asked, 'Is this going to take long? I'd like to get up to the hospital as soon as I can.' Little emotion.

'We'll do our best to be quick. It helps make things go faster if you speak clearly and distinctly,' Tómas said, and explained to Karl that he was being treated as a witness.

The tape recorder started. Ari Thór wrote a few words and passed a note to Tómas.

'Would you give me your jacket?' Tómas asked.

The question seemed to take Karl by surprise and his eyes widened.

'Your jacket. Can you take it off? Give it here.'

Karl obeyed, apparently just noticing the little stain that Ari Thór had seen, but saying nothing. He passed his jacket to Tómas.

'This will have to be sent away for examination.'

Ari Thór nodded and fetched an evidence bag for the jacket.

'Blood?' asked Tómas.

Karl didn't seem upset by the question. 'Probably.'

Tómas sat in silence and Karl did the same; they were eyeing one another, almost daring the other to speak first. Karl was the winner, as Tómas looked down, shuffled in his seat and began his line of questioning.

'Do you know how it got on your jacket?'

'I took it off when I found her, used it to cover her, to keep her warm. There was blood everywhere. The paramedics put it to one side when they arrived and tried to revive her.'

'When did you last see Linda?'

'This morning.'

'She went to work?'

'Yes, she had a shift until six.'

'Do you know if she went home early?'

'No idea.'

'Have you heard from her today?'

'No, not a word. Could I give the hospital a call?'

He sat quietly, as anyone with nothing to hide would. Ari Thór's instinct was that they were wasting time on the wrong person.

'I'll speak to the doctor shortly. Weren't you at home at six?'

'No,' he said and lapsed again into silence.

'Where were you?'

'Playing poker with the boys. Every Wednesday. We meet at five, five-thirty, when they've all finished work, and we play into the evening. Not too late, though. A couple of beers, a few hands of cards.'

'They'll confirm that you were there before six?'

'Yes,' Karl said and hesitated. 'You want their names?'

'Yes, please,' Tómas said, handing him a pen and paper.

Karl handed back a list. Tómas looked at the names.

'I'll make the calls. I know them,' he said to Ari Thór.

I know them, and you don't. Out-of-towner.

Tómas stood up.

'Can you call the doctor?' Karl asked.

Tómas nodded and left the room. Ari Thór wasn't sure if he should continue the investigation or keep quiet. Maybe just chat about something else. The result was an uncomfortable silence.

'Coffee?'

Karl shook his head. 'You're sharp. The jacket and the blood on it. I hadn't noticed anything.'

Ari Thór wasn't sure how he should take this and wondered why Karl was complimenting him. Was the man trying to establish a rapport?

Should he be saying thank you?

They were silent and then he asked, 'Sure about the coffee?'

'Quite sure.'

'That's a nasty cut to your forehead,' Karl said.

Silence again.

'What happened?'

'Nothing serious,' Ari Thór said shortly, and the uncomfortable silence resumed.

'Lousy weather. I suppose you're not used to this.'

Ari Thór tried not to let himself get distracted, but it was not easy to hide the effects that the unremitting snow, the winds and the bone-shattering cold had on him. He certainly didn't want to be where he now found himself. He would much have preferred to be in Reykjavík.

Karl seemed to have understood his thoughts and acknowledged that he'd touched on a sensitive point. 'It can be terrible. It's even tough for me to get used to it, and I was brought up here. It's like the walls are closing in on you when the weather's like this,' he said with a careless smile.

Damn it. Couldn't Tómas hurry up?

Ari Thór kept quiet and tried to think of something else. The minutes passed. Maybe Tómas was deliberately delaying his return, giving Karl time to sweat? If that was the case, it didn't seem to be working.

The ring of Ari Thór's phone shattered the silence.

He looked at his phone's screen.

Kristín.

He picked up the phone and set it to silent. This wasn't the time or the place to answer.

Kristín. He hadn't heard from her for a few days and wondered what she wanted. He longed to call her back and cursed her bad timing.

The distance between them was starting to take its toll. Their emails were becoming fewer, the calls far less frequent. He missed her and dearly wanted to lie close to her at night, when his spirits were at their lowest ebb and when the isolation was at its worst. But he was still upset with her – upset by her reaction to his moving north, upset that she hadn't gone with him to Siglufjördur that first weekend, upset that she hadn't called him on Christmas Eve. Admittedly she had called on Christmas Day . . .

Damn it! Your girlfriend should call on Christmas Eve. Elderly aunts are the ones who call on Christmas Day!

The door was opened suddenly.

'A word, Ari Thór. Out here.' There was determination in Tómas's voice.

'I've spoken to them all,' he said, when Ari Thór had shut the door behind him. 'The whole poker school.'

There was a dramatic pause, indicating that there might be something of an actor in Tómas.

'They all say the same thing. He was there the whole time, turned up around five and was doing well. He didn't leave until the phone call, when the neighbour called him.'

'When did Linda leave work?'

'Around six-thirty. I spoke to the nurse who was on the same shift that Linda was. She finished her shift and had something to eat at the hospital. That seems clear enough. He didn't do it.'

'Anything from Hlynur?'

'No. We'll leave him to get on with it for a little longer.'

Tómas peered out of the window. The visibility was practically zero. Ari Thór was grateful that he hadn't had to handle the crime scene.

'I'm going to try and get hold of the doctor. Wait for me and we'll get back to the interview.'

Ari Thór could feel his phone ring in his pocket. That would be Kristín again. He wondered if something might be wrong. Tómas was on the phone so he took the opportunity to answer. For a fraction of a second he thought of Ugla's beautiful face, but quickly shrugged off the distraction.

'What's going on?' Kristín demanded immediately, her voice cold and determined. She sounded curious, even excited.

'What?'

This wasn't the greeting he had expected. No *darling*, no warmth.

'This woman – you know. The woman in the snow.'

What the hell?

News clearly got around fast.

'How did you know?'

'I saw it on the Web,' she said and mentioned the Web site by name. 'Are you involved in the investigation?'

He went to the computer.

Woman found naked and unconscious in Siglufjördur . . .

'I can't say anything . . .' – *my love*. The words dried up before he said them. Words that had been so normal a few weeks ago had become something terribly distant. All the same, he longed to say something pleasant, something affectionate, but she had clearly called simply to ask about the breaking news. His irritation intensified.

'I can't talk now. I have to get back to work.'

He could hear Tómas about to finish his own call.

'I reached the doctor,' he said, coming over to Ari Thór. 'He's going to call again later. She's still unconscious. She had probably been there around three-quarters of an hour or so, he thinks. It's unbelievable that she's still alive, but thank God she is.'

He smiled, obviously relieved not to be dealing with a murder case. Not yet, at least. His expression changed when he saw the computer screen and the report on it.

'How the hell did that happen?'

'No idea. My girlfriend called and told me about it.'

'That's despicable! First Hrólfur and now this! Everything goes straight into the papers! We can't get any peace to work.'

'You don't think this has anything to do with the accident at the Dramatic Society, do you?' Ari Thór asked mildly.

'What? No, hardly. But it's bloody infuriating. Completely unacceptable that we have to handle two cases like this in a row.'

Even more 'infuriating' for Hrólfur and Linda.

Ari Thór remained silent, and then Tómas's phone rang.

'Hello?' Silence. 'No, dammit,' he said furiously. 'You can just leave me to get on with my job!' There was a short silence. 'No. I don't have time. No comment. Did you get that?' He ended the call.

'Bloody journalists. Come on, we'll finish the interview. There's no reason to keep the man hanging around here,' Tómas said angrily. 'This is going to turn into a nightmare. We have to get to the bottom of this right away, otherwise people are going to be terrified.'

Ari Thór glanced quickly out of the window before they went back into the office. It was still snowing. This peaceful little town was being compressed by the snow, no longer a familiar winter embrace but a threat like never before. The white was no longer pure, but tinged bloodred.

One thing was certain. Tonight people would lock their doors.

26

SIGLUFJÖRDUR: WEDNESDAY, 14TH JANUARY 2009

'I'll talk to the boy and his mother in the morning,' Tómas said. 'We need to get a first-hand account, but that doesn't change the fact that Karl is not a suspect. I didn't believe that he could be the perpetrator. I remember him as just a boy, when his mother and father decided to move to Denmark. That lot were always struggling, always short of cash as far as I remember, and there wasn't a lot of work to be had here. I think they did well for themselves abroad.'

'And Linda, is she Danish?'

'Danish-Icelandic. They met in Denmark.' Tómas's thoughts appeared to be elsewhere and he seemed worried, as if more than just the pressure of work preyed on his mind. 'Listen. You mentioned Hrólfur just now . . .'

'Yes?'

'Keep your eyes peeled. We can't afford any mistakes. Understand?'

Ari Thór nodded his agreement. 'You think there could be a link?'

'It's unlikely, but it's not something we can rule out. Two deaths in suspicious circumstances . . .' Tómas said and his voice died away as an embarrassed look appeared on his face. 'Sorry. She's still alive, of course. What worries me is how quickly one incident followed the other, and with Karl and Leifur both at the rehearsal on the evening Hrólfur died.'

'Leifur? What does he have to do with Linda?'

'He lives in the apartment above Karl and Linda. Can you go and talk to him?'

'I'll do that.'

'There's something else about that incident in the theatre. There's some kind of webcam that sends out pictures of the Town Hall Square, some sort of live camera broadcast from the town for the benefit of people who have moved away. You understand? Maybe something might have been recorded that evening, people who came and went. Check it out, would you?' he asked, passing Ari Thór a slip of paper with the Web address.

A phone rang, this time Tómas's mobile.

He didn't say a lot during the short conversation, little more than 'Yes, OK.'

His expression said more than many words could have and he dropped the phone back into his pocket.

'She's still unconscious. There'll be an emergency flight to take her south. Hopefully the weather will clear up enough for them to fly tomorrow,' he said. 'There's something else the doctor mentioned. We need another word with Karl, right away.'

||||||||||||

The heavy drifts had risen higher than any snow Ari Thór had experienced in Reykjavík and he had no doubt that they would deepen further in the coming days.

Karl had answered the phone when he had called a second time. He was still at the hospital.

Visibility was poor. The little police 4×4 bumped along the snow-filled streets towards the hospital, its wipers working overtime to keep the windscreen clear. The snow lit up the darkness, reflecting the lights that shone from every window. Most people had chosen to stay indoors that evening and there was a palpable feeling of brooding uncertainty.

Karl sat placidly in the waiting room, leafing through a newspaper. He nodded to Tómas and Ari Thór before returning to the paper.

'A word with you.'

He turned the page as if nothing had happened.

Tómas raised his voice. 'We need to talk to you.'

Karl looked up and peered at them through half-closed eyes. 'Why? What's going on?'

'You have to come with us.'

'Hadn't we already been through everything?' he asked, a new edge to his voice. 'I'd prefer to stay here, close to her.'

'Come with us.'

Karl stood up hesitantly and patted Ari Thór hard on the shoulder. 'All right, then.'

The pain was unbearable.

Damned shoulder.

Clutching their coats tightly against the driving winds, Ari Thór, Tómas and Karl reached the 4×4, setting off once again in the blinding snowstorm.

'I spoke to the doctor,' Tómas said, when they were sitting in the office at the police station. He waited for a response, but none was forthcoming.

'Have you knocked her about?'

The question arrived like a thunderbolt.

'Have I what?' Karl demanded with a hostile glare at Tómas, and then another directed at Ari Thór. At first he seemed taken by surprise, but this quickly turned to shock, and then anger.

'Do you beat your wife?' Tómas's voice was louder and harder. Ari Thór glanced sideways at him.

'Are you out of your mind? Of course not.'

Before Tómas could ask his next question, Karl interrupted, as if he could see it coming and wanted to head it off. 'She took a tumble yesterday, she was dusting something in the living room and slipped, or so she said. Is that what you're asking about?'

Tómas didn't answer directly. 'There are clear bruises on her back, as if from a heavy blow or a fall.'

'Exactly,' Karl said coolly.

'Is that the first time you've done this to her?'

Karl rose to his feet and looked hard into Tómas's eyes. 'I've never laid a hand on her. You hear that?'

Tómas remained still. 'I'd appreciate it if you'd sit down. You're telling me you've nothing to hide?'

'Nothing at all,' Karl said, sitting down, his anger cooling, leaving him pale.

'Wait here a moment.'

Tómas stood up slowly and a look at Ari Thór told him he wanted a word in private.

'He beat her,' Tómas said when they were outside. 'He hit her, or pushed her, but we can't be sure of that without talking to her. I want you to go to Hlynur and find out how he's getting on. There might be something there that could give us an idea of what happened. Karl has given us permission to examine the property.'

'Exactly because he gave us that permission, there's not likely to be anything there to find,' Ari Thór said.

'You're probably quite right, unfortunately.'

ıιιιιιιιιιιιιιιι

Ari Thór stood in the driving snow outside the house on Thormódsgata. It was late in the evening, but there were lights on in both upstairs and downstairs flats. He went straight to the back garden, where Hlynur was bent over as he searched in the snow, looking for the weapon or any other clue. Ari Thór tapped him on the back. There was no point in calling out to him in this weather.

Hlynur looked up.

'Nothing. Nothing so far,' he yelled through the storm.

Ari Thór nodded acknowledgement and pointed towards the house.

Hlynur came closer. 'Take a look inside. I've been through the flat and taken pictures. Didn't find anything there except her shirt – a red T-shirt on the floor,' Hlynur said. 'It's in an evidence bag in the car.'

The shirt she was wearing when the attack took place?

Ari Thór stepped into the warmth of the flat through the back door, and it was as if he'd gone back a couple of decades, judging by the quaintly colourful furniture and fabrics. There was nothing here that went properly together, at all – although, in a weird sort of way, it did make some kind of cohesive whole. Had she been attacked inside or outside? Could it have been someone she knew, someone she had invited in?

There was no sign of a struggle inside, nothing to be seen in either the living room or the little kitchen. The bright yellow paint on the kitchen walls and cabinets screamed at him, as if it had been cut from some over-the-top, mid-seventies magazine. There was a cheap set of tired kitchen knives next to the stove, with slots for five knives, three small and two larger ones. There were only four knives to be seen; maybe a coincidence, or maybe not.

Ari Thór looked into the bedroom, pausing at the picture of Jesus that hung above the old double bed and letting his mind wander back to his days studying theology. *The Reverend Ari Thór.* He was certainly better off in the police force. What had God ever done for him, other than take away his parents before there had been a chance to get to know them properly?

He looked out of the window.

The snow had stopped falling, as if a tap had been turned off.

That was when he saw the phone, a small, red mobile phone next to the pillow on the unmade bed. Her phone? Probably. He was gripped by a sudden discomfort, a sudden stab to the guts, and his heart beat faster. He put the phone in an evidence bag and placed it in his pocket.

Could it be what he thought it was?

No, hardly. Damn it.

Ari Thór went out through the front door, up the steps and rang Leifur's doorbell.

Leifur looked tired, but not surprised to be getting a visit from the police so late in the evening.

'I'm sorry it's late,' Ari Thór said. 'I won't keep you long; I imagine you have work in the morning.' He smiled, making an effort to be amicable. The Reverend Ari Thór would undoubtedly have been on the best terms with his parishioners.

Leifur's voice was dark and low. 'It's all right. I have a day off tomorrow.'

A labrador barked at the sight of Ari Thór and came over to greet him. A pleasant, friendly dog, he thought.

There was a smell of freshly sawn wood in the hall, and Ari Thór could smell it again in the living room, reminding him of woodwork classes at school and the things he had knocked together for his parents. The living room was sparsely furnished and had a cold energy – a blank, soulless room almost the diametric opposite of the explosion of colour downstairs. Nothing hung on the walls. A single photograph, of a youngster dressed for his confirmation, stood in a frame on top of the television.

'Coffee?' asked Leifur.

'Tea, if you have it.'

He didn't feel the need for any overblown courtesy in this place, in this raw, everyday environment with no room for any shred of ceremony.

'You made the table?' Tómas had told him that Leifur was a carpenter.

'S'right.'

Ari Thór could sense there was something on Leifur's mind.

The tea soon arrived and Leifur sat on the grey couch, the dog at his feet.

'You've been home all evening?'

'I came home around six. I work at the petrol station.'

'And you've been here since then?'

'Yes. I was working on something, like I do most evenings. I have a workshop in there and get some jobs now and then to bring in a little extra cash.'

'It doesn't bother the neighbours?'

'It might well do, but I try and finish before ten. The television drowns out any noise before that.' He took a sip of the tea that he'd made for himself to keep Ari Thór company. 'We have a tacit agreement. I pretend I don't hear their rows and they let me work in peace.'

'Rows?'

'Yep. A hell of a racket, and it happens all the time. Mostly Karl, you get me? He makes the noise and Linda doesn't often shout back.'

'Was there an argument yesterday?'

'They were at it hammer and tongs yesterday, not that there's anything unusual about that. There was some damage as well, or so it seemed.'

At last, a step in the right direction, although an account of an argument wouldn't be enough. It certainly now appeared less likely that she had fallen, but still . . . it wasn't enough.

'Do you think he knocked her down?'

'I don't know. Maybe. But listen, I don't take a lot of notice anymore. I just reckon it's an ordinary enough argument. To tell you the truth, Karl doesn't strike me as the type to beat his wife,' he said, and lapsed into silence. 'So what happened tonight?'

'Did you see anything?'

'No. Nothing. I was in the workshop and there's no window looking out onto the garden. I'm in a world of my own when I'm in there. Of course I had a look from the kitchen window when things started to get busy, when you appeared, and then I saw something about it on the Web,' he said, and repeated his question. 'Do you think Karl did it?'

'No, there's nothing to indicate that.'

'Is she going to make it?'

'It's impossible to say . . . Speaking of arguments . . .' It was as well to make use of the opportunity, and Tómas had practically given him carte blanche. 'I hear there was an argument during the rehearsal when Hrólfur died. Were you aware of that?'

The question about the Dramatic Society didn't seem to take Leifur by surprise, either.

'Did I ever! Nobody could have missed it. They had a proper row; Hrólfur was a little drunk and Úlfur was argumentative. Nothing unusual there.'

'Well, Hrólfur falling to his death was something out of the ordinary.'

'Of course. But it's not as if anyone would have given him a push.'

'Did you leave during the dinner break?'

'I did.' A touch of fear now appeared in Leifur's eyes, as it seemed to dawn on him that he could be a suspect in two police investigations. 'I always do that, take a walk and go home. I went out that back door and had a word with Nína before I went. She said she was going to clear up in the basement during the break.'

Ari Thór stood up. There was little more to be found from this visit and he felt it might be best to leave on friendly terms, as the Reverend Ari Thór would have done.

'Thanks for the tea,' he said, then pointed at the confirmation photograph. 'You haven't changed.'

Leifur looked stunned. 'That's my brother,' he said and hesitated. 'He's dead. Died in a car crash.'

'A long time ago?' Ari Thór asked, the sympathetic clergyman coming out again.

'Twenty-three years,' Leifur answered without having to think about it. 'Twenty-three years tomorrow. That's why I have a day off. I always take the fifteenth of January off.' He was silent, but it was obvious that he had something to add. 'You never caught him.'

Me? We? Was Ari Thór supposed to be responsible for the sins of others?

'Caught who?'

'The driver. A friend of my brother's was a passenger in the car. He survived, just, and he described what had happened. He said that there was a car coming the other way, in the middle of the road, that's why their car rolled over. It wasn't my brother's fault. The weather was bad . . . and this . . .' Leifur was clearly struggling to control his fury. '. . . this man forced them off the road. The car rolled over.'

Silence.

'The police never found him. It was difficult for my brother's friend to identify the car, other than that it was dark – red, perhaps, hard to be sure. Nobody came forward and the case was closed. It's probably at the bottom of some drawer at the police station.'

Ari Thór stood in silence. There was nothing he could say.

He offered his hand. Leifur grasped it with his own calloused hand, a carpenter to his boot heels.

Outside there was a carpet of snow over everything and the town felt peaceful. A small cat scampered from under the car, hurrying home to somewhere warm. A few flakes still fluttered down, so light that they could hardly be seen. Ari Thór looked up and took a deep breath.

Maybe everything will work out for the best.

He heard Hlynur calling as he was getting into the 4×4.

'Ari Thór!'

He turned round.

'The knife. Found it.'

The knife had been behind a shrub in the garden of the house next door. There was no doubt that it was the missing kitchen knife.

'He must have hidden it as he ran off,' Ari Thór said.

So, he had been right about the knife.

Well done.

He hoped he wasn't right about the phone.

||||||||||||||

Tómas had no idea when he would next get a chance to sleep. All he knew was that he wouldn't be going home that night. He wanted to take the opportunity to lie down at the station, which would show his wife what things would be like once she moved south. Then she'd have to sleep alone, or so he hoped.

'I don't imagine there'll be any prints on the knife,' he said with a sigh. 'Send it to Reykjavík anyway, just in case.'

He poured hot, strong coffee into a mug.

'We'll have to let Karl go soon, won't we?' Hlynur asked, yawning.

'There's an emergency flight on the way. It's just as well the weather's clearing so they can land. Linda still hasn't regained consciousness and we can't be sure that she'll be able to tell us anything. What's your take on all this, gentlemen?' Tómas looked at Hlynur, who seemed too exhausted to reply.

'It doesn't look good,' Ari Thór said.

'You two go home and get some sleep. We'll meet in the morning and go over everything again. Ari Thór, you keep an eye open for anything to do with the Dramatic Society, just in case. Maybe you ought to have a word with Pálmi tomorrow if you get a chance. He knew Hrólfur well and he'd know if there's any aspect of this we ought to look into.'

Ari Thór nodded.

'I found her phone,' he said. 'I haven't had a chance to find out what number she was using.' He showed Tómas the red mobile. 'All right if I use it to call my phone?'

Tómas nodded his agreement.

Ari Thór pulled on gloves and punched in a number.

His phone began to ring. He picked it up.

'I think I recognise the number,' he said. 'I think it was her who called me.'

Tómas frowned, he didn't understand the connection. 'Called you?'

'Yes, on Christmas Eve.'

'The prankster?' Tómas's stomach flipped over, as he suddenly realised what Ari Thór was implying.

'Maybe it wasn't a prank.'

'Look it up,' Tómas instructed.

'Right away,' Ari Thór said and went to the computer. He came back a moment later. 'Same number.'

Tómas took a deep breath. Had he made a mistake? He had

assured Ari Thór that it wasn't anything to worry about, just someone playing a joke on the police.

'I think we'll have to keep Karl here overnight,' Tómas said decisively. 'The plot thickens by the minute. Of course he'll want to go to Reykjavík with the emergency flight, but in light of what you've just shown me, I don't think we can release him right away. First the assault on Linda and now this damned phone call. Let's see if he makes a clean breast of it in the morning.'

Tómas tried to sound confident, but privately felt certain that Karl would do no such thing.

||||||||||||||

It was a perfectly ordinary kiss; gentle, soft, short and pleasurable. Ari Thór sat stunned for a few seconds, the taste of the kiss on his lips, delighting in the moment. He sat still and thought of Kristín. What the hell had he done?

Had he really done anything? He sat motionless, tired after the long day, his shoulder still sore. He had only meant to stop by for a coffee or a cup of tea and a pastry after a tough day.

It wasn't his fault. She had kissed him. *She* had kissed *him*. He didn't even get a chance to voice an opinion on the matter.

Kristín would go wild if she found out.

Ugla had sent him a message as he was walking home from the station, asking after Linda. He had called her and she invited him to drop by for a coffee. *No, I mean tea*, she corrected herself with a good-natured laugh. The pain in his shoulder was obvious, so she offered to massage it for him. He said yes, which of course he shouldn't have. He shouldn't have agreed to drop by at all.

Then she had kissed him, and he didn't return the kiss, only stood up clumsily. He didn't say a word about Kristín, just said that he had to go. Ugla stared at him in astonishment and disappointment, but didn't say a word.

He had felt guilty all the way home; guilt over the kiss, and also for having discussed Linda's and Hrólfur's cases with Ugla. He was painfully aware that Ugla was, strictly speaking, a potential witness, and might even be seen as a suspect, if it was indeed a genuine investigation. He wasn't sure that it was. On the other hand, she had been extremely helpful, telling him about the argument between Úlfur and Hrólfur, and this time she had mentioned that it might be worthwhile paying a visit to a lady called Sandra at the old people's home. Sandra was in her nineties, as strong as a horse, relatively speaking, and had known Hrólfur longer than most people. He had made a habit of visiting her once a week, Ugla said.

Ari Thór tried to convince himself that Ugla's information was enough to balance out the fact that he'd disclosed and discussed official business with someone outside the investigation.

But he didn't try to use the same logic to justify the kiss.

He went to sleep, not sure whether Ugla or Kristín would feature in his dreams.

27

SIGLUFJÖRDUR: THURSDAY, 15TH JANUARY 2009

He was at the pool, deep below the surface with the warm water coursing around him, a little breath left in him and a few more strokes to go. Two more, then one more. He had to breathe, fill his lungs with air, get up to the surface. He swam upwards, higher and higher, his eyes and face emerging to see snow everywhere, thick, heavy snowflakes that peppered his face, filling everything, snatching the oxygen from him; he could find no refuge, nowhere to take a breath. He had to dive back down. Back down deep into the pool, with no air in his lungs and the water smothering him. Up again, still snow and no air. He jerked upright, felt for a moment that he was unable to breathe in bed, could see nothing out of the snow-caked window. And, at last, a little oxygen. His heartbeat slowed and he breathed steadily as the increasingly familiar nightmare faded away.

It had snowed heavily in the night. Ari Thór had overslept

and it was already half-past nine. He skipped breakfast and hurried to the station.

Tómas and Hlynur were there before him.

'Just as well the Reverend shows up at last,' Hlynur said with a smile. 'Tómas has been here all night, looking after our guest.'

Tómas was clearly in no mood for joking, even though the joke had been at the new boy's expense. His tone was serious: 'We're going to have to release him. He's not going to do her any harm now that she's been taken to Reykjavík. The flight finally went last night. No change to her condition. The whole thing is inexplicable. There's every indication that he had subjected her to violence and threats, but he has witnesses who confirm that he simply could *not* have assaulted her unless he was in two places at once.' Tómas leaned dangerously far back in his chair. 'We'll have to release him,' he repeated and it was clear that this was far from being to his liking. 'I asked him to stay in town, otherwise I'd be looking for custody. He agreed to stay, but if Linda's condition worsens he said he'd want to go south. Truth is, he'd struggle to get to Reykjavík at the moment. The roads are terrible, practically impassable.' Tómas paused and mopped his head, his frustration evident, before continuing. 'I went to see the lad this morning, the little boy who found Linda. Nothing new there. I've seen better witnesses. He's just a little boy, after all.'

'Shouldn't we be on our way?' Hlynur asked.

Tómas stood up and turned to face Ari Thór. 'I'm going with Hlynur to check the flat. We need to take another look around. I think we also need to consider the possibility that Hrólfur's death wasn't accidental, open up a formal investigation but keep it low-profile – can you start working on that?'

Hlynur grinned and preened a little, obviously happy to be working on the more prestigious case.

Being asked to play in the sandbox while the adults deal with the real case, Ari Thór thought to himself. Although he still believed that Hrólfur's death might not have been accidental, there was no denying that Linda's case was more important at the moment.

'No problem.'

Tómas placed a hand on Ari Thór's shoulder.

Hell. His shoulder wasn't getting any better.

Tómas accompanied him to the door and spoke in a low tone so that Hlynur would not overhear. 'That call . . . on Christmas Eve, we did the right thing, don't you think? We agreed, didn't we?'

Ari Thór clearly recalled just how unnerving that call had been, the whispered voice . . . When he called back, the person, whom he now believed to be Linda, had said that there was nothing to worry about. But, all the same . . .

'Yes, of course.'

Really?

'There was nothing we could do,' Ari Thór added. And what could they have done? The number had been unregistered, and there was no way of finding out who the caller might have been.

There was nothing we could do.

When Tómas and Hlynur had gone, Ari Thór took the opportunity to check the webcam showing the Town Hall Square, watching someone walking across the snow-filled square towards the Town Hall, in real time. It was difficult to identify who it might be on the little computer screen so it wasn't likely that the webcam would be much help to them, even if there were any recordings from Friday evening. He found the number of the webcam's owner.

'Sorry to bother you, my name is Ari Thór, I'm calling from the police.' He tried to be formal and courteous.

'Yes, the new guy, right?' The owner of the webcam was a local man whom Ari Thór had heard of yet never met.

'I was wondering, your webcam . . . ?'

'Yes, what about it?' the guy replied rather grumpily.

'Is it possible to get access to past recordings?'

'From my webcam?' The guy laughed heartily. 'Do you think I run some sort of surveillance operation? Nothing is recorded, it's just a live feed from the square. Why do you ask? Is it about Linda, the attack?'

'Sorry, can't really comment. Thanks for the help.'

A frustrating dead end. He would really have liked to show Tómas some progress. If only he could call Ugla and get more background information on the theatre group. But that was hardly possible at this point. Since the kiss he had heard nothing from her. That was no surprise considering how quickly he hurried off that night, almost as if he had been bitten rather than kissed. The next piano lesson was on Sunday. Should he turn up as if nothing had happened? How should this relationship be allowed to develop? Kristín was in Reykjavík and he mustn't forget that or let the distance blur his thinking. It was almost a week since he had spoken properly to her. He always assumed that she would call, that she wasn't as busy as he was. And now, after that kiss, how could he speak to her? He had crossed a line, inadvertently perhaps. The kiss wasn't just a kiss out of the blue, he knew that he had been flirting with Ugla, that he had kept his relationship with Kristín hidden from her. And, worst of all, he thought he might be developing feelings for Ugla . . . No, he wasn't prepared to call either Ugla or Kristín at this moment.

He would have to start by approaching other members of the Dramatic Society, starting with the playwright, Pálmi.

|||||||||||||

Pálmi lived in a smart detached house off Hvanneyrarbraut that was probably too big for a single man and too small for a family. He was smartly turned out, in a checked shirt and grey flannel trousers. He seemed surprised to see Ari Thór.

'Good morning, Pálmi. Mind if I come in?'

'What? Yes, but why? I have visitors. Can't it wait?'

Ari Thór avoided the question and nodded towards the interior of the house. He had been given an assignment and intended to carry it out conscientiously.

'This won't take long,' he said with one foot inside the door and a smile on his face. 'We're speaking to everyone who was at the rehearsal on Friday evening.'

Pálmi appeared to be taken by surprise. 'Oh? Why's that?'

'Nothing serious. Just some loose ends that need to be tied up so we can close the case.'

A little white lie there.

'Come inside, then.'

'I'm sorry for intruding.' Ari Thór looked around. 'You have guests, you said?'

'Yes. They're staying in the flat in the basement.'

'I see. Out-of-towners?' Ari Thór asked, speaking as if he wasn't a newcomer himself, but not sure he sounded convincing.

'Yes . . .' Pálmi said uncertainly, as if wondering how much information to share with the young police officer. 'An old friend of my father's, from Denmark. She's visiting with her son. A pilgrimage to Iceland.'

'Your father lived in Denmark?'

A little chat didn't do any harm and it had worked with Leifur. Pálmi appeared ill at ease and it was probably best to tread carefully if he was going to get him to reveal any secrets regarding Hrólfur and that fateful night.

Pálmi looked visibly more relaxed. 'That's right. He moved there when I was very small. I don't remember him.'

They were now seated in the living room, Pálmi on the sofa and Ari Thór in a matching armchair, both upholstered in eighties-style shiny brown leather and remarkably underused, given their age. In fact, the whole room looked like an advertisement from an old furniture catalogue with little that bore witness to the owner's own taste, other than the paintings on the walls. On the walls of Ari Thór's flat, which he shared with Kristín on Öldugata, and which now seemed so far away, there was just one painting. Inherited from his grandmother, it was a magnificent original by the Icelandic master, Kjarval. He recognised the artist's brushwork in four of the canvases on Pálmi's walls.

'That's a fine art collection.'

'Thank you. It's hardly a collection, just a few works.'

'Good all the same. I have a Kjarval myself. Are these heirlooms?'

'No, I collected them myself. I put my savings into the house and art over the years. I'm not one for trusting banks.'

'Quite right, considering what's been happening.'

'Well, there's that, of course, but I've never trusted them –

something inspired by my mother. She was the type who preferred to keep her savings under the bed, although she died without much to show for it. Maybe that's not the ideal way to hang on to your pennies.' He smiled and the atmosphere lightened.

'I wanted to talk to you about Hrólfur. You knew him well, didn't you?'

'Yes, pretty well. But he tended to keep people at arm's length.'

Ari Thór decided to go straight to the heart of the matter. 'Do you know of anyone who might have had a reason to, well, push him down the stairs?'

Pálmi looked up, clearly surprised by the question.

'What? You don't think that someone might have pushed him?'

'Actually, no. But it's a little too coincidental that Linda should be assaulted only a few days afterwards. It's given us reason to look more closely into the fatal incident at the Dramatic Society. I understand that he and Úlfur were at loggerheads?'

'No, I wouldn't go that far, but they weren't always in agreement,' said Pálmi, biting his lip. 'There's an artistic temperament there, but they normally parted on good terms.'

'Were you up in the balcony that evening?'

'I went up there a couple of times. Most of the time I was watching from the auditorium.'

'And you came home in the dinner break?'

'Yes. I needed to make some changes to the script, so I came straight here.'

'Did anyone see you?'

'What do you mean?'

'Is there anyone who could confirm that?'

'Well, no.'

'How about your visitors?'

'No, as I said they're using the basement flat. I didn't see them during the dinner break.'

'Did you and Hrólfur meet often?'

'Not often. But occasionally he would invite Úlfur and me for coffee, or a glass of red wine. He kept a magnificent wine cellar.'

'Expensive?' Ari Thór felt like he was clutching at straws, looking for a motive – but it was better to leave no stone unturned.

'Quite.'

'Do you have any idea what will happen to that wine now?'

'The wine?'

'Who inherits it?'

'I have no idea. To tell the truth, I don't know any of his relatives, or even if he had any living.'

'Had he made a will?"

'Not that he ever mentioned to me,' Pálmi said, with apparent sincerity.

'Who did he speak to or see regularly in the town, apart from you and Úlfur?'

Pálmi paused, lost for a moment in his thoughts. 'Hmm. He used to visit an old lady called Sandra every week.'

Sandra. Ari Thór recalled that Ugla had also mentioned her, suggested that he visit her.

'She's been in the old people's home these last few years. She's not as strong as she used to be, although she's as sharp as a knife. I think she must be ninety-five, bless her.' Pálmi paused for a moment. 'Then there's the girl.'

'Girl?'

'Yes. Ugla.'

Ari Thór felt his pulse quicken. He tried not to catch Pálmi's eye, fearing that he might give himself away.

'Ugla. Yes, of course.' He knew he would have to pursue this line of questioning to counter any suspicions that he knew Ugla better than might be thought appropriate. 'Did they meet often?'

'So I gather. She rented his basement but she continued to visit him after she moved out. Now she lives . . .' Pálmi thought. 'Yes, on Nordurgata, I think.'

'That's right,' Ari Thór said without thinking.

Damn.

Pálmi didn't seem to have noticed his slip, and it was obvious that he wanted to get rid of Ari Thór as quickly as possible.

There was a faint knock on the door and a very old lady appeared, accompanied by a tall man with a full beard, in his sixties, Ari Thór guessed.

These had to be the guests from Denmark. Pálmi switched to Danish to introduce them. 'Rosa and her son Mads. Ari Thór is from the police.'

Ari Thór stood up to shake their hands and spoke in English, not daring to try his Danish. He had taken Danish at school for many years, but had a hard time speaking it, although he could read it with little effort. The old lady spoke for both of them and her English was excellent although heavily accented. Mads stood behind her in silence.

'What has Pálmi done?' she asked curiously and looked deep into Ari Thór's eyes with a warm smile.

Ari Thór smiled. 'Nothing. Not a thing. We're investigating the death of the author Hrólfur Kristjánsson. He lost his life in an accident at the Dramatic Society's rehearsal.'

'I had heard that. Pálmi told us. We had intended to go to the theatre at the weekend,' she said. 'I met Hrólfur in Copenhagen many years ago. They were friends, Hrólfur and your father, weren't they?' she asked, looking at Pálmi.

'Acquaintances,' Pálmi replied. 'They were in Denmark at much the same time.'

This time the old lady's words were directed at Ari Thór.

'He was a handsome young man, that Hrólfur, if I recall correctly. He spent a lot of time with Páll, Pálmi's father, when he was on his deathbed. I don't think Páll knew many people in Denmark and it can be lonely on your own in a strange country.' She looked at Pálmi. 'I hope I was able to make your father's life easier in the months we had together.' She smiled. 'I met Hrólfur at the hospital. I hadn't seen Páll for a few months as I'd had to go to the country to work with my family. I hurried back when I heard that he had been taken ill, and by the time I made it there he was pretty far gone. I didn't even have the heart to say goodbye. It would have been too difficult for both of us.' A tear ran down one wrinkled cheek.

'Are you treating this as . . . as a murder investigation?' Pálmi asked, switching to Icelandic.

'We are.' Ari Thór was there on Tómas's authority, in the pursuit of his duties, so it seemed the most straightforward answer.

Pálmi stood in thought, seemingly unsure of whether or not

he should add anything. Then, with a fleeting look of guilt in his eyes, as if he were about to reveal some terrible secret, he said, 'There's maybe one more thing you ought to know.' He paused and the silence was heavy with expectation, which even Rosa seemed to sense, in spite of the language barrier.

Mads stood still, an uninterested look on his face, as he inspected one of the Kjarval paintings.

'I heard it said that Hrólfur had a child, out of wedlock, of course. He never married, but there was a child born after he returned from Denmark, maybe during the war or possibly later. That's something to look into.'

28

SIGLUFJÖRDUR: FRIDAY, 16TH JANUARY 2009

'Sweet Brother Jesus' echoed through the common room, where those senior citizens at the old people's home who were in robust enough health had come together for the morning gathering. Some joined in wholeheartedly, while others appeared more inclined to take it easy and watch. Ari Thór recognised the young woman who led the singing, remembering her from the theology faculty at the university in Reykjavík; he knew the face but didn't know her well enough to speak to. So they had both moved north to Siglufjördur? She was presumably in training for the priesthood while he had given up.

The previous day had been quiet. The knife from Karl and Linda's flat had been sent south for examination. Ari Thór was still in the process of digging for information that could shed some light on Hrólfur's death, and had stunned Tómas with the news that Hrólfur might have had a child.

Ari Thór stood in the doorway and watched the singing. The

nurse he had spoken to had said there was no reason he couldn't speak to Sandra, but asked him to avoid interrupting the morning gathering. She pointed out an old woman in a wheelchair with a crocheted blanket over her knees, singing with feeling.

Ari Thór hadn't enrolled in theology because of his strong faith or beliefs, the exact opposite really – maybe more to try to regain his faith, or simply to find a purpose in life. He felt a need to find answers to questions which philosophy – the subject he had previously given up on – could not supply. Or maybe he had simply tried to pick a path as different as possible to his late father's, who had been an accountant. Plato or God – anything but Mammon. When it became apparent that theology wasn't providing him with any real answers, Ari Thór had still persevered, stubbornly trying to convince himself that he could finish his studies without any faith at all.

Ari Thór could pinpoint the time that he lost any faith he might have had – it was at the age of thirteen, on the day his father disappeared, and was confirmed later that same year, when he was told of his mother's death in a road accident.

His theology studies had done nothing to move him closer to the Almighty. The academic debates, the often-bloody history of the church and of religion in general had all helped to reinforce his belief that nobody was watching over him or looking out for him. As he had for much of his life, Ari Thór felt very much alone.

The singing continued, this time a tune that was familiar from Sunday school many years ago. Would it be his fate to be forced to sing hymns again when he was shipped off to a home in his old age? Would he have to sing hymns without a shred of belief in the words?

Ari Thór's former fellow student led a short prayer and announced in ringing tones that coffee was ready for those who wanted it.

Sandra had a cup in her hand as Ari Thór introduced himself in a clear, loud voice.

'Don't talk so loudly, dear boy. I can hear perfectly well. It's my feet that are the problem,' she said and smiled at him. She had a finely chiselled face and a soft voice, speaking clearly and gently. She sipped her coffee delicately.

Ari Thór looked around for a spare chair.

'We don't have to sit here, you know. I have a room of my own along the corridor. Can you push?'

He steered the wheelchair slowly.

'How old are you, dear boy?'

'Twenty-five,' he said, adding, 'later this year.' It felt wrong to tell the old lady a lie, even if it was just a white one.

Her room was furnished with a drab bed, old chest of drawers and a stool. A few pictures stood on the top of the chest of drawers, some in colour, others faded and old.

'My late husband,' she said pointing to a black-and-white photograph. 'Children and grandchildren in the other pictures. I've been very lucky over the years.' She gave him a thin, understanding smile.

Ari Thór perched on the stool by the bed. 'Should I ask someone to help you onto the bed?'

'Good grief, no. I'll sit here as long as I can with my handsome young visitor.'

Ari Thór gave her a polite smile, anxious to get down to business.

'How are the roads?' she asked. 'You didn't have any trouble walking up here?'

'I drove here,' Ari Thór said. 'In the police jeep.'

'Tell me something,' she said, looking straight into his eyes with a serious expression on her face. 'Why does everyone in the town now have to have a big jeep? I don't understand it. In the old days people didn't have these huge cars. Hardly anyone even *had* a car, and we managed well enough.'

'Hmm. I suppose people want to be able to leave town, even if there's snow on the roads.'

'What for?'

'What do you mean?'

'What do they need to leave town for?'

He had no suitable reply to this question.

'You've come to ask me about Hrólfur?' she asked eventually.

Ari Thór nodded.

'I thought as much, dear boy. The poor old fellow. He didn't have many friends. Maybe I was his closest friend, these last few years.'

'Did he visit you often?'

'Every week at the same time. He lived not far from here – on Hólavegur, a decent walk for him.'

'What sort of a man was he?'

'Why do you ask?' She looked at him with suspicion dawning in her eyes. 'It was definitely an accident, wasn't it?'

'That's what we're investigating. I don't expect it to have been anything other than an accident, but we have to make sure.'

'Hadn't he . . . well . . . had the old fellow had a drink?'

She had guessed shrewdly. Ari Thór decided there was no

point hiding it from her. 'Yes, he appears to have drunk a small amount.'

'A small amount. Yes, well . . . Hrólfur was a complex man, I can tell you, and I could never fully understand him. I remember him from the old days, before he left Siglufjördur. Then he became this world-famous author and that went to his head. There was so much ambition there, a determination to stand out from the crowd and see the world, and that's just what he did. He travelled a lot after his book had been published.' Her tired eyes closed as she rested for a moment. 'Then he came home again. People always return home, don't they? By then he was better known here than in the south. Have you read the book?'

'Actually, no. I have a copy that has been lent to me.'

'Then read it. You won't regret it,' she said. 'Anyway, you're not a local boy, so what did you move up here for? There's no herring anymore.'

'I was offered a job here.'

'Talking to old women in rest homes about dead authors . . . is that exciting? You should have been here when there was herring. Those were the days, I can tell you. I started work in the herring when I was thirteen; salting herring was what I did. My children started even younger – the youngest was eight when she started salting. That wouldn't be allowed today, would it? It was like an adventure when the herring came, and it was a nightmare when it didn't.'

There was a faraway look on her face and her gaze was no longer on Ari Thór but on the past; it was as if the old Herring Waltz had started playing in the background.

'I was twenty minutes salting a barrel of herring when I was at my fastest, just twenty minutes. There were plenty of people

who were envious of that. I was worth something back then.'
She smiled. 'You should have seen the boats as they were coming
in, loaded to the gunwales, so full of herring that they were only
just afloat. That was a wonderful sight. Have you been up to the
mountain, Hvanneyrarskál?'

Ari Thór shook his head, relieved that she fixed her eyes on
him again, after being lost in memories of the herring boom all
those years ago.

'I've heard the songs about it,' he said sheepishly, regretting
not having found the time to go there himself.

'Go up there in the summer. Plenty of romantic adventures
started up there.'

He nodded dutifully. 'Tell me, about Hrólfur . . .'

'Of course. I'm sorry, my boy. I forgot myself completely
there.'

'That's all right.' He smiled. 'Tell me if there's any reason you
can think of that someone could have wanted to push Hrólfur
down the stairs? Did anyone hold a grudge against him?'

'Yes and no. I can't imagine that anyone wanted to do him
harm, although there were plenty of people he didn't get on
with. There was an arrogance about him and he could be awkward when he had been drinking, he wanted everything to be
done his way. I can well imagine that he was pretty overbear-
ing as the chairman of the Dramatic Society,' she said, and
hesitated. 'Please excuse me for speaking ill of the dead. But I
do want to help, if it's the case that someone may have pushed
him.'

'Understood,' Ari Thór said, falling quiet again to give her
an opportunity to continue.

'Actually . . . there's one thing that could be important. He mentioned to me before Christmas that he was on the track of some secret. I think that's how he worded it – "some secret". Some members of the Dramatic Society were keeping something from him. He grinned when he told me and it sounded like he was delighted that he had unearthed this secret. He had eyes like a hawk, the old boy.'

'A secret?'

'That's it, a secret,' she said, her voice dropping almost to a whisper.

'Do you have any idea of what this secret was?'

'Not exactly. But I gathered from him that it was . . . that it could be something . . .' she said, winking. 'If you get my meaning.'

'Something romantic? Adulterous?'

'That's the impression I got, or something along those lines.'

Ari Thór made rapid notes. There might be something in what the old lady had to say.

'Do you know if he made a will?'

'It's not something he ever mentioned to me. But he should have made one. I don't know that he has any close living relatives, just distant cousins, but I do know that he will have left quite a number of worldly goods behind. Not like me – all I have left is this old chest.' She laughed, and gestured towards an old wooden casket, the wood discoloured and polished smooth with use, probably dating back to a period before Sandra had even been born.

'It's my understanding that there might be a child.'

'A child?' She squinted as she peered at him in amazement.

'Yes, it's been suggested that Hrólfur fathered a child after the war.'

'Good heavens, that's a story I've never heard. Where did you get that from?'

'From Pálmi, Pálmi Pálsson.'

'I know him, of course. He and Hrólfur were good friends, so maybe it's something they talked about. I have to say it's a revelation to me. But that's life, it keeps taking you by surprise. The poor old fellow.'

'Hrólfur?'

'No. Pálmi. He lost his father so young, a real tragedy. His father was a special character, very artistic, and struggled to put down any roots. He left his wife and young son to go to Copenhagen, but then he caught tuberculosis and died. I have a suspicion that he got to know a few ladies before he met his end. He wasn't the type not to stray.' Again, Sandra winked suggestively.

'An old friend of his from Denmark is staying with Pálmi at the moment.'

'You don't say?' Sandra said. 'Pálmi has done well enough for himself, the dear boy. His mother died far too young, only sixty-five or sixty-six; a stroke,' she said and asked suddenly, 'You eat herring?'

'Well . . . no.'

'Those were good years,' she said, and the distant look was back. 'And in the old days people certainly knew how to cook it.'

She smiled as her eyes focused somewhere in the past, and Ari Thór waited patiently.

'Those were good years,' she repeated. 'I always have this, just in case,' she said, and reached for a book from the chest of drawers. It was an old notebook, creased and much used. 'We didn't buy recipe books in the old days. There were no pennies to waste then. This is where I wrote down my recipes.' She handled the book as if it were precious, and opened it at the middle. 'See, my boy? These are herring recipes. Food fit for a king.'

Ari Thór peered with difficulty at the small, careful handwriting.

'Tell me. What happened to Linda? How is she?' Sandra asked, as she laid the book in her lap.

'Did you . . . ?' He stumbled and started again. 'Do you know her?'

'I know who she is. She works at the hospital. A lovely girl, but I can tell you there's always some kind of sadness in her eyes.'

'She's in intensive care in Reykjavík. She's still unconscious.'

'I heard you arrested Karl.'

'No, that's not right. We needed to speak to him as he was the one who found Linda after the assault.'

'He's innocent. I'm sure of that.'

'Really?'

'Such a sweet boy.'

'You know him well?'

'I knew him well in the old days, before his parents decided to move to Denmark. I often used to meet him in the Co-op when I was working there. He came across so well, and I have no doubt he still does. He was working for Pálmi's mother then, helping her with housework for pocket money. He did anything, whatever she needed doing – went shopping for her, fixed things around the house, even turned himself into a rat catcher when needed; whatever. A lovely boy.'

We'll see about that.

Ari Thór just smiled, keeping quiet about a terrified Linda

having called the police on Christmas Eve; keeping quiet about the rows and the bruises.

'Did Hrólfur have any other friends? Close friends, I mean?'

'He always spoke highly of Úlfur and said he enjoyed a good argument with him, said there was some real character there. But he also said that Úlfur ought to stick to directing and tear up that play of his.'

'Play?'

'Yes, play. He supposedly wrote a play,' she said with a smile, and then a yawn. 'Well, my boy. I'm starting to get tired.' She sipped her coffee, which had to be cold by now. 'That'll do for now, won't it? Come back and see me again another time.'

Ari Thór looked over at the elderly woman, her eyes starting to close as her head tipped back in her seat. His heart was beating quickly. There was certainly more to the Hrólfur story than met the eye.

29

SIGLUFJÖRDUR: SATURDAY, 17TH JANUARY 2009

Saturday was another day of relentless snow. It formed icy crags in gardens and the knee-high drifts in the town made it almost impossible to navigate the streets without wading.

Ari Thór felt that the snow had given the town a cosy feel in the weeks leading up to Christmas, almost a holiday atmosphere, while in Reykjavík December was normally a month of rain. But now this endless snow was becoming oppressive. Granted, it did lighten up the darkest period of the year in this northerly fjord, but it made everything difficult. Even the police 4×4 sometimes struggled in the streets, and walking around would guarantee wet shoes, wet socks and wet trousers.

Ari Thór stood outside Siglufjördur's imposing church with Tómas and Hlynur, who were both on duty that weekend. At the station they had talked over his interview with Sandra, with plenty of speculation over what Hrólfur's secret might be, but no conclusions. Ari Thór was not in uniform, but wore a suit as a mark of respect for Hrólfur, a man he had never met. Sandra had hit the nail on the head when she described him as a complex man. He had reached respectable heights in his own career, but refused to fade away when his fame dwindled. He had friends and acquaintances, as well as those who envied him. He had been an awkward customer when the mood took him, but could be a kindly and amiable personality on other occasions. His relationship with Ugla was case in point.

Ugla.

Ari Thór thought of the book he had borrowed. He would have to take a look at it soon; it might give him a little insight into the dead author's thoughts.

They sat on an empty pew in the centre of the church. Once inside, the church seemed small compared to its towering height. It was a peaceful place with its stained glass windows, a shelter from the snow. Ari Thór had bumped into Ugla outside; they had exchanged glances but no words. Since the kiss they had not spoken, and it continued to worry him.

He had slept badly, struggling to nod off. Now he was careful always to lock the outside door. Nobody had admitted to the break-in and Tómas had pushed it to one side while they were concentrating all their efforts on Linda and Karl. But Ari Thór always felt a twinge of trepidation as he closed his eyes; the horror of waking up to find someone in his house meant that he felt far from safe there. The nightmares, the panic attacks that he had been experiencing before the intruder had visited, became darker and longer. At work he felt the effects of the lack of sleep, but still gave it everything he had. On top of it all, he was worried that his relationship with Kristín seemed to be gradually fading away. Although they had been together a relatively short time, he had been sure she was the one, and in a way he still felt the same, but his attraction to Ugla was confusing.

The church was gradually filling with people, many of them now familiar faces. Úlfur and Pálmi both sat on the front pew with the other pallbearers. Leifur was near the front, clearly alone and his mind on other things, as if he were wishing he could be somewhere else; working, maybe, anywhere but at a funeral.

Karl sat two rows in front of Ari Thór, next to Anna. Ari Thór wondered if he should try and speak to her at the reception after the funeral; he intended to speak to everyone who had been at the rehearsal, but it was taking longer than anticipated to fit it all in.

Jealous. That was how Ugla had described Anna, jealous at having missed out on the lead role. Ari Thór reminded himself that he was apt to treat everything Ugla said as completely truthful, and wondered if he ought to doubt some of what she had to say, or simply be thankful that he had access to an insider at the Dramatic Society – someone whose word he felt he could trust.

The church was practically full when the service began. It was possible that not everyone present had known the author personally, but his unexpected death had gone some way to breathing new life into his reputation, a reminder of his past fame. Everyone who was anyone was among the congregation. Ari Thór had heard that two former government ministers had meant to attend to pay Hrólfur their respects, but they had not made it. Travel was still treacherous, and the road into Siglufjördur was nearly impassable, with a blizzard raging on the high ground above the town.

The funeral service was formal – Icelandic folk songs blending with classics, while there was a reading from *Verses for Linda*. The magnificent altarpiece by Gunnlaugur Blöndal, of Jesus appearing to sailors in peril on treacherous waters, made a poignant backdrop, a reminder of Siglufjördur's losses over the years and the proximity of the merciless sea. The requiem was dramatic, but Ari Thór was not able to see any evidence of tears. Hrólfur may have been respected by many, he thought, but missed by few. The question was, had he been really hated by anyone?

||||||||||||

Life hadn't been easy for Nína Arnardóttir. For reasons she could never understand, she had never managed to march in time with her contemporaries, or perhaps they had been out of tune with her. Now she had more or less missed the bus, the years had swept past her, leaving her alone in this dark little flat. She often wondered why she had never pushed herself forward and taken life by the scruff of the neck – built relationships, had a family, lived like other people lived, surrounded by others. She had fallen in love once, only once, and it was a pure love. The man, who was older than she was, had rejected her, had very kindly, warmly, said that it wasn't meant to be, but that he still felt affection towards her. She had really only loved him more after that, but never acted on it again – and she never really opened up her heart again, either; never gave herself the chance to fall in love for the second time. And now she just spent her days at home in the dark and read by the light of the lamp or watched the television. The years had passed in a tedium of routine existence, and suddenly she was sixty.

At the moment she was without a proper job, living in social housing and relying on benefits for her entire income, while doing voluntary work for the Dramatic Society. That was easy and convenient, simple enough to look after the ticket sales and the occasional odd job. Being part of a crowd wasn't something she had ever been comfortable with, but she was prepared to put up with the people for the chance to be part of the Dramatic Society.

Nína was robustly built, stout and big-boned. She was well aware that advancing age hadn't robbed her of her strength. In her youth her physique had made her the butt of numerous jokes at school. But in spite of her physical strength, she had never fought back when her stepfather raised a hand to her, never daring to do anything other than cover her head and take the blows as they came. It was worse when he stopped beating her; that was when she began to feel real fear. Sometimes he'd leave, or lie on the sofa and pass out in a drunken stupor. Sometimes he would be quieter, and instead of the rain of blows there would be groping hands. Then she would close her eyes and disappear into her own darkness. Those were the years when she had always felt best in the dark, under the bed or in the wardrobe, where she could be in peace. That was where she went when she heard him, learning to recognise the smell of booze and the clink of bottle and glass. She developed an instinct, knowing within seconds when she needed to flee, hide herself away. She knew that the other children at school played hide-and-seek, but never for the same high stakes. When she had grown up she could never understand why nobody had ever come to her aid. Why had her mother, a victim herself, ignored the violence that took place? Nína had once tried to complain about him, but her mother had looked the other way and said it was bad to tell lies about people. After that she never again broached the subject.

It puzzled her still that the teachers never said anything when she turned up at school with bruises. Did they really believe she had just 'fallen over' yet again? Why did nobody lend a hand or even notice when she stopped wanting to speak to any of the other pupils, withdrawing deeper into her dark, lonely little world?

Instead, her teachers repeatedly reported she had a problem with concentration, suggesting that she couldn't learn. She did poorly in exams. For a long time, indoctrinated by her teachers' beliefs, she believed that she didn't have an intellect suited for study. Her fear of books grew, and it soon became clear that college would be out of the question, as would any thoughts of university. Her teenage years were the toughest, staying in Siglufjördur and watching her contemporaries disappearing – some to Akureyri and some to Reykjavík, off to exciting futures. She spent long hours alone in her room, in the dark, even when *he* was finally dead, courtesy of the bottle.

Eventually her mother gave way under the pressure, the strain of seeing her daughter spending wordless hours alone in the dark. Nína was placed in an institution in Reykjavík and those two sequestered years remained a blur. She recalled the identical days melding into one, without a single visit from her mother. But when she finally came home to Siglufjördur, Nína didn't ask her why she never visited. She discovered that her mother had explained her absence by saying that she had been with relatives in the south for those two years. Nína never knew if anyone in the town found out the truth, and she didn't really care.

After this terrible upbringing she never thought she could find true love, but when it presented itself, she clung to it, even after the object of her affection had gently dismissed her approaches. She kept loving him from afar, staying close. Loving him.

|||||||||||||

'There have been some stories about Nína,' Tómas said to Ari Thór before the funeral. 'Try and talk to her at the reception. She disappeared for a couple of years when she was quite young, sent to Reykjavík. I recall my mother and her friends talking about it at the time. Her father was a heavy drinker and she was always very introverted.'

Ari Thór wondered what tales would be told of the Reverend Ari Thór once he had moved away. Or were there stories already being told? Gossip about him and Ugla? He would presumably be the last one to hear it.

Nína sat at a table in the upstairs hall of the church, enjoying traditional twisted doughnuts with a glass of orange juice. She was looking across the hall at Pálmi and Úlfur, who stood together in conversation. She was startled as Ari Thór came and sat by her side.

'Looks like it's slippery underfoot,' he said, pointing at Nína's right foot, which was in plaster.

She looked back at him solemnly. 'There's ice on the ground,' she agreed.

'It pays to tread carefully,' he said cheerfully, unwilling to jump straight in with questions about Hrólfur. He cast his gaze around the assembled guests. Nobody would be going home hungry, as the tables groaned under the weight of cakes, dough-nuts and pancakes.

She didn't comment, but looked at the assembled people in the hall.

'Did you speak to Hrólfur often?'

'What? No. He'd spit out orders now and again. That was about it,' she replied, obviously uncomfortable with the thought of speaking ill of the deceased right after his funeral.

'He liked to give the orders?'

'Yes. He could be difficult with some people. Not everyone. Either he liked you or he didn't,' she said.

He took it as a simple statement of fact, considered and with-out any regret or bitterness. 'Do you think he liked you?'

'I don't think he had an opinion. It doesn't matter now, does it?'

It was clear that she wasn't expecting a reply.

'I gather that Hrólfur was curious. Could he have come across something that he ought not to have heard about? Maybe to do with someone at the Dramatic Society?'

'Someone who might then have pushed him down the stairs?'

Her directness took Ari Thór by surprise, although it made a pleasant change. She appeared to be the first person he had spoken to in connection with Hrólfur's death who didn't have something to hide, apart from Ugla, of course. Ugla wouldn't hide anything from him, even though he hadn't been as open with her as he could have been.

He hadn't mentioned Kristín.

Ugla was seated at the next table, by Leifur. He shot a quick glance in her direction, ensuring she wouldn't see him looking. Her eyes looked puffy, as if she had been crying. Maybe Ari

Thór's assessment that there had been no tears for the old man had been wrong.

'Yes. Maybe,' he answered, pulling his thoughts back to Nína and the case.

'No. To be quite honest, no. I think he got on people's nerves but I can't imagine that anyone would have wanted to do him harm,' Nína said. She still hadn't answered his question about Hrólfur having come across some information he shouldn't have, secrets at the Dramatic Society, so Ari Thór repeated his question.

She thought for a moment, as if weighing her thoughts. 'No,' she answered shortly, and looked across the hall to where Pálmi and Úlfur stood, as if she would prefer to be talking to them. Her eyes were blank and her face expressionless.

He stood up and thanked her for chatting.

Tómas and Hlynur were talking to people he didn't recognise. Everyone here knew everyone else and he felt like a gate-crasher; maybe that wasn't far from the truth? He hadn't even known the deceased.

He looked around, hoping for a chance to speak to Anna, but she was nowhere to be seen – and neither was Karl.

30

SIGLUFJÖRDUR: SATURDAY, 17TH JANUARY 2009

The black jacket didn't suit her, so she had taken it off, along with her T-shirt, by the bed in the basement flat. She glanced at the window to make sure the curtains were drawn – not that it mattered in this blizzard – and peeled off her trousers. Black wasn't her colour.

As so often before, they had gone to her place. Little could be seen through the falling snow, which provided cover for them. Siglufjördur wasn't the most convenient place to carry on an affair and caution was everything. On the other hand, she didn't have experience of adultery in a larger place, but she imagined that it would be a lot easier. Here, everything had to happen under cover of darkness, and even then nobody was safe from the watchful eyes of neighbours, with their twitching curtains. There was no hotel where a couple could register under assumed names. The manager of the town's only hotel was an old friend of her parents' and she had been at school with the reception manager.

The reality was that this was complete madness. But wasn't that the attraction? The excitement of clandestine meetings in the dark and feverish lovemaking. Both of them being involved in the rehearsals did make things easier for them, as it meant there was an innocent reason they could be seen walking together, but they had to take care going to her place; always one at a time, always in darkness. Fortunately, the door to her basement wasn't on the street, but hidden away at the side of the house. Her parents generally left her to herself and didn't make a habit of calling in unannounced, undoubtedly hoping that she would put off moving back south if they left her in peace – even though she was living in their basement. It had certainly never occurred to them that she might have a lover, least of all a lover who was already living with another woman. Whatever way you looked at it, the situation was inexcusable. She could hardly find words to describe how much she hated herself for what she had done. But she couldn't stop. There was always one last time, and when he held her in his tight embrace it was as if she forgot what the word 'conscience' meant.

Even now, right after the funeral, she couldn't resist. He'd ensnared her with a penetrating glance after the service, whispering so sweetly in her ear.

'Not in the middle of the day, not now. Someone will see us,' she protested unconvincingly. She might as well have asked him just what they were waiting for. All the same, she knew it wasn't the timing that was the worst part of it. It didn't matter that it was daytime or right after the funeral of a man neither of them had liked. The worst part was that she couldn't say no, even knowing what had happened to his wife.

'Are you just going to stand there?' he asked. His voice was gentle, but it carried an authority that was so seductive she melted every time she heard him speak.

'What about Linda? This is just so . . . wrong. For God's sake, Karl, she's in intensive care in Reykjavík!'

'Come on, don't be like that. You know that it was all over between me and Linda long ago.'

'But she is your wife, and she's still critically ill.'

'I can't do anything about that, and the police won't let me go down south,' he said. 'I wasn't the one who assaulted her,' he added, somewhat defiantly.

No. I hope not. She only had his word for it.

'I didn't attack Linda,' Karl repeated. 'You know that, don't you?'

Anna looked at him. She wanted to believe him, but she wasn't entirely sure. She had to conceal her doubts.

'Of course, sweetheart. Of course I know that.'

She longed to ask him to leave, but it was all too exciting; everything was so fantastically inappropriate that she couldn't resist the temptation and slipped into bed beside him.

It would be nothing short of catastrophic if someone were to come in now, she thought. What sort of person had she become? What would her parents say? The story would spread like a virus around the town. It wouldn't matter so much for Karl – he could just move away, maybe back to Denmark. But she had no other home than Siglufjördur for the moment, and she stood a decent chance of getting a long-term job at the school. All this she was placing in jeopardy, everything wagered on the single turn of a card and a few minutes of passion with Karl. It was just as well that she could trust him to keep his mouth shut.

She'd asked herself more than once if she genuinely knew anything about him. She knew that he was far too old for her; in the summer he'd be forty-three to her twenty-four. Twenty-four; it had struck her when the priest had described Hrólfur's life that he had been just twenty-four when his masterpiece was published. When he had been her age his greatest achievement was already behind him. Her only achievements so far were to finish university and sleep with another woman's husband.

Karl was certainly too old for her, although she knew her friends in the south went out with men of that age – older, even. But adultery was another matter.

How the hell had she got herself into this?

A phone rang, Karl's mobile. He didn't even look up.

'It might be something about Linda. Aren't you going to answer it?

'Not now, darling. We're busy.'

How could she be so entranced by a man who was so indifferent to his own wife's wellbeing?

This time her phone rang and she reached for it on the bedside table.

'Don't answer it, darling,' said Karl.

But Anna had already picked it up. 'Hello? Anna here.'

It was Úlfur. He sounded business-like. 'Anna. I'm calling the whole company together. Can you come to the theatre this afternoon? Say, three o'clock? We need to go over things.'

'All right. I'll be there.'

'Good. Have you seen Karl, by the way? I didn't see either of you at the reception.'

Anna paused before saying, 'No, I haven't seen him.'

'That was Úlfur,' she said, ending the call. Then smiled weakly, a stab of concern deep inside, worrying that someone might put two and two together. It was a thought she didn't dare dwell on.

|||||||||||||

Úlfur entered the theatre to find he was alone.

The auditorium was probably the only place in the town where he was able to exclude entirely the turbulent outside world and retreat into a dream world – into a fantasy where nothing had gone wrong, a world where the chairman of the Dramatic Society had not fallen to his death a week before and the male lead's wife had not been found in the snow, close to death in a pool of her own blood.

He looked out over the auditorium.

He suddenly felt old; a lonely, old man, crushed by how much he missed his work, his ex-wife and even his late mother. Although he would presumably be asked to run the town's Dramatic Society, all at once it hardly seemed to matter.

|||||||||||||

'Damn! Damn!' Tómas shouted in fury. He banged his cup down on the table in front of the computer, where he had been reading the latest report on the investigation into the fatal incident at the Dramatic Society.

Ari Thór had accepted a lift to the station in the police jeep, even though he was still wearing his suit. In spite of being off duty, he had no desire to be at home. This was the kind of thick winter weather that called for company. He sat in the coffee corner with Hlynur and started when Tómas's anger boiled over.

'Hell and damnation!' Tómas swore a third time.

Ari Thór stood up while Hlynur sat still, as silently as he could.

'What's the matter?' he asked, hardly daring to speak.

'How do they find out this stuff? How the hell do they sniff it out? Look at that.'

Ari Thór read the headline.

Murder at Siglufjördur Theatre?

According to reliable sources, the police in Siglufjördur are treating the death of Hrólfur Kristjánsson as suspicious . . .

'Has either of you talked to anyone about this?' he shouted at Ari Thór accusingly.

Ari Thór shook his head and Hlynur mumbled something.

'What?'

'No, Not a word to anyone,' Hlynur said.

'I asked Nína earlier, not directly, of course, but I can hardly imagine that she could have called some journalist,' Ari Thór said.

'You can never tell. It's a bloody nuisance.'

Tómas read through the news item a second time.

'It's the same journalist again, the same one who wanted to know about Linda. By rights I should call him and give him a piece of my mind, but we need to tie up this bloody investigation, and as quickly as we can. I think we have to release a statement to say that the Hrólfur investigation is over and that it was an accident. Ari Thór, have you spoken to everyone who was at the rehearsal that night?'

Ari Thór thought quickly. If he included the chat with Úlfur in the hot tub and the private conversations with Ugla, then there was just one person he still needed to speak to.

'Everyone except Anna.'

'I was at school with her father. A good guy and a petrolhead like you.'

Ari Thór cursed himself for incautiously admitting that he had a fondness for cars; it had become part of his persona, along with the theology. The Reverend Ari Thór – priest and petrolhead. He wondered if it would be possible to become 'just' Ari Thór again, without the labels?

'You ought to go and have a look at that old jeep of his. It's a real beauty, still with the original number plates. You don't see many cars with those anymore. He bought it from Karl years ago, before he moved to Denmark. Karl had saved for ages to buy her, and then he had to pull up stakes and move with his parents. My guess is that he's never stopped regretting the fact that he was forced to sell her.'

Ari Thór looked at his colleague with something bordering on bemusement. Was there any hope of getting to the bottom of this case in a place where everyone knew everyone else so intimately? Old schoolchums, former workmates, friends and relatives; everyone seemed bound together with innumerable links.

'I'll call Anna and see if I can meet her,' Ari Thór said, side-stepping the discussion about Karl and the car. *Anything to get me out of here.*

||||||||||||||

'The show must go on.'

Anna sat at the back of the auditorium, not far from Karl and Pálmi. Nína had arrived unusually late and sat next to Pálmi. Leifur stood by the wall with his head in the clouds, studiously ignoring everything around him. Úlfur clearly hadn't succeeded in grabbing everyone's attention.

Anna had been careful to sit as far as she could from Karl.

'We said our farewells to Hrólfur today, but he is still watching over us,' Úlfur said.

It hadn't escaped Anna's notice that being on stage did not come naturally to Úlfur. He was nervous; his hands fidgeted incessantly and his eyes flitted in every direction, but mostly down at his feet. 'Hrólfur would have wanted to carry on regardless. I propose that we open next weekend, on Saturday. We'll have one dress rehearsal during the week and then put on the finest performance that Siglufjördur has ever seen. I spoke to Karl just now. He's ready to continue to play the lead, in spite of . . .' He hesitated. '. . . Linda's situation. This demonstrates commendable commitment and courage, I have to say. I admire the man.'

He smiled warmly at Karl, but got no response.

Nobody said a word.

'Well, now. We meet here on Thursday. That will be the final rehearsal. Any questions?'

There was a moment's silence again, before Anna stood up and spoke in a low voice that was clear enough to be heard throughout the auditorium.

'I saw a report that Hrólfur might have been . . . murdered.'

Úlfur jerked in alarm and he shook his head sharply, muttering under his breath. But then he raised his voice so it filled the hall. 'Stupid! Damned stupid! Isn't this just some wicked gossip? Speculation?' he shouted. 'There's all kinds of idle talk when someone well known passes away under unusual circumstances.' He took out a handkerchief and mopped his forehead. 'Shall we call this meeting to an end? Let's all be on our way home before we're literally snowed in.'

Anna's phone rang. It was a number she didn't recognise but she answered it. 'Yes . . . I'll be home shortly,' she said. 'You know the address? That's right. I live in the basement.'

She could feel the sweat start to rise on her skin. Her fingertips were suddenly damp. The police.

Had they found out about the affair?

If not, maybe she ought to use the opportunity to ask them about Karl? She had to be sure of him. Should she mention the life insurance? That could cause him problems, but only if he was guilty.

She knew she had to be sure.

31

SIGLUFJÖRDUR: SATURDAY, 17TH JANUARY 2009

The weight of snow on the road was almost too much for the little police 4×4 to cope with. Maybe it would have been more sensible to stay at home and become gradually cocooned as the drifts piled up. The houses all looked the same through the falling snow: shadowy detached buildings hidden in the swirling snowflakes driven by the northery gale. Having parked the car once, only to find it was outside the wrong house, Ari Thór finally found the right one. It looked spacious, a two-storey dwelling with a basement and a double garage.

There was no mistaking Anna's nervousness when he arrived. She shook his hand, her palm sweaty and her eyes darting from side to side, avoiding his gaze as she tried to muster a smile. Ari Thór watched her carefully.

The basement flat was dark, with every curtain drawn.

'Best to keep them closed,' Ari Thór said to break the ice. 'There's no need to watch all that snow piling up.'

She laughed awkwardly.

'Well . . . actually, I love the snow. I could sit by the window and watch it all day. I just wish I was still eight years old and could go and sled down the slopes.'

'Of course,' he said, wishing he could feel as positive.

They sat at the kitchen table, which presumably doubled as the dining table; a potted plant that he didn't recognise stood in the middle of its dark wood surface.

'This won't take long,' said Ari Thór. 'I just need to ask a few questions about Hrólfur.'

She sat in silence.

'It has been rumoured that Hrólfur may have come across something that, well, he'd have been better off not knowing about.'

She looked at him apprehensively.

'Do you have the feeling that there might be something behind this? Is there anyone in the company who might have something to hide?'

Her eyes immediately gave her away, but he could see she was trying to remain calm.

'Nothing that I am aware of,' she said nervously.

'You're sure?' He looked hard at her as she dropped her eyes, wringing her hands.

'I'm completely sure.' She put one hand on the table and lifted it again, leaving a damp palm print behind. 'Completely sure,' she repeated, and tried discreetly to mop her forehead with her sleeve.

'Do you think someone could have pushed him? Was there anyone who might have wanted to get rid of the old man?' Now his voice was sterner; her discomfort had succeeded in making him almost uncomfortable. 'Some secret that mustn't become public knowledge, whatever the price?'

She stood up. 'I'm sorry. I need a glass of water.' At the sink she turned on the tap before answering. 'There's nothing I can think of.'

'You got on well, did you, you and Hrólfur?'

'Yes, of course.'

Ari Thór had a suspicion where Anna's sensitive spot might lie and aimed for it.

'Do you have the lead in the production you're rehearsing now?'

'No.'

It was a short, sharp answer.

'Really? . . . The out-of-town girl got the part instead of you?'

'You mean Ugla?'

'Yes, exactly. Ugla.' Ari Thór waited for her to sit down again.

She clasped the glass of water between her hands.

'Was that Hrólfur's decision?'

'Yes . . . I mean, it was probably a joint decision, between him and Úlfur.'

'Surely you weren't happy with that?'

She continued to hold the glass tight. 'No.'

Ari Thór was silent, waiting.

'No,' she repeated. 'It was very unfair. She didn't deserve it. But Hrólfur had a great fondness for her.'

'In what way?'

Ari Thór could breathe a sigh of relief that not *everything* became public knowledge in this small town. News of his friendship with Ugla had clearly not reached Anna.

'She rented his flat. I think he had almost started to treat her as his own child.'

'Didn't he have children of his own?'

Anna looked perplexed. 'No, I thought you knew that.'

Ari Thór steered the topic back to its former course.

Strike while the iron's hot.

'So it could be argued that your position is better now that he's gone?'

'What do you mean? Do you think I pushed him?'

Instead of becoming angry, she was more obviously unsure of herself.

'Not at all.'

Ari Thór longed to ask her straight out if she had done it, but held back. He mustn't let his own temper lead him into a mistake. He also had to admit it was highly unlikely that a young woman would have pushed an old man down the stairs simply to get a part in an amateur production in a small town. On the other hand, she obviously had something to hide. The question was whether or not it was something to do with Hrólfur's decision not to cast her in the lead role. Was this something she was trying to avoid discussing? Or was there something else, some other secret that she was hiding?

At last she took her first sip of water.

Ari Thór would probably have accepted a glass if it had been offered. The little flat was hot, with every window closed.

He noticed that she had changed her clothes since the funeral; not that he remembered what she had been wearing, but it certainly wasn't the red wool sweater and the black tracksuit bottoms she was wearing now. Ari Thór was stuck in his black suit, like being caught in the grip of a nightmare.

He had asked enough aggressive questions. Now it was time to reduce the tension and hope that she would let something slip.

'Are you working – or studying perhaps?'

'Working. I finished university in Reykjavík.'

'Haven't I seen you in the Co-op?' he asked in an amiable tone.

'That's right. I work there, and at the hospital.'

'So you must know Linda?'

'We work together. How is she?'

Her question seemed to be sincere, he thought. 'No change, I'm afraid.'

'Do you have any idea who might have attacked her?'

'The case is under investigation,' Ari Thór answered shortly.

'Did he do it? Karl?'

'No, he's in the clear.'

'Really? You're sure?'

Ari Thór wondered whether the question stemmed only from straightforward curiosity.

'Yes. The indications are that he was elsewhere at the time. Why do you ask?'

'Well, no reason, really. I was just wondering about . . . about the insurance.'

'Insurance?'

'Yes. But that's all right if he's innocent.'

'What insurance are you talking about?' he repeated, trying not to let his interest show.

'There was a salesman who was up at the hospital in the summer. We all bought life insurance.'

'Including Linda?'

She nodded.

'You know who the beneficiary is . . . if she dies?'

'Yes, of course. Karl, obviously. Linda and I talked about it when we decided to go for it.'

'And Karl knows about this?' Perhaps she wasn't the right person to ask, but he posed the question all the same.

'I haven't a clue,' she said, with more animation than the question warranted.

'A large amount?'

'A few million, I think.'

This case was constantly taking new directions, and again the spotlight had shifted to Karl, the man who seemed to have the perfect alibi. *Damn it.*

Ari Thór stood up. 'Thanks for your time, Anna.'

'Yes . . . sure.' She seemed slightly nervous again.

'I'll see you around.'

He was struggling not to show his excitement at the new information.

Winter greeted him again at the door. Winter in all its majesty, if that was the right word.

The freezing darkness swallowed him up.

32

SIGLUFJÖRDUR: SUNDAY, 18TH JANUARY 2009

The snow had continued to fall through Saturday evening and far into the night. After dozing fitfully for a few hours Ari Thór finally managed to get to sleep. The weather was affecting him badly. Usually he was able to read before turning in, but now he couldn't focus, thinking only of the darkness closing in on him. He had tried to listen to classical music to drown out the deafening silence of the incessant snowfall, but it was as if the music magnified the gloom.

Night after night, his dreams dragged him into dark and treacherous places where he struggled to breathe, held under by an unknown force that could only have come from within. He would be training at the pool, practising diving, with a mask on his face – swimming deeper and deeper until he reached the bottom, where he looked up and enjoyed the moment. When it was time to push upwards he felt as if his feet were stuck fast to the bottom of the pool, trapped and as heavy as lead; he watched other swimmers break through the surface, while he stayed down below, unable to move. And so it continued. Yet again Ari Thór awoke, suffocated and crushed, the sensation of drowning unbearably real, as if his lungs were actually filling with water. As fear gripped him, and paralysed by sleep, he stretched out a hand for someone – Kristín, maybe, some kind of warmth.

Once again, it was impossible to return to sleep – sleep that became less restful as the dreams became increasingly relentless, like the blizzard outside his windows. To make matters worse, his injured shoulder still caused him considerable pain. He was on his feet very early on his day off, despite his intention to catch up on some sleep, shake off the debilitating exhaustion and relax after a tough week. Peering out the kitchen window, he could see that the snow had not let up, menacing in its evident desire to bury the town of Siglufjördur. He sat at the kitchen table, staring at the so-called view outside.

Does spring ever come here?

He soon gave up and pulled the curtain across the window, and then drew them over every other window as well.

It wasn't until midday that he turned on the radio to hear about the night's events. An avalanche had fallen on the Siglufjördur road, on the other side of the mountain, closing off the only route into town. He felt physically bruised by the news. Nobody had been hurt, fortunately, but this meant that there was no way in, no way out. Nobody would be leaving by land, and travelling by sea was hardly an option. He felt both shaken and deflated; the situation sucking out of him what little energy remained. He tried to breathe slowly, deeply, but it made no difference and his heart hammered wildly in his chest. He heard the presenter announce that there would be no attempt to try to clear the road that day, and possibly not even the next day, as a result of the forecast of more poor weather. After that, the news turned into white noise, incomprehensible words that blurred into one.

Ari Thór's thoughts spun in his head as he tried to convince himself that everything would be fine. It was a temporary situation and the road would re-open in a day or two. He opened the door, intending to meet the weather face-to-face, reassure himself that it was not an enemy. The wind had gained strength and a snowdrift had formed halfway up the door. He closed it quickly.

It'll be fine.

Pulling himself together, he called the station to see if he was needed – more as a distraction than anything else.

'Just checking in.' Ari Thór tried to sound casual. 'Need any help?'

'We're busy as always,' Tómas said warmly. 'But you need the rest, my boy. Nothing we can't cope with.'

'OK, just wondering, you know, because of the news. It's pretty horrible.'

'The news?' Tómas sounded surprised.

'The avalanche . . .'

'Oh, the avalanche. That's nothing unusual, happens every year, more or less. It fell on the road in the middle of the night, so no one was injured, thank goodness. On a more positive note for us, it's clear now that Karl can't go anywhere. He's stuck here.'

After speaking with Tómas, Ari Thór went back upstairs and lay down again. With his eyes closed and his body still he courted sleep for many hours. It was evening by the time he switched on the radio again. The road was still blocked and would be until Tuesday at the earliest.

He hadn't eaten much all day, and the only thing in his fridge was a herring fillet, which he had picked up from the fishmonger after he had spoken to old Sandra. He had felt he needed to try and get a taste of the good old days. He had found a simple recipe, frying the herring in a pan; lightly salted to bring out the flavour. The result was surprisingly good, different from other fish he had tasted, with a slight taste of fat, but decent enough, and he only wished he had someone to share it with.

He picked up his phone. He needed to hear Kristín's voice – anyone's voice.

He listened to the ringing, about to hang up when it was finally answered.

'Hi.'

It was a sharp greeting, as if she didn't have time to talk to him, yet this was their first call in over a week.

'Hi. How are you?'

Ugla.

The kiss and his conscience were all troubling him. How could he act as if nothing had happened? *Ugla.* The name echoed through his head, booming and overwhelming.

'Listen . . . I'm at work.'

Again. She was always at work, with never a moment for anything else.

'All right,' sighed Ari Thór, before blurting out, 'It just snows and snows nonstop here. There was even an avalanche last night.' It felt good to say the word out loud. *Avalanche.*

'Yes, I know.' She sounded distracted. 'I heard it on the news. There isn't any threat to the town, is there? I thought it was somewhere else in the district, on the road to Siglufjördur? To tell the truth, I wasn't really worried about you.'

Everything she said was true and it sounded so innocently sensible in her voice that he felt instantly calmer.

'How are things with you?'

'I'll have to call you back later. I can't chat while I'm at work,' she said, straight to the point as usual.

'No, of course. I'll speak to you later.'

It was Sunday. Piano day. Ugla. Would she be expecting him? Could he turn up after that kiss, after having scuttled away? He put off making a decision, and tried to close his eyes again.

Hell. There was nothing to lose. He stood up from the bed, pulled on his down anorak, tugged the hood up around his head and wrapped a scarf around his neck before venturing out into the blizzard, over the drifts and through the almost impenetrable walls of snow, eyes half-closed against the stinging wind. His phone was in his pocket, in case Kristín should call him back; *if* Kristín called him back.

Ugla greeted him as if nothing had happened; wearing the same navy jeans and white T-shirt as usual, she beamed at him and asked him inside.

They sat in Ugla's living room long into the evening, talking about nothing and everything, the piano lesson forgotten. The flat was warm and welcoming; through the open curtains, he could see the drifts building remorselessly, while the tenderness of her voice dampened the fear, the ache inside him.

'A glass of wine?' she asked when they had chatted for a while.

'Sure, just not too much, I have to work tomorrow.'

She returned with two glasses and a bottle of red. When she had poured the wine, she fetched a couple of candles and lit them. The scene was set.

'Any news on the investigation?' Ugla asked. 'Or should I say investigations?'

'Not really, we're still working on it. I have a feeling someone is hiding something in relation to Hrólfur's death.' Ari Thór believed that he could trust Ugla, speak to her openly about the case, in full confidence. The only thing not up for discussion was the kiss, but it hovered in the background as if imprinted on the living room walls.

'I have to admit that this stuff really gets to me,' she said. 'The attack on Linda, and Hrólfur's death. It's all a little bit too close to home. I mean, can I be sure that I'm safe?' She sounded genuinely scared.

'I'll look out for you,' Ari Thór replied.

'I think most people now believe that Hrólfur was killed. That's a terrible thought, isn't it? I can sense the fear in town, and it has become worse by the day since Linda was attacked.'

Ari Thór longed to put his arms around her and tell her that everything would be fine.

The bottle was quickly emptied. Ugla fetched another one from the kitchen and sat on the sofa next to him, her body pressed close to his. He could smell her clean hair and found himself wanting to bury his face in it.

For a while, they sat in silence, sipping their wine, and then Ugla placed a hand carelessly on his knee. Her touch stirred him, and he struggled to answer when she asked him if he liked the wine.

Ari Thór smiled, turning towards her, knowing what was coming as she kissed him lightly on the lips. He backed away, torn by the feelings he was experiencing.

One more kiss wouldn't do any harm? He ran his fingers through her long, sweetly scented, fair hair, put his arms around her and returned the kiss, a long, passionate one.

There was a warming energy about her that was not only a much-needed antidote to the suffocating snow outside, but also to the emptiness that had been growing in his heart.

Her invitation to the bedroom was too strong to resist.

After that evening he wondered, more often than he liked to admit, at what point a betrayal had taken place. Did it really matter whether he had slept with her or not? When he had taken her hand and followed her into the bedroom, shutting the door behind him, hadn't the crime already been committed?

Was the avalanche an excuse? An avalanche on the far side of a huge mountain and so far away that he didn't even hear a murmur of it, yet so close that he hadn't been able to think straight all day?

Did he genuinely have an excuse? More to the point, did he care?

33

SIGLUFJÖRDUR: MONDAY, 19TH JANUARY 2009

There was a brief break in the snowfall as Ari Thór waded through the banks of fresh white powder that had collected overnight to get to work on Monday morning. He was deeply confused, his mind on both Ugla and Kristín, and what the latter's reactions might be.

Tómas was on duty, as usual, well before his shift was due to start. Ari Thór had the occasional suspicion that Tómas's marriage might be in trouble, as he so obviously lived for his work. He reflected that this was a job that provided him with no shortage of challenges, and was now giving him the opportunity to vent his anger at the impertinence of journalists before calming down with a mug of coffee in his hand.

'They don't stop calling,' were the first words he uttered as Ari Thór came in, stamping the snow from his feet. 'Damned journalists. They won't leave us in peace.'

'I hear that after all the news coverage people believe Hrólfur was murdered. Have you heard that as well?'

'Just a bit. I've also heard the theory that Hrólfur's killer is
the same person who assaulted Linda. What do you think of
that?' Tómas asked, the journalists apparently no longer an irritation.

Ari Thór had a feeling that he secretly enjoyed being the
centre of attention.

'I doubt it . . . I'd suspect.Karl, but it looks like he's innocent, of the attack on Linda at any rate.'

'I've rarely seen a guiltier man,' Tómas said. 'Our bosses in
Akureyri have been in touch, asking to send a man to help us
with the investigation.' His expression showed what he thought
of the suggestion. 'I couldn't really argue. They'll be in touch
when the roads are cleared. I tried to convince them that it's all
under control.'

Ari Thór nodded, struggling to concentrate. On top of everything else he still felt the pain in his shoulder. He had swallowed a couple of painkillers that morning, but they weren't
having any effect. He thought of booking an appointment with
the doctor, but decided to wait and see if it would heal by itself.

Tómas poured himself another mug of coffee and sat down.
'Listen. While I remember . . . Old Thorsteinn called me yesterday. Could you go and see him today?'

'Thorsteinn?'

Tómas seemed to expect that Ari Thór would automatically
know everyone in Siglufjördur by name.

'Sorry. Thorsteinn's a lawyer. He had a practice in Akureyri
years ago, but he moved back home when he retired. He still
has a few clients, but they're gradually dying off.'

'OK,' Ari Thór agreed, still wondering why he needed to meet this lawyer.

'He called me yesterday,' Tómas said. 'He has the old man's will and said that he held off opening it until after the funeral. He reckoned we might be interested in the contents, not least as "Hrólfur had been murdered", or so he said! As far as I could make out, he was very pleased that he has something to offer us in the middle of such an exciting murder investigation . . .' Tómas smiled for the first time that morning. The coffee appeared to be working.

'A will?' Ari Thór said in surprise. 'I can hardly believe it. I thought he hadn't made a will.'

'Life constantly takes us by surprise,' Tómas said, sipping his coffee and sighing theatrically.

||||||||||||

As far as the eye could see the world was white, the streets bleached with silvery snowdrifts piled across the pavements. The mountains sparkled, their pearly surfaces broken by the occasional fleck of black. The pale sky was an indication that the next fall of snow was not far away. It was as if nature had called a temporary truce, although everyone knew that sooner or later the weather would close in once again. There were no plans to clear the Siglufjördur road, at least not that day, leaving the inhabitants prisoners of the snow. Ari Thór tried to concentrate on the will and the meeting with Thorsteinn, trying to avoid, as so often, thinking about the snow.

The lawyer lived on Sudurgata, in an imposing, pale-coloured house that looked like it was built in the twenties or thirties.

It was surrounded by a large garden, the branches of its trees bowed down under the weight of the ice and snow; from a distance, it formed an exquisite, picturesque winter scene.

Thorsteinn answered the door almost as soon as Ari Thór had rung the bell, as if he had watched him approach.

'Welcome. Come inside.'

He looked to be around eighty, with thick glasses perched on his nose and thin grey hair. His formal suit and checked waistcoat were stretched over his portly frame, and he seemed a little overdressed, even for a meeting with the police.

'Welcome.' An older lady appeared in the hall and took Ari Thór's hand. 'I'm Snjólaug, Thorsteinn's wife,' she said with a smile. 'How nice to have a visitor.'

The impression was that visitors were a rarity.

'Can we offer you anything? Coffee and cake?' Thorsteinn asked.

'Thank you, but no,' Ari Thór said, keen to get to business.

'Shall we sit in my office?' the old man suggested, gesturing down a narrow hallway, where a couple of old framed photographs of Siglufjördur hung on the walls; they appeared to be fading at the same rate as the wallpaper.

The office was more of a study, with three of its walls lined with books. The lawyer's reddish-brown desk was carved from heavy wood, and a green lamp on its surface provided an almost surreal glow – the only light in the room, with the curtains drawn and the main lights switched off. A red-leather folder occupied the centre of the desk and there was no computer to be seen, not even a typewriter in this room where everything seemed to be done the old-fashioned way. Thorsteinn sat in a large office chair, opened the folder and then reached down to take an envelope from one of the desk drawers.

Ari Thór took a seat opposite him. He was about to ask his first question when Snjólaug came into the office with a tray that she placed carefully on the edge of the desk. There were two cups of steaming coffee, a plate of freshly baked pancakes and a small sugar bowl. There was clearly no point refusing hospitality in this house. Ari Thór thanked her, smiled and sipped his coffee.

'Would you like milk?' Snjólaug asked.

'No thank you. Black is fine,' he answered and she departed with a nod of her head.

The single wall of the office not lined with books from floor to ceiling was split in two, the upper part covered by wallpaper patterned with pale-blue flowers, while the expanse of wall below the dado rail had been painted black. There was also a brass wall light and the room's only window, its ivory frame just visible behind dark curtains.

'Is your investigation making progress?' the lawyer asked, his expression weary but also clearly suggesting that he thought he could make a contribution to the case.

'It's getting there, a step at a time, although it's most likely that it was an accident. So Hrólfur had made a will?'

'Absolutely, absolutely,' Thorsteinn said with the envelope in his hands, as if waiting for the right moment and unwilling to play his trump card too soon. 'Have a pancake,' he said, taking one for himself. He sprinkled it with sugar, folded it and ate it in a single mouthful.

'I can't do this every day, not at my age. I have to be careful what I eat,' he said, mouth still full.

Ari Thór nodded weakly, and attempted to guide the conversation back to the will. He suspected the older gentleman was lonely. 'Did Hrólfur make his will a long time ago?' he asked.

'Well, no. Not that long. About two years ago. I met him by chance and he mentioned that he wanted to sort out his affairs once and for all. He said he was so damned old, the time had come!'

Thorsteinn smiled. His smile was a tired one. 'While I remember, would you like a little stiffener in your coffee?'

He turned to the bookcase behind his desk. Most of the books looked to be legal, volumes of supreme-court judgments in bound tomes filling several shelves. He took the 1962 volume from its place on the shelf and reached for a whisky bottle tucked away behind it.

Ari Thór grinned. 'No thanks. I'm driving.'

And on duty.

'Up to you.' Thorsteinn poured a small measure into his coffee, and avoided Ari Thór's eye. 'Now, to continue . . . He asked me to prepare his will, as I've been handling a few legal affairs since I closed my practice in Akureyri. It doesn't do any harm to keep yourself up to date.'

'Nobody has mentioned this will before. So it has certainly been kept quiet,' Ari Thór said, his statement more a question.

'Indeed. Hrólfur asked me specially to keep the contents of his will confidential. He made it quite clear that he wasn't going to tell anyone about it, least of all the beneficiaries. Only we four know about this will.'

'Four?'

'Yes. Hrólfur and I, my wife, Snjólaug, and Gudrún, who is

a nurse at the hospital. Gudrún and Snjólaug were witnesses and I trust them both completely, so don't worry. Gudrún is an old friend who visits us regularly and has done so for many years. I can assure you that nobody except myself, Hrólfur and the witnesses knows about the will.'

We'll see about that.

If there was anything Ari Thór had learned during his short time in Siglufjördur, it was that secrets were liable to spread with astonishing speed in such a small community.

'Was Hrólfur a wealthy man? Who *are* the beneficiaries?' Ari Thór's patience was wearing thin and he wanted answers.

'Wealthy? Well, when is anyone wealthy?' Thorsteinn asked, as if expecting an answer.

Ari Thór sat silent and Thorsteinn continued.

'He was fairly well off, but as far as I could see he knew how to enjoy himself. He travelled and lived life to the full. If he had continued to write and had spent less time having fun, then he would have doubtless died a wealthy man – which begs the question, "Which is the more sensible course of action?"' He laughed lightly. 'So, enough chat,' he said, to Ari Thór's relief. 'To business.' He opened the envelope.

'Everything is divided between friends and relatives.'

Ari Thór opened his notebook, ready to record details.

'Let's see. He had several bank and savings accounts, with a few million in each one. The money goes to a fairly distant relative, a great-nephew in Reykjavík, the only one of his relatives with whom he had any contact. He has a wife and children, and they've been struggling financially, I believe. So Hrólfur reckoned it would help them.'

'Hrólfur had no children of his own?'

'No. No children.'

'You're sure of that?'

'Yes, well, as sure as it's possible to be. Do you suspect that might not be the case?'

He sent Ari Thór a hawk-like look, just as if he were playing the part of a defence counsel in front of a courtroom.

'No,' Ari Thór lied. 'Not at all.'

The lawyer's brows furrowed and he continued.

'Then there are the rights to his books, or rather, book. His short stories never sold much, and neither did his poetry.'

'And who gets the rights?'

'Old Pálmi. Well, old and not that old. He's younger than I am. You know him?'

'Yes, I know him. Do you have any idea why Hrólfur chose him?'

'No, I don't have a clue, and there was no explanation.'

'And are these rights worth anything?'

'I couldn't say. There might be a few sales now that he's gone, but his time had passed and I can hardly imagine that there'll be much to be made from the rights, at least nothing signifi-cant, probably small amounts now and again. Nothing like it was in the old days when he was in demand with literati all over the world.'

Ari Thór sighed. It didn't seem that this had given Pálmi any strong motive for pushing an elderly author down the stairs.

'Is there any more?' he asked.

'Of course there's the wine, one of the finest cellars to be found in the town, or probably anywhere in these parts.'

Ari Thór waited. The lawyer paused for a long moment, just as he might have done in a courtroom.

'Úlfur gets the wine,' he said, and it seemed like he longed to add something – *The lucky old dog* – but decided against it. 'Those bottles are worth millions, but I somehow doubt he'd try and sell them. It would be a sin to sell such a cellar.'

'And the house? He must have owned the house?'

'Most certainly, and mortgage-free.'

'And does that go to his relatives?'

'No, actually it doesn't. This did take me by surprise, I have to say, and I'm not easily surprised these days.'

His heart leaped as Thorsteinn named the beneficiary.

'Her name's Ugla,' Thorsteinn repeated. 'She's just a young woman.'

Ari Thór sat in silence and almost in shock.

'It's inexplicable, to say the least. She gets the house, the contents and the old Mercedes. That's probably not worth a lot these days but the house is magnificent.'

Ari Thór hardly heard the rest of the conversation. He could only think of Ugla. Had she known about this? Had she been leading him on, tempting him down the wrong avenues of investigation? It was obvious that if anyone in the town would gain from Hrólfur's death, it was Ugla.

But he couldn't think of her except with warmth. He knew that he would have to meet her again, in spite of everything. But how was he going to negotiate a situation that was fast becoming an ethical dilemma? It went without saying that the investigation had to take priority. He couldn't sacrifice his job for a passing fancy. Or was there more to it?

Should he let Tómas know about their meetings? That would mean admitting he had shared more information with her than might be seen as acceptable.

He thanked the lawyer for the meeting, and it was obvious from Thorsteinn's expression that he would have liked Ari Thór to stay on for a while, to get more information about the case, a little more gossip.

As Ari Thór left the house, it occurred to him how much it had felt like a real home, filled with warmth and kindness, so different from the place on Eyrargata he was trying his best to call home. His thoughts returned to Ugla, again.

What have I got myself into?

The same thought had flashed through his mind when Tómas had first told him how uneventful things were in Siglufjördur. The reality had turned out to be very different. There were too many problems, and he had put himself at the centre of the investigation in a way that was far too personal. He wanted to yell at the encircling mountains that hemmed him in on all sides, but now that the blizzard had again set in, they were blotted from view. A perfect time to hide away.

What the hell have I got myself into?

34

SIGLUFJÖRDUR: MONDAY, 19TH JANUARY 2009

Nína sat alone in the darkness, not for the first time and not for the last.

There was no rehearsal today, and she had stayed at home rather than going to the theatre to be there alone. In any case, it was unlikely she would meet him there until the next rehearsal, on top of which she struggled to get about on crutches. Damned bad luck to break a leg like that.

She felt at home in the darkness, where she saw nobody and nobody could see her. She had been so distressed these last few days. She had made a mistake and could only blame herself. *Damned bad luck.* But it wasn't over yet and there was every chance that the mistake would never be discovered. She had at least done her best.

She counted the days, even counting the minutes until she would meet him. In a way, she was glad that nothing had ever happened between them, and never would. She liked loving him like this, any thought of intimacy scared her. Maybe it would have been different if her mother had done something to help her, other than send her to Reykjavík, the easy, cheap way out.

But now they would be bound together forever, in a way. A shared secret, and not just any secret: a murder.

||||||||||||

Ari Thór couldn't bring himself to speak to Ugla, not right away.

Thorsteinn had held off informing the beneficiaries of the bequests, but they would now be contacted by him.

The question of whether or not Ugla had known about this inheritance nagged at him constantly. Was there anyone in this town he could trust?

Tómas had asked him to follow up, see what the beneficiaries had to say, test the water.

Pálmi looked tired when he answered the door, and didn't seem overly surprised to see Ari Thór standing there.

He could hear the mutter of voices from the kitchen and guessed that the old lady from Denmark was in conversation with her son.

'I imagine you'll want to talk about the inheritance,' Pálmi said with no preamble. 'Thorsteinn called just now.'

'Yes, if you have time,' Ari Thór said, rapidly taking on the priest's persona, courteous and warm. It was a part he played, just a part.

They sat in the living room.

'You knew about this?' Ari Thór asked.

'About the inheritance? No, it had never even crossed my mind.'

All the same, there was something elusive about his eyes, something that was difficult to pin down.

'He had never hinted at it?' Ari Thór asked, unwilling to give up.

'No, never,' Pálmi said with the same expression on his face. 'I understand from Thorsteinn that it's not worth a great deal. There are no huge royalties on these books anymore.'

'So it's symbolic as much as anything?'

'Well, yes. I suppose so.'

The elusive eyes again. Ari Thór was silent, waiting.

Pálmi yawned. 'Excuse me. I'm not completely awake.'

'The opening night's not far away, is it? Long rehearsals?'

'Yes, well. No, no. Just plenty to do. They're still here, the Danes, as I imagine you can hear, and they keep me awake.' He tried to squeeze out a smile. 'They can't leave town because of the avalanche.'

'Why do you think Hrólfur chose you? He had a relative in the south.'

'No idea,' he said, still sounding tired, still with the odd look on his face. 'Maybe he wanted the rights to stay with someone in Siglufjördur, and there aren't many of us left who knew him well.'

'Úlfur got the wine cellar.'

'Úlfur?' he asked in amazement.

'That's right.'

'Well. I suppose the bottles will stay in the town. Unless he's planning to sell them?'

'I haven't heard from him,' Ari Thór said, rising to his feet.

The old lady and her son came in from the kitchen as Ari Thór was about to leave. He greeted them.

'How is your investigation going?' Mads asked in English.

'We're making progress,' Ari Thór replied. 'Are you staying long?'

'We had planned to leave today, but because the weather is so bad we will have to spend a few more days here.' He had a hangdog look on his face that indicated he would have much preferred to be somewhere warmer, where the sun didn't stay hidden behind the mountains all day.

||||||||||||||

Ari Thór called Hrólfur's great-nephew in Reykjavík, who was delighted with the news of the inheritance, saying that, although he would naturally miss his uncle, he and his wife had been on the point of losing their flat. There was no indication of any links between this man and Siglufjördur, or anyone who had been at the rehearsal that evening, not that anything could be ruled out. Úlfur was next on his list, and Ugla would have to wait. He couldn't meet her, not yet.

'Apologies for the questions the other day. The hot tub wasn't the right time or place,' Ari Thór said to Úlfur. A little humility could sometimes pay dividends.

They sat at the kitchen table of Úlfur's house in Sudurgata, not far from the Town Hall Square. Ari Thór had already got as much information about the director as he could from Tómas. Úlfur was a former diplomat with roots in the town, whose father had been lost at sea when Úlfur had been very young. He had then moved back to the north when his mother had died at an advanced age. He had few friends in the town.

'He's a divorced man – pretty lonely, I'd imagine,' Tómas had said, strangely concerned.

'Don't worry yourself about it, Reverend,' Úlfur had said, leaning forward to slap Ari Thór's shoulder, the sore shoulder. *Hell*. He would have to get it seen to.

The storm hammered at the kitchen window, although the weather didn't seem to affect Úlfur in any adverse way. Quite the opposite – he seemed to be in a good mood.

'It's going to take you a while to drink all that wine,' Ari Thór observed. 'I understand there are a lot of bottles.'

'Yes, and each undoubtedly better than the last.'

'It must have been a pleasant surprise.'

'You could say that. I certainly hadn't expected anything at all from the old boy. But that was Hrólfur in a nutshell. He always had to have the last word,' Úlfur said and grinned. 'I bitterly regret arguing with him that evening. I used to let him get on my nerves too often.'

'You didn't always agree?'

'Good heavens, no.'

'I understand he wasn't happy with your play.'

'No, he wasn't,' Úlfur answered, almost automatically, before taking in what had been said. 'What do you mean?'

'Aren't you writing a play?'

'Yes, but where the hell did you hear that?' he demanded, suddenly angry.

'I gather he wasn't impressed by it.'

'True. He preferred Pálmi's writing,' Úlfur said, now looking more embarrassed.

'Well,' Ari Thór said, getting to his feet. 'I don't suppose that'll be a problem now.' He tried to sound careless.

'Problem? What do you mean?' Úlfur's temper flared again.

'Your play. Hrólfur won't block it from being produced now.'

Úlfur shot to his feet and the stool almost fell to the floor behind him.

'What the hell are you implying, boy? You think I killed him? Do you think I killed him to get a play staged?'

'Let's not forget the wine,' said Ari Thór, with a wink.

'You get out now, you hear me.' Úlfur strode out of the kitchen and into the hall where he opened the front door, which led out into the storm.

What's got into me? Ari Thór asked himself as he made for the door without saying goodbye.

He decided it was easiest to blame the weather.

35

SIGLUFJÖRDUR: TUESDAY, 20TH JANUARY 2009

Ari Thór was at work early, after another battle with the incessant storm.

'The road won't be cleared today,' Tómas told him, without being asked.

'Soon, though, I hope,' Ari Thór said, trying to sound cheerful.

'The forecast looks bad for the rest of the week. So we're stuck here, whether we like it or not,' Tómas said with a lighthearted laugh.

The woman from the insurance company called later that morning. Tómas had asked Ari Thór to check on the insurance angle and he had contacted Linda's insurer the previous day, so he'd been expecting a call to confirm the details.

'I'm sorry it took a while, we've been busy,' she apologised.

'No problem.'

We're just the Siglufjördur cops, nothing important.

'We sent a salesman around the north last autumn and he travelled to Siglufjördur and made presentations in several workplaces, including the hospital.'

'And she bought a policy, the woman I asked you about yesterday?'

'Yes, Linda Christensen. She took out a policy. Has she died?'

'No, but we're looking into a connection with a case we are investigating.'

'Hey, is this the woman in the snow? Wasn't that in Siglufjördur?'

'I'm afraid I can't comment. What pay-out are we looking at here?'

'Ten million krónur.'

'And her husband is the beneficiary in the event of her death?'

'Karl Steindór Einarsson it says here, but they aren't married and aren't even registered as living together. His legal residence is in Kópavogur.'

'But he's the one who benefits, isn't he? Karl?'

'Yes, that's quite clear.'

'And it presumably doesn't make any difference if the insured person dies of inflicted wounds, or under suspicious circumstances, if we assume that is the case?'

'No, it makes no difference.'

'Could you send me the terms and conditions?'

'I should be able to do that. I'll have it scanned and email it to you later today. I hope she makes it, the woman in the snow.'

'Thanks for your help,' he said, replacing the receiver.

Ari Thór turned to Tómas. 'Ten million.' Tómas looked up. 'He gets ten million if she dies.'

'So do you think he did it?'

'If he did, I can't figure out *how* he could have done it,' Ari Thór said thoughtfully. 'But it looks bad for him, I mean to be getting a pay-out if she dies.'

'There's so much that looks bad for Karl, but he has kept his cool right from the start.'

'Shall I have a word with him again? Ask him about this life insurance?'

'Wait a bit. Let's not rush into anything. This whole case seems to be in limbo at the moment. It's as if the snow is slowing everything down.' Tómas seemed more relaxed than his words might have indicated; accustomed to heavy winters and not one to let the weather upset him. 'The town goes into semi-hibernation when the weather's like this, especially if the road is blocked.'

'We ought to ask Karl about the rumours that Sandra heard from Hrólfur – the secret at the Dramatic Society,' Ari Thór said, after a moment's thought. 'She hinted that it might have been something to do with a clandestine affair, or something along those lines.'

'Hmph. Karl would be a strong candidate for that. Karl and that girl from the west, Ugla. It seems she gets about,' Tómas said.

Ari Thór felt the hurt rise inside him. He tried to count silently to ten, and pretend nothing was wrong.

He stood up quickly and felt the familiar stab of pain in his shoulder.

'Dammit,' he muttered.

'You all right?'

'Yes, it's just my bloody shoulder. It's been painful since . . .' he said, and paused. 'Since the break-in.'

Sounds better than since I fell over in the living room.

'You're going to have to go and get it checked.'

'It'll sort itself out.'

'Get it seen to right away,' Tómas ordered, and this time there was a firm tone in his voice. 'We can't have someone on duty with an injury – what would happen if you got caught up in an altercation?'

'All right. I'll go up to the hospital later this week.'

'No. You're going right now, and that's final.'

|||||||||||||||

The time passed so slowly, so painfully slowly. Nína had tried to put on the light this morning, to sit by the window and read, but found she couldn't concentrate. The anticipation was so strong. It was getting closer to when they could be together, the two of them, alone in a world of their own.

She kept the evidence under the bed. It was a good hiding place, as she knew from her own experiences in the old days, back when she had needed to flee.

He would be so pleased with her. She had taken it away so he wouldn't be caught. She practised the conversation over and over in her head; anticipating telling him how she had done it, and how she had tried to go one better, but that it hadn't worked out. *Where the hell had she gone wrong?* She was furious with herself. Hopefully he wouldn't be angry.

No, of course he would be pleased with her.

And then . . . then she would invite him home for dinner.

The excitement was killing her.

||||||||||||

Tómas had called ahead to the hospital, asking the doctor on duty to find time for Ari Thór, even though he didn't have an appointment. There was no point protesting any longer. Tómas needed to keep the 4×4 at the station, so Ari Thór walked to the hospital, although eddies of snow made it almost impossible to get anywhere. Although the storm had abated, flurries contin-ued to swirl around him – almost violently – forcing him to close his eyes against their angry blasts.

The doctor he was due to see was busy, so he took a seat in the waiting room, still breathless from his journey. His shoulder wasn't at the top of his list of concerns right now. He flipped through gossip magazines, dog-eared and long out of date. After a while he stood up and asked the receptionist if Gudrún, the nurse Thorsteinn had mentioned as a witness to the will, was on duty.

'Yes, she is,' the receptionist replied.

'Could I have a word with her while I'm waiting?'

'I'll get someone to fetch her.'

The police uniform certainly had its uses.

They sat at a table at the end of the waiting room, away from reception and the only other patient waiting to see the doctor. It was best to take no risks.

'I'm sorry to disturb you at work,' he said, trying to put her at ease.

A middle-aged woman with a friendly look about her, Gudrún seem unperturbed by the request to talk to the police, and she smiled openly.

'Don't worry about it,' she said. 'What can I do for you?'

'I wanted to ask you about the will that Hrólfur Kristjánsson made. I understand you witnessed it.'

'That's right. It was at Thorsteinn and Snjólaug's house. All I did was sign it as a witness.'

'I expect that everything was done properly. Hrólfur was present in person, wasn't he?'

'Yes, of course.'

'Do you know who the beneficiaries of the will were to be?'

'Good heavens, no. I didn't ask, and it was none of my business,' she said, flushing.

'Did you mention to anyone that Hrólfur had made a will?'

'No, I didn't. He made it very plain that this was to be kept confidential, and I take that kind of thing seriously.'

Ari Thór felt she sounded convincing. 'Of course. I don't doubt that.'

'Was he . . . murdered?'

Ari Thór didn't get an opportunity to reply. His name was called.

'Sorry, have to rush. Meeting the doctor.'

'Yes, OK. I hope I've helped.'

'Indeed,' he said, although it wasn't exactly truthful. 'Thanks for seeing me.'

He hurried to his appointment.

The doctor was a young woman, tall and authoritative, with short black hair.

'What seems to be the trouble?' The tone of her voice made

it plain she had no time to waste. 'Tómas mentioned something about your shoulder?'

Ari nodded. 'This one.' He pointed to the injured shoulder. 'I fell on a table in my living room.'

'The home can be a dangerous place,' she observed, kneading his shoulder. 'Does this hurt?'

He winced with the pain. 'Very much.'

After a brief examination she gave her verdict: 'Nothing serious. Just some badly pulled muscles. It will hurt, and it should get better in a few days. You need to take some time off work and put the arm in a sling.'

He wanted to decline, but didn't have the energy, not right now. He left with his arm in the sling, determined to take it off as soon as he reached the station, and then cursed his own stubbornness. It could be just as well to give his shoulder a rest.

He wasn't far from the hospital when he suddenly turned around and retraced his steps. There was something he wanted to check at the hospital, hoping that it might lead him one step closer to finding out who had broken in that night.

||||||||||||||

The information he got at the hospital fitted into his theory about the break-in, although the picture wasn't yet fully clear. He weighed the possibilities in his mind on the way back to the station, his mood lighter and more optimistic. He had ideas of his own about who his nighttime visitor had been, but he still didn't know why. What could he have of such value, presumably in relation to the investigation? And then suddenly it dawned on him. Could it be the camera? He was so excited that he almost forgot his injured shoulder and the doctor's instructions to rest.

He went straight to the computer without a word to Tómas and immediately found the folder of pictures taken at the cinema.

'The Reverend has his arm in a sling?' Tómas said amiably.

'Hmm? Yes. The doctor said the muscles have been badly pulled. I just need to take it easy for a few days.'

'I thought so. You can switch with Hlynur. I'll ask him to come in tomorrow and take this week's shifts and you can come back at the weekend.'

'I'd prefer to be at work, if you don't mind. It's not like I have anything else to do.'

Except think about work, Ugla and Kristín.

'We'll do what the doctor says, shall we?' The paternal tone reminded Ari Thór of his own father. It was just what he would have said.

'Fair enough. But I expect I'll be around anyway.'

'Up to you. But you aren't on duty. Let's make that clear.'

Ari Thór looked back at the screen and searched the pictures. He wanted to be sure before explaining his theory to Tómas, and he had a ways to go yet.

What had eluded them? He scanned the pictures again and again, but nothing presented itself. Hopelessness swept through him.

One possibility was to show them to Ugla, assuming she was the only one he could trust. Maybe she would spot something? But it wasn't that simple.. There were things they had to discuss . . . and then there was the will; which was quite apart from the fact that it was inappropriate to show her pictures of a crime scene connected to a case in which she might also be a suspect.

He saved the pictures onto a CD and dropped it into his pocket.

He decided to do it – to go and meet Ugla. He had to find out what she thought.

IIIIIIIIIIIII

Hlynur had changed as the years passed, matured. When he looked back he wondered how he could have been so, well, evil, when he was a younger man. Evil. And quite vile.

He had always been tall for his age – and strong. But instead of using his strength to help the children at school who needed it, he found that teasing them was a better outlet for his energies. Teasing wasn't quite the right word, though.

It was bullying, or torturing was probably a better description. Sometimes he'd wake up in the night bathed in sweat, thinking back to old sins.

I'll go to hell for this.

That was all in the distant past, and he was a grown man now. He had moved to a new place, north to Siglufjördur. He tried to forget those years many times, but it was always difficult to push aside the memory of those he had treated so badly. He remembered every name and had tried to make contact with his victims in recent years. He had apologised to them. Most of them had taken it well, some better than others. Some appeared to have got over it all, on the surface at least. Others were less willing to forgive.

He had reached all but one. He hadn't been able to find him in the phone directory, or in the national registry. There was no sign of him at all, until he had the idea of searching through old

newspapers on the Internet, and the name came up in the obitu-
aries. He read them again and again, and it was obvious that the
man had taken his own life. Surely it wasn't the bullying . . . could
it have been his fault? Surely not, not after all this time? He still
hadn't been in touch with the man's family. Even the thought of
it brought him out in a cold sweat. He wanted to talk to them, to
reassure himself that something else had pushed him into suicide, but still he hesitated. He was terrified that they might confirm what he suspected deep inside. This particular boy had been
hit the hardest. Hlynur remembered how he had held him
underwater in the school swimming pool, a little longer each
time, threatening to drown him. The poor boy was petrified, yet
Hlynur had kept at it. He had been small, stout, shy, never capable of defending himself, and that simply made Hlynur more
eager to continue the torture, even resorting to giving him the
occasional beating. The boy had finally become a man, and killed
himself. Ever since Hlynur found out about his death, he had
been contemplating going the same way, finding it increasingly
difficult to live with himself and his conscience.

Why had he been such a . . . such a bastard?

His only saving grace at the moment was the fact that he
had been able to build a respectable relationship with one former classmate, one he had also treated badly. That man was
now a journalist in Reykjavík. They had met over a coffee a few
years ago to talk over old times, and they had met once or twice
more since then. The weight of his conscience was sometimes
more than he could bear and he wanted to do anything to make
this man's life easier. He wanted to help those he could still
help – a penance for his old misdeeds. In some cases, one at
least, it was too late.

Sometimes he had to bend the rules a little to make up for his past. He didn't regret leaking information to the journalist; it was the least he could do. These were the first big cases in the town since he had moved up north, and he couldn't miss the chance to allow his old schoolmate to be first with the news.

He did it, even if it meant betraying Tómas and having to listen to him going on about it. He admitted to himself that this gesture of kindness to an old victim was one of the few things standing between Hlynur and suicide. This kept him alive.

Hlynur looked out of the window. He had a day off. He sat for a while and watched the snow continue its inexorable fall. The drifts deepened, and the darkness moved in.

||||||||||||||

'It doesn't look good.' Tómas put the phone down with a despondent look on his face. With no reason to go home, Ari Thór was still at the station.

'What's that?'

'Linda. She's still unconscious and the doctors haven't seen any improvement. Quite the opposite, in fact. Her condition seems to be getting worse.'

'Have they let Karl know?'

'They're in regular contact with him.'

'And what was his reaction?'

'He said he'd be on his way to Reykjavík as soon as he can. He was overwhelmed, the doctor said, although I reckon that's maybe not the right word.' He looked at Ari Thór with a serious expression.

'He doesn't care in the least about her.'

Ari Thór watched for his superior's reaction.

Tómas nodded. 'I think you're right. I just don't understand it,' he said.

'He's hiding something,' Ari Thór said, and turned back to the computer, hearing Tómas mutter something as he did so – maybe to him, or maybe something to himself. *Hiding something.* He looked up an email address from a list of cooperating police forces in other countries. Now was the time to try and dig out some more information about that man.

Ari Thór wrote his email quickly and sent it off. He would have to wait. If this provided them with any results, he would have a trump in his hand.

Ugla popped back into his thoughts.

Ugla and Karl? Was that the secret that Hrólfur had stumbled across?

No. Hell, no. Not Ugla.

For a second he doubted his own judgement, but then shook his head and mentally excluded Ugla from the picture.

But what about Anna? He thought back to her positively odd behaviour when he had visited her. She definitely had something to hide, just as Karl did. Were those two hiding the same guilty secret? At the same moment he realised that he had seen neither of them at the reception following Hrólfur's funeral. Not that it necessarily meant anything, but all the same . . .

Had Karl pushed Hrólfur down the stairs to hide his affair with Anna?

Or Anna herself?

'I was wondering,' he said, turning to Tómas. 'This rumour about Hrólfur having a child during the war or just after. Could it be true?'

'I doubt it, my boy.'

'But it's possible, right?'

'Anything is possible. But even if so, I don't see it having any bearing on our case.'

'Could it be anyone from the Dramatic Society?' Ari persevered. 'Born during the war . . . someone who would be about sixty-five now, give or take? Pálmi? Úlfur?'

'Hardly. Pálmi would be too old, and Úlfur – well everyone knows who his father was. The sea took him. No . . .' Tómas said, contemplating. 'Nína, on the other hand . . .'

'Nína?'

'Yes, she's a little older than I am, probably born around '45.'

'Why does she come to mind?'

'Sorry. Sometimes I just assume that you know everything I do, everything about everyone . . .'

Get to the point.

Ari Thór watched Tómas with impatience, until he finally spoke.

'Nína was brought up by her mother and her stepfather, and she took his name. Her mother moved in with him not long after she became pregnant and I have no idea who Nína's real father was. If I remember correctly, her mother lived down south during the war, so it was some soldier, I'd imagine.'

|||||||||||||

Ari Thór called on Ugla that evening.

'Hi.' She seemed a bit shy. Beautiful as always, warm and enchanting. 'Look at you!' She pointed gleefully at the arm in its sling.

He sensed from her reception that their relationship was changing, developing into something he had not expected when they had first met. Not that they discussed anything, and hopefully she wouldn't push him for a serious conversation now. He still needed to talk to Kristín, and he still hadn't decided what he genuinely wanted.

He had tried to convince himself that Kristín's interest in him had dissipated, that it was all over between them. They had talked very little and the last phone call had ended fairly abruptly, as she was busy at work. A part of him knew that this was just Kristín's style; she had never been overly emotional.

He felt good near Ugla. There was a contentment that came over him when he was in her company. He needed warmth and reassurances now more than ever. His nightmares were getting steadily worse; and the same could be said about his claustrophobia. To begin with he had simply feared being snowed in, but now that it had actually happened in this remote spot, he almost felt that he couldn't take much more. And this bloody darkness didn't help either. He had to keep working just to stay sane. The road was still closed, and another avalanche, smaller this time, had fallen that evening. He desperately needed someone.

'About the . . . inheritance . . .' Ugla said when they had sat down. 'Honestly, I had no idea. You have to believe me.'

'I do, Ugla. Of course. Hrólfur was an unpredictable character. And there's nothing to be ashamed of; you treated him kindly, you were his friend. Why shouldn't he do this for you?'

'It's way too much. I feel very uncomfortable with it.'

'Don't. This can change your life, in a way. You can live for free in a huge house, and even rent out the basement. Or rent out the whole house and use the money to go back to school.'

'I know,' she said, rather ill at ease. 'I've thought about all those options. I'm just so thankful to him.'

'You could even sell the house, if you can get a good price,' Ari Thór suggested.

'No way, I would never do that to Hrólfur. I'm keeping it as it is, with the furniture and everything. But what will people think . . . ? Word will get out about this . . .'

'Don't worry about other people's opinions.' Ari Thór moved closer and put his arm around her.

After a moment's silence she said: 'There's something I have to tell you, something that has been on my conscience.'

He felt his heart miss a beat. Was she about to confess to something? And if it had something to do with Hrólfur's death, would he ever feel comfortable about reporting it to Tómas?

'I sort of told you a lie . . .' she said, and Ari Thór waited in agony.

'It's about Ágúst, my boyfriend, the one who died,' she continued. 'I told you he had been hit in the head by an out-of-towner, but that wasn't entirely true. The guy who killed him – unintentionally though – was someone I knew. Someone I was having an affair with . . .'

Like I'm having now, Ari Thór thought.

'And that's why I had to leave Patreksfjördur. Not only because of Ágúst, but because of this other guy, who still lives there. A constant reminder of my horrible mistake. Of the part I played in Ágúst's death . . .'

Her tears were starting to flow, so he tried to comfort her the best he could.

She shook herself, trying to recover.

When he was sure she had, he thought he could discuss the matter that had prompted the visit in the first place.

'Do you think you could do me a favour?'

'Of course.' She smiled. 'Anything.'

'I have a few pictures from the theatre, from the night of Hrólfur's death, which I'd like you to take a look at. I think someone may have tried to steal my camera when I had the break-in, but I can't imagine why.'

He borrowed her computer and showed her the pictures from the CD, asking her if she could spot anything unusual.

She took some time to go through them, then went back and checked one picture more carefully. She spotted something, a detail, but an interesting one.

It was the name that she mentioned that took Ari Thór by surprise. He would have to do a bit more digging, to give him a clearer picture. Or was he going in the completely wrong direction?

He left Ugla with a kiss, schoolboy butterflies again fluttering in his stomach.

36

SIGLUFJÖRDUR: WEDNESDAY, 21ST JANUARY 2009

Ari Thór's mind was full of the investigation as he lay down to sleep on Tuesday night. All he could think about were the people at the Dramatic Society, Karl and Linda, and old Sandra. For once, however, he slept soundly, free of the suffocating dreams, the usual feelings of helplessness. Maybe he was acclimatising, albeit gradually. He woke up refreshed, with a new clarity. A particular idea had been sparked in his mind. He revisited his conversation with Sandra, and began tentatively to put together some of the facts he'd gathered in the investigation so far.

Could a terrible crime have been committed in the town many years ago? A crime that nobody had even noticed at the time?

It was time to talk to Sandra again, and half an hour later he was out of the house and on his way to the rest home. His spirits lifted as he took in the beautiful winter's day. The snow had ceased its persistent hammering and the air was still. It had become a beautiful winter's day. His arm was back in its sling and the ache in his shoulder was starting to abate.

Sandra welcomed him, a merry delight in her eyes.

'I knew you'd be back. We had such an interesting chat last time.' She lay in bed, but propped herself up on her elbows to speak, shyly smoothing down the covers. 'It's just a shame I'm not a little more presentable.'

'I hope you're well,' said Ari Thór, trying to set her at ease.

'Not so bad. I'm still here.'

'There's something you mentioned the other day that I wanted to ask you about.'

'Really? Go on, then.'

Ari Thór asked his question.

The old woman looked confused, and a little dismayed.

'Say that again?' she asked quietly.

Ari Thór repeated it.

'I thought I hadn't heard right at first. Why on earth do you want to know about that?' said Sandra, visibly puzzled.

'I'm trying to work out if a crime was committed a long time ago.'

Her look of curiosity changed to one of horror as she suddenly realised what Ari Thór was implying. She gave herself time to think before replying.

'You don't think . . . ?' she asked at last.

'Yes, that's what I'm beginning to suspect,' he confirmed. 'It was nice seeing you again. I'll be back, if you need the company,' Ari Thór said with sincerity.

'Absolutely, you're always welcome, dear boy.'

When he was about to leave, he heard her muttering to herself: 'Well, I'll be damned . . . And in our peaceful town!'

||||||||||||

Ari Thór took the opportunity to call at the hospital, of which the rest home was an extension, and asked for a word with the doctor. The answer he was given to his hypothetical question fitted perfectly with the theory that had formed in his mind.

So many things were becoming clear, he felt that he was within touching distance of solving the mystery of Hrólfur's death. Ari Thór's instinct had been to blame Karl, but the photograph Ugla had shown him pointed in a quite different direction, towards a person he had not seriously suspected before.

||||||||||||

Bundled up in a thick down parka and jeans, Ari Thór called at the police station that evening. The storm had returned with a vengeance, surpassing its former strength and hurling snow that piled up anywhere there was a little shelter from the biting wind.

Ari Thór, having thought that his feelings of claustrophobia and anxiety were starting to wane, realised that he was still some way from having made a full recovery.

Hlynur was alone on the evening shift, a mug of coffee in his hand. Ari Thór took a seat in the coffee corner.

'Those demonstrators down south burned the Christmas tree. Did you see it?' Hlynur asked.

Ari Thór stared at him curiously. 'The Christmas tree?'

'Yep. On Austurvöllur Square by the Parliament building. Your giant Christmas tree, the one the Norwegians always send over.'

'What? The Olso tree? That's unbelievable.'

'I couldn't imagine anyone setting fire to our tree on the square here. Think of the uproar. We get our Christmas tree from Denmark. Don't think they'd send us a tree next year if that happened.'

'Maybe the demonstrators were just cold,' Ari Thór suggested wryly. 'Things are quiet, are they?' he said, changing the subject.

'Yes . . . who's going to be out breaking the law in this weather? Oh, they called from Reykjavík just now, just after Tómas had gone home, about Linda.'

'Saying what?'

'They found something on the knife. Some faint traces, wool, probably. But no prints.'

'Right. Traces from her clothes, probably?' Ari Thór asked, at the same time remembering that she had been found half-naked.

'No, it didn't match her shirt, which we found in the flat. It was some blue material. I think they said wool. We'll have to check it out tomorrow.' He yawned. 'I'll tell Tómas in the morning.'

Ari Thór felt the prickle of sweat breaking out. Blue wool, a dark-blue wool sweater. The snow and a motionless body in its halo of blood.

Karl.

That bastard Karl.

At last there was something to connect him to the case; or at least something to link him to the knife.

'Interesting,' he said, biting back his excitement. It was probably best not to say too much for the moment.

Ari Thór sat at the computer and saw that the emails from the insurance company had come through with the policy's terms and conditions. And there was another message in his inbox, one from abroad. This would be the answer to his query from the day before. He read the message and the attached file as quickly as his language skills would allow and printed them both with his heart beating faster.

He returned to the message from the insurance company, and printed out the policy, then sat back to read it.

Now there's a surprise . . .

His heart was hammering. Trying to mask his growing excitement, he waved a friendly goodbye to Hlynur and pulled up the hood of his anorak. The pieces were falling into place, one at a time, and this evening would reveal the truth.

He stepped out into the white darkness and set off; somewhere in the furthest recesses of his mind he sensed a warning voice whispering to him to tread carefully and wait until the morning, reminding him it wasn't clever to be going alone to meet a man who seemed to have a great deal on his conscience.

The weather deteriorated with every step he took, the wind picking up the fallen snow and throwing it into the fresh fall to create a freezing vortex. A warning from nature. He could hardly see, but Ari Thór knew precisely where he was going and how to get there. Nothing was going to stand in his way.

37

SIGLUFJÖRDUR: WEDNESDAY, 21ST JANUARY 2009

Karl opened the door with a look of exhaustion on his face, which was quickly replaced by surprise when he saw Ari Thór standing on his step. He shook his head and frowned.

'What do you want?'

There was no suggestion of any courtesy here. Maybe people were only polite to the police when they were in uniform. Had Karl been playing a part all this time, with his friendly manner and show of concern for Linda? Was the real Karl now in evidence?

Ari Thór could smell the alcohol immediately. Not drunk, but not sober either, he decided, and probably from something stronger than a can of beer on a Wednesday night. It occurred to him to turn around and let it wait until the morning. He wasn't on duty and the man he had come to talk to was in no state to be interviewed. Nevertheless, he remained determined to get to the heart of the matter.

'Could I have a word?'

Karl looked him up and down, his face wary, but curious. He shrugged his shoulders before replying, 'Why not?'

He stood aside to let Ari Thór in. It was cold in the flat. Not as cold as outside, but noticeably chilly.

Karl went ahead of him into the living room, and turned down the volume on the television. He sat down in the leather armchair that he had obviously occupied before Ari Thór had knocked. There was a small glass on the wooden table, a bottle of tequila, a lime cut into segments and another uncut lime next to it, a sharp knife and a salt shaker. There were knife marks in the wood of the table. Ari Thór noticed with disquiet that Karl was between him and the door, like a guard dog. He sat on the old yellow sofa, still piled with the oddly decorated cushions. He felt awkward, unsure of himself in Karl's territory. Karl shifted his chair and stared at Ari Thór.

'I want to ask a few questions,' Ari Thór began.

'What?' Karl asked, taking a long drink, which seemed to relax him.

Ari Thór gathered his wits and strengthened his resolve. 'A few questions, I said.'

Karl sat silent.

Ari Thór took out his notebook and pretended to leaf through it, although he knew precisely what he was about to ask.

'Your legal residence, Karl – is it correct that you're still registered in Kópavogur?'

Start small, gather courage.

Karl laughed. 'Is it correct? What a question! Don't beat about the bush, Ari Thór. Of course I'm registered in Kópavogur, and you've already checked. What you want to know is the reason.'

Ari Thór nodded in reply.

'I owe a bit of money, half a million or so. I'd prefer not to let them know where I live right now.'

'Who? The bank?'

He laughed again, and this time he seemed genuinely amused. 'The bank? No, these are gentlemen who don't use conventional methods. They've probably forgotten about me by now. Who's going to follow me all the way to Siglufjördur? No one in their right mind comes to Siglufjördur in the dead of winter,' he said and paused. 'Except for you, a fuckwit from down south,' he added with a grin.

Don't let him wind you up.

'I gather you've been seen with another woman.'

Straight in at the deep end, drop the bait. Sometimes it paid off to be elastic with the truth.

Karl grinned again.

'Well, it was going to happen sooner or later. Hide-and-seek gets tiring after a while, but it's fun as long as it lasts. So who saw us?'

'Hrólfur,' he said, reflecting that it could well be true.

'Hrólfur! That old bastard? Spying on his neighbours.'

Neighbours? Anna?

'You're still seeing each other? You and Anna?'

'Ach, what the hell does it matter? Do you really care who I sleep with?'

Karl fell silent and suddenly appeared to realise the implications of what he had said.

'Ah . . . so you reckon I pushed the old man down the stairs?' he laughed loudly, his face a mask.

'Did you?'

Karl glared at him. 'No.'

'You're not ashamed of being unfaithful?'

'Ashamed? No. It wouldn't have been all that great if Linda had found out. She's the one who paid the rent. But now . . . Now I don't care either way, now that she's dead, or as good as dead.'

Ari Thór felt a fury build up inside him, wondering how the man could say such a thing.

'And Anna? I don't suppose she'd want this to be widely known?'

'No, definitely not. She's planning to stay here and teach.' He smirked. 'That's not my problem. I'm leaving. I have a job to go to in Akureyri.'

He stared out of the window, silent as the storm raged around them. Ari Thór waited, listening to the baying of the wind.

'Did you come here to ask me if I'd murdered the old man?' Karl asked at last.

Ari Thór fixed his gaze on Karl, determined not to let himself be side-tracked. He was in the lion's den now and intended to see this through to the truth.

'You think I killed Linda as well?' Karl asked, mocking him now.

'No,' he said, holding Karl's gaze.

'Really? Then maybe you're not as stupid as you look.'

'I know perfectly well that you didn't assault her. I know about the life insurance.'

Karl's jaw dropped, and he struggled to rearrange his features. 'How the hell did you find out about that?'

'So you obviously knew about the insurance?'

'No point denying it now.'

'There were threads from your sweater on the knife.'

He smiled. 'You're as smart as hell, Ari Thór. Maybe I should just admit it to get rid of you.'

'You're quite obviously innocent of the assault. But you can wipe that grin off your face because I know what you did.'

'Really? Tell me, then. I can hardly wait.'

'You moved the knife. You hid it behind the bushes so it wouldn't be found near her, so it would look as if someone else had done it.'

'And why would I do a thing like that?' Karl asked, his voice measured, as if speaking to a child.

'I'm guessing that you read the terms and conditions of the life insurance policy, or at least had an idea of their contents. You don't stand to get anything if she commits suicide so soon after the policy starts.'

The look on his face said it all.

'Do you think she intended to commit suicide?' Ari Thór asked.

'I don't have a clue,' Karl said, looking away. 'She was always whining. She couldn't stand the weather, didn't like the darkness. If she'd wanted to do herself in, then she would have cut her wrist or something. I think it was just attention-seeking. She talked about it sometimes, doing herself harm, playing with the kitchen knives. I told her to shut her trap and grow up.' He was quiet for a moment. 'Something went wrong, she must have cut too deep and lost too much blood. Damned stupid. She probably wanted to tempt fate, cut herself to draw blood in the snow. She could be a proper drama queen. But you have to admit it makes a great contrast, blood red on white, and she had an artistic side to her.'

This cold analysis told Ari Thór that this man had no fondness for Linda.

'Then on top of that it was all Hrólfur's fault,' continued Karl.

'Hrólfur's?'

'After he tumbled down the stairs. She got much worse, more unstable, especially after the rumours that he had been murdered.'

'But you admit you moved the knife, because of the insurance?'

'I never admit anything. It's not worth it. I'd get nothing from that . . . I just play along when there's something to be won . . . I admit it's a pain in the neck to be with someone who does shit like that. What does it say about me?'

He stopped, and was quiet, before continuing in a more aggressive tone.

'I can see you were hoping to stick something serious on me. But you won't put me behind bars for moving a knife . . .'

No, unfortunately.

Ari Thór took some folded sheets of paper from his pocket and laid them on the table. His phone rang as he did so. He took it from his trouser pocket and looked at the screen. Ugla. He placed the phone on the table and switched off the ringer.

'What's that? What have you got there?' Karl asked, stuttering slightly, his composure wavering. He didn't go so far as to stand up, instead reaching for a lime and cutting it into slices. It didn't seem to bother him that he was cutting more grooves into the surface of the old table.

Ari Thór didn't answer right away.

'What the fuck is all that stuff?' Karl asked again.

'Documents that were sent to me by the Danish police.'

Karl's face was expressionless, but the force he used to slice the lime increased visibly.

'You lived there for a while, didn't you?' Ari Thór asked.

'You know that already. What are you trying to dig up, you bastard?'

'These are old police records. It looks like you had a few altercations with the law.'

'So what? There was never anything serious.'

'One incident was more serious than the others, and it seems you were interviewed as a suspect in a very significant case . . . Strongly suspected, but no proof.'

No reaction.

'Shall I refresh your memory?'

Silence.

'There was a break-in at the home of a woman on the outskirts of Århus . . . Stolen jewellery. Does that sound familiar?'

Karl's expression was as cold and hard as stone. He stopped slicing the lime and, as if by rote, he laid the blade against the sofa and ran it slowly up the arm, scarring the leather.

'A woman was assaulted. I guess you know the rest of the story, don't you?'

Karl grinned and Ari Thór shuddered at the chill it sent creeping up his spine.

'Yes, I know the story.'

38

She tried again to open the door, her heart hammering as she could hear him approaching, sense him coming closer.

The click was the most wonderful sound she had ever heard. The door was unlocked, and she pulled it inwards, taking a step back so she could swing the door open and make a run for it, run as fast as her legs would let her. She would run for her husband, run for her children and grandchildren. She would run so she'd be able to go back to the Indian takeaway again and get chicken, with rice this time.

||||||||||||||

He was livid when he realised she was trying to get away. His fury gave him an additional burst of energy and he raced for the door with the knife in one hand and his phone in the other; he ended the call to his friend, the one who had pointed the house out to him as an *easy target – a woman frequently home alone. In exchange for the information, he would take a share of the proceeds.*

He had killed before, but not in circumstances like these, and never with violence. Killing hadn't affected him at all; it had simply been a necessary piece of work to achieve an aim. Why should it be different this time?

There was no hesitation, not even a stab of conscience, as he drew back the knife and plunged it deep.

||||||||||||||

Her back turned, she didn't see him, feeling only a stinging pain. She looked over her shoulder with difficulty, and saw him pull the knife from the wound. She closed her eyes, missing the second plunge of the knife. And then she saw nothing more.

||||||||||||||

He had been right. He didn't feel anything; not a shred of remorse – only anger that he had given her the opportunity to run, and, of course, frustration that he'd never claimed the contents of the safe. That didn't matter now. The important thing was to get away.

He made his way out into the warm darkness of the Danish evening and vanished among the imposing suburban houses where people took care not to notice anything.

39

SIGLUFJÖRDUR: WEDNESDAY, 21ST JANUARY 2009

Karl stared at Ari Thór in silence.

'Nobody was ever charged with that murder,' Ari Thór said at last, without dropping his eyes.

Karl shrugged. 'I don't know what that has to do with me,' he said, picking up the knife and continuing to slice the lime.

'You're handy with a knife.'

'I learned young how to handle one.' He scowled and then chuckled. 'You don't have anything on me. A wet-behind-the-ears fuckwit from down south, coming here and trying to scare me. No chance.'

There was determination in his voice.

We'll see.

Ari Thór had been right so far. He was sure of it, even though Karl hadn't really confirmed his suspicions. There was one more thing he wanted to clear up, and then it would be time to let fly.

'When did you move abroad?'

'To Denmark? 1983. I wish I had never bothered coming back.'

'That summer?'

'No, that autumn.'

'I gather your family had a tough time in Siglufjördur in the old days.'

'What are you getting at?'

'Your parents weren't that well off, were they?'

'My bloody parents were always too poor to give me anything.'

'All the same, you were able to buy a car at that time . . . the jeep. The jeep that Anna's father owns today.'

For the first time a look of concern flashed across Karl's face.

'And what the hell does that have to do with anything?'

'A beautiful vehicle,' Ari Thór said, not that he had actually seen it.

'It was a great car. A crying shame I had to sell it.'

'Why did you move?'

'That's none of your business,' Karl said, and thought for a moment, obviously deciding to play the good guy. 'To find work. Dad couldn't find work here.'

'You're sure that was the only reason?'

'What are you trying to say?' He lifted himself in his chair, still holding the knife. The lime lay forgotten.

'How come you could afford such an expensive car?'

Karl said nothing.

'Surely the old lady didn't pay that well?'

This time Karl went pale, but said nothing.

'The old lady, Pálmi's mother. You were working for her, weren't you? I heard you'd done odd jobs for her, cleared up, killed vermin, and when I asked about that a few other things popped up. The old lady I spoke to worked at the Co-op at that time and she remembered you buying rat poison; she just assumed that you were going to poison rats for the old woman.'

Ari Thór took the opportunity to pause and watched Karl squirm in his chair.

At last.

'Pálmi told me that his mother had never trusted banks and kept her savings hidden away . . . but when she died, there was barely enough to cover her funeral. That's a little odd, don't you think?'

Ari Thór waited. Karl rose to his feet. He stood motionless, the knife clasped in his hand.

'Suppose she had trusted you enough to tell you that she kept her savings in the house. Or let's say you came across it when you were clearing up. Either way, she died suddenly in the summer of 1983, of a brain haemorrhage. I spoke to a doctor and asked if rat poison could produce the same symptoms as a brain haemorrhage, and he confirmed that it would. At the time nobody suggested a thing. A woman of sixty-seven suffers a brain haemorrhage and dies. An amiable youngster who had worked for her buys himself a smart jeep soon afterwards . . . Were your parents the only ones who made the connection?'

Karl said nothing. The fury was clear on his face. Ari Thór pressed on, regardless.

'It's obvious, Karl. You killed the old lady to get your hands on her cash. How much was it? Enough to buy yourself a jeep, we know. Was there any left over? You managed to fool her just as you fooled me; innocent on the surface, friendly, polite. But your parents saw through you. They left the country so the truth wouldn't come out. You couldn't fool them, could you? They knew what you were like inside, what you were capable of doing.'

Karl was suddenly at the table, the knife still in his hand.

Ari Thór sat still. Only the table was between them.

'You bastard! You don't say a word to anyone . . . or else . . .'

'Or what?'

He regretted the question the second he had asked it. He knew precisely what was being threatened.

Karl reached quickly over the table and grasped Ari Thór's shoulder, the injured shoulder, his arm still in its sling.

The pain shot through him and he was gripped with fear; a rat in a trap, cornered.

'I ought to sort this out right now.' Karl's eyes blazed with madness and he lifted the knife closer to Ari Thór.

Ari Thór stood up, smartly and without warning, his fist clenched. His punch was enough for Karl to lose his balance. Staggering backwards, he dropped the knife, as Ari Thór leapt over the table. Leaving his phone where it lay he made for the door at the end of the corridor.

He could hear Karl getting to his feet with a roar.

He yanked open the door and ran out into the storm, into the darkness, as the driving snow blinded him. His feet were as heavy as lead, just as in his worst nightmares.

He took a short cut across the old football pitch in the centre of town, buried under layer upon layer of snow. It was years since he had run across a field like this; he had been a small boy in Reykjavík.

He wouldn't allow things to end like this. He had to reach his destination. Karl couldn't be far behind him and he was desperate enough to do anything. Ari Thór knew that if he stopped, his life would end there, alone in a pool of blood in the snow.

He took a jump over a deep bank of snow and onto the pavement that fronted the town's liquor shop. He had to run faster, avoid the urge to stop and look behind him. The thought that they could now put Karl behind lock and key boosted his energy.

He was in the Town Hall Square. If he ran straight over it and round the corner he would reach the police station.

He pushed himself to go faster.

He was going to make it. Almost there.

He had to get there.

40

SIGLUFJÖRDUR: WEDNESDAY, 21ST JANUARY 2009

It wasn't long until opening night.

That was when Nína was determined to make her move.

She had already waited long enough. She had offered to volunteer for the Dramatic Society just to be close to him, the man she loved.

Even though he had told her they couldn't be together, she always felt that they would, in one way or another, end up as a couple. He had always been so kind to her.

She was going to speak to him at the reception after the opening night, ask him out on a date, like a teenager.

She'd missed out on her teenage years. She had waited for life for far too long, watching it shoot past her like a landscape seen from behind the windows of a moving car, driven much too quickly.

Nína felt the flutter inside her.

She was so excited.

||||||||||||||

It wasn't until Ari Thór reached the police station, his mind and body overcome by exhaustion, that he finally dared to look over his shoulder. Nobody there.

Hlynur jumped to his feet and stared at Ari Thór as he staggered in through the door, cold and bedraggled – his eyes wide and pleading. It was a while before he could get a coherent sentence past his lips.

'Karl . . . the bastard . . . tried to kill me. He's armed and dangerous. I found out he murdered Pálmi's mother, and a woman in Denmark.' Ari Thór spluttered and coughed as he struggled to make clear the impending threat.

'Calm down, Reverend.' Hlynur took the news calmly, almost as if he had expected Ari Thór to appear in just this state. 'Sit yourself there and get some coffee down you. I've called Tómas.'

'Tómas?' Ari Thór took the mug Hlynur handed him. 'You've already called Tómas?'

'Karl called, a couple of minutes ago.'

'Karl?' Ari Thór yelped. 'What the hell for?'

Hlynur laid a hand gently on his shoulder, the good shoulder. 'He called because he wants to make a formal complaint.'

'A complaint?' Ari Thór could hardly form a complete sentence. He felt overwhelmed, besieged by Karl's treachery. He buried his face in his shaking hands and exhaled. The murderer was going to complain about him?

'Calm down,' Hlynur said amiably. 'Don't worry . . . We know what Karl's like and nobody's going to believe him. But the complaint will have to go through the proper channels, for formality's sake.'

Ari Thór sat speechless.

'He said you pushed your way in and started interrogating him, even though he'd obviously had a drink and you weren't on duty. He wants you charged with assault. Smacked him, did you?'

'He was trying to kill me!'

Ari Thór jumped to his feet and hurled the coffee mug to the floor where it shattered into pieces, splashing coffee in every direction.

'He was going to kill me, the bloody murderer. You hear me?'

'Let's wait for Tómas, shall we?' Hlynur said, his voice oddly comforting.

'No, you go get Karl right away!' he yelled. 'He may try to escape, do you hear me?!'

'He won't get anywhere.'

'Are you kidding me, Hlynur? Are you going to believe him or me? You have to go over there and arrest him! Do you hear me?' Ari Thór said furiously.

'Take it easy, Reverend,' Hlynur said. 'I'll get you another cup of coffee.'

|||||||||||||

'Tell me again what happened.' Tómas tried to keep a calm and quiet voice. Ari Thór was noticeably upset and spoke incoherently. 'Did you attack him?'

'No, of course not. He had a knife, I had to hit him to get out of there! I confronted him with my theories. That Linda had tried to commit suicide, and that he had covered it up when he found the body, by moving the knife.'

'Why?' Tómas asked.

'Because of the insurance terms. He wouldn't get the ten million if it had been ruled as a suicide,' Ari Thór said anxiously.

'And did he admit to it?'

'More or less. He didn't deny it.'

'I don't think that will do, my boy,' Tómas said calmly. 'And anyway, it would hardly be more than a misdemeanour, interfering with a police investigation.'

'And then . . . I think he killed two people.'

'Really?'

'Pálmi's mother. The old lady, Sandra, mentioned that he had done all sorts of stuff for Pálmi's mother, including exterminating vermin. I asked her about it in more detail: she remembered him buying rat poison in the Co-op. Pálmi's mother died shortly before Karl moved away with his parents, and just before he bought the jeep, she died penniless. They must have hurried away when they found out what he did. And . . .' Ari Thór tried to catch his breath between words. 'And, the symptoms of rat poisoning could be the same as her alleged cause of death, a haemorrhage.'

'It's a theory, my boy,' Tómas said. 'I believe Karl is capable of anything, but do you have any real evidence? Anything concrete? Maybe you're putting two and two together and getting five, just because you want to.'

'He didn't really deny it!'

'He may be playing games with you, Ari Thór, winding you up.'

'Anyway, the last thing is dead certain . . . I've seen the police records from Denmark, I have them printed out on my desk. He was the prime suspect in the killing of a woman in a break-in, some jewellery went missing.'

'Again, what can we do now? The Danish police have surely done their best. You should go home, get some rest.'

'Aren't you going to arrest him?!' Ari Thór looked outraged.

'I'll have a talk with him. You say he pulled a knife on you?'

'Well . . .' Ari Thór hesitated. 'He had a knife when I came in, slicing a lime.'

'Okay, that's enough for now, my boy.'

It was Ari Thór's word against Karl's, Tómas thought to himself. The boy had been off duty, probably slightly unbalanced. And he had apparently hit a suspect. He had made more than one mistake that night. But he had also drawn some interesting conclusions, even though most of it could probably never be proven. Yes, the boy had potential, but he needed to be more careful.

||||||||||||||

Tómas had interviewed Karl at the police station while Hlynur had searched his house.

Karl was calm and self-possessed, answering in monosyllables or with silence. Tómas told him he was being interviewed as a possible suspect, and could have a lawyer present, or listening in via telephone. Karl said that there was absolutely no need for a laywer.

After Karl had flatly denied having anything to do with the death of Pálmi's mother, Tómas shifted the interview to Linda.

'We found traces of dark-blue wool on the knife. The evening you found the body you were wearing a dark-blue wool sweater. Linda had life insurance and you stood to gain financially from her death. So tell me . . .' Tómas looked steadily at Karl. 'Tell me why I shouldn't arrest you here and now for attempted murder?'

Karl sat silent for a while.

'She had the knife in her hand when I found her. You can't pin an assault charge on me, no way.' He seemed to be in total control of the situation.

Tómas sat still and waited.

'I don't know what came over me. I hid the knife in the garden next door to, well, so as not to damage her reputation. It was a lack of judgment on my part, of course.'

'And because you knew you wouldn't get a penny if it was shown to be suicide.'

'I didn't know that.'

He grinned in the certain knowledge that no copy of the insurance policy would be found in a search of the house.

Tómas pursued a line of questioning about the earlier reports of domestic violence, despite having nothing more than suspicion and Leifur's testimony that Karl and Linda had argued frequently. According to the latest reports, there was nothing to indicate that Linda was likely to regain consciousness and bear witness against Karl.

'Did you threaten Ari Thór with a knife?' he asked, trying to wrong-foot Karl.

'I certainly did not. I had a knife in my hand when he barged in on me. I gave him a chance to speak, though he was obviously quite unstable, and when his accusations became outrageous, I stood up and asked him to leave. That was when he attacked me. I hope that my complaint will be dealt with properly.'

'Of course,' Tómas said. 'I need to ask you to wait here for a moment.'

He left the interview room and made a call to the police lawyer on duty, seeking advice on the next steps.

'It doesn't sound like you've got any real evidence linking him with the attack on Linda,' the lawyer said after Tómas had gone over the situation in detail. 'As to the other cases, the older ones, I don't see that anything can be done about that. Pure speculation. No grounds for custody, in my view.'

Tómas waited for Hlynur to finish the search, which proved fruitless, and subsequently informed Karl that he could leave.

'But don't leave town for the next few days,' he added as a warning.

'I'm not likely to go far with all the roads closed,' Karl smirked, as he stepped out into the darkness, the snow eddying around him. The smile and walk of a man, thought Tómas, who knew that he had escaped justice; because he'd done it before.

41

SIGLUFJÖRDUR: THURSDAY, 22ND JANUARY 2009

Fish.

It all started with the fish.

If there hadn't been fish in the sea then nobody would ever have thought of living here. The first house would never have been built and Ari Thór would never have come to live here. Now he couldn't be sure that he would keep his job, and he was facing an assault charge.

That bloody fish.

Shattered by the events of the evening, Ari Thór had slept soundly that night. He stopped at the bakery on the way to the station to buy himself a roll and felt that every eye was on him – in the bakery and on the street – searching, inquisitive eyes, as if his altercation with Karl had become common knowledge. He tried to steady his breathing. Of course nobody knew. He had to get his bearings, get his feet back on the ground. There was no all-encompassing conspiracy of townspeople against him.

'Good morning. Sleep well?' Tómas asked cheerfully.

Ari Thór nodded and glanced towards Hlynur. 'Apologies for all the excitement last night.'

'Excitement? It doesn't even compare with the news from down south,' Hlynur replied. 'These protests are boiling over and I hear our colleagues had to use tear gas to get it under control.'

'That's how it goes,' Tómas said. 'At least there's not much in the way of protest going on up here.'

'Didn't you say the other day that you missed out on the boom years up here? Maybe you should have protested about that at the time,' Ari Thór suggested. 'Anyway, did you speak to Karl last night?'

'We did, and we had to release him,' Tómas said. 'For the moment.'

It was what Ari Thór had expected, but he still felt a stab of disappointment. It was an uncomfortable feeling knowing that Karl was a free man.

'I spoke to the insurance company this morning,' Tómas said. 'I told them that the case is under investigation as an attempted suicide. If Linda dies, which unfortunately doesn't seem to be unlikely, then Karl won't get a penny. So there's a little justice there. Then I had a word with the sheriff in Akureyri as well. We're commended for an efficient investigation into Linda's case. They won't be sending anyone to help us out after all, the case is more or less cleared up,' he added.

Ari Thór had printed out a version of the information from Denmark the night before. Karl had been interrogated as part of the investigation at the time. The woman's husband had arrived home early in the morning to find the body by the outside door, with two stab wounds in her back. It had been deemed that she had died instantly on receipt of the second wound, and the case remained open.

'You asked Karl about this affair in Denmark?' Ari Thór asked.

'There's no way he can be convicted on the basis of what we have,' Tómas said in a serious voice. 'There's no new evidence. It doesn't matter how convinced you are that he's guilty, Ari Thór, or what you feel you deduced from his manner, unfortunately. But I'm convinced that you're right.'

'What about Pálmi's mother?'

'It's a damned good theory, very convincing . . . But I reckon it's far from likely that he'll ever admit anything. He wouldn't answer any questions yesterday. He's not the type to break down under questioning, but we'll certainly try and look into this. I've asked Hlynur to interview Sandra and ask her to make a statement regarding the rat poison.'

Ari Thór felt his spirits lift.

'But don't get your hopes too high. Karl will never be sent down for this murder; I'm sure there's insufficient evidence for a conviction. But we might check on his parents, who still live in Denmark, and see where that leads us. If your theory's right and they left the country to keep him out of harm's way, I doubt they'd let him down.'

'I'm prepared to do my best to put him away.'

'Sorry, my boy . . . You're not going to be part of this investigation, not with an official complaint hanging over you. It has been sent to the state prosecutor, but don't worry about it. I don't doubt that the case will be thrown out once the context is taken into account. The man had a knife in his hand, after all.'

Being left out of the case was something that had not occurred to Ari Thór. He had been set on making up for his mistakes by putting every ounce of energy into the investigation. He was silent, disappointed and dissatisfied.

'But it *was* clumsy on your part,' Tómas said. 'Not clever at all. We might have to give you an official reprimand, but we'll see . . . Let's hope we can get away without that. While I remember, we need to let you have another phone. Yours is part of the evidence.'

Ari Thór nodded, accepting that he had no choice in the matter. The night before he had told Tómas that he'd forgotten his phone at Karl's, having had to run for his life.

'And the car?' he asked earnestly.

'Car? What car?'

'Karl's jeep. The one he bought with the money stolen from Pálmi's mother. Can't you check and find out if he paid for it in cash?'

Tómas made a note.

'I'll do that, my boy.'

‖‖‖‖‖‖‖‖‖‖‖

The tale spread rapidly once a news Web site in Reykjavík posted the story, painting it in suitably lurid colours.

Man suspected of 25-year-old murder in Siglufjördur.

Reportedly based on "reliable sources", the story even mentioned that the man in question had been suspected of a murder in Denmark and that his wife was the woman found more dead than alive in the snow only a week before.

Hlynur had not mentioned to his journalist acquaintance

that the case of the woman in the snow was being treated as attempted suicide.

Nothing about Karl and Anna's relationship had reached the media. The reason was a simple one; Hlynur preferred as far as possible to shield the innocent.

· ||||||||||||

Leifur watched as Úlfur timidly made his way up onto the stage in the old theatre. This time the director had everyone's undivided attention.

Standing by the wall close to the stage, Leifur looked over the room. Nína stood in the doorway, not far from where Hrólfur's corpse had been found. That now seemed so long ago.

Pálmi sat near the front, Anna and Ugla farther back, but not side by side. Pálmi looked despondent and weary. The young policeman from down south had managed to uncover a murder from years back, something nobody had ever suspected. Pálmi's mother had been deprived of her twilight years by a ruthless killer, or so it seemed, although it hadn't been possible to prove anything.

Leifur had no answers. Someone had forced his brother off the road, wrecking the family's happiness. Every day, little by little, he was coming to terms with the fact that the hit-and-run driver would never be found; that some questions would remain unanswered.

Úlfur cleared his throat.

The words "the show must go on" hung in the air, unspoken, and hardly fitting the occasion. Instead he mumbled something as if to himself, and looked up into the auditorium.

'We have to find a way to manage things with . . . Karl's situation. I can well imagine that not all of us are keen on treading the boards right at this moment, but I'm sure it would do us all good to hold the opening night this coming weekend. I . . . I have spoken to Leifur. He has thought it over and is prepared to take the lead, even at such short notice.'

His eyes rested on Leifur, who smiled shyly and looked out again over the auditorium. Pálmi's expression remained unchanged; he had presumably known of this already. The others murmured in surprise, never having expected Leifur to have the confidence in himself to take on such a part.

'Well, I think I can manage,' he said.

He had made up his mind the evening before. He knew the script well enough, having learned it as Karl's understudy, but he had taken a few days off work to prepare himself. He was determined to shine.

He thought of his elder brother, who would now have been proud of him.

Leifur felt his self-esteem growing inside him. Maybe he ought to take the opportunity and have a word with Anna after the opening night? There was something captivating about her.

42

SIGLUFJÖRDUR: FRIDAY, 23RD JANUARY 2009

The town was still under a heavy layer of snow when Ari Thór walked down to the pontoons by the harbour in the early morning, his face drawn after a restless night. Fences had been engulfed by the snow and in many places it reached as high as the windows of the houses. A thrush perched on a post in one garden. A closer look revealed that a flock of thrushes had gathered to feed on the seed that a warm-hearted householder had scattered for them.

Ari Thór walked out onto the dock and looked over the troubled sea, the majestic mountains. Summer seemed a long way off. Would he still be in Siglufjördur when it arrived? Or would Tómas have sent him home in disgrace by then? Even if everything worked out here for the best, if Karl's official complaint were to come to nothing, would he still want to be here?

He was proud of what he had achieved, despite having been

unable to unravel the mystery of Hrólfur's death. He still believed there was something sinister about it.

After all, he probably was where he should be in life at this point. Police work suited him. If he were to keep his job, then he would have to give Siglufjördur a chance.

Then there was Ugla. He wasn't sure if he was in love with her, and he wanted to make sure.

She had done her best to persuade him not to give up on the town.

'Give it until the spring,' she had said. 'Sometimes, in spring or early summer, you wake up and see the mist lying on the fjord – you can't even see the sea, and there's just a glimpse of one or two mountain peaks, just as if they're floating in the air. Then it all changes suddenly, when the sun appears. The beauty of the place is breathtaking. It's when you've experienced those days that you find you never want to leave.'

She had been very persuasive.

He had stepped over the mark with Ugla, first the kiss and then the invitation into her bedroom. He had wanted to sleep with her, but then his conscience had taken over. He felt he couldn't be so disloyal to Kristín. First he wanted to be sure of where they stood.

Hell, but it had been hard to leave Ugla lying practically naked in bed. She was beautiful in jeans and that figure-hugging white T-shirt, but irresistible once her clothes lay in a heap on the floor.

He felt like the world's biggest fool when he told her he wanted to wait, without any mention of why. Ugla didn't know about Kristín, and that was going to be a tough conversation.

Ari Thór looked up to the mountains. In Reykjavík, he'd always felt that he lived in the shadow of Mount Esja, but now he really knew what it meant to live under the shadow of a mountain. Esja was so far from his place in the centre of town; here the mountains were right on top of him.

In Reykjavík, right in the centre of town and not far from his flat, with the government close to falling, it had been impossible to avoid hearing of the protests. These were historic times that he would have experienced at first hand if he had not moved north. But none of this seemed relevant now. All those things were happening far away, almost in another world.

He gazed out over the fjord, imagining the water as still as a mirror on a bright day. He took a deep breath and exhaled slowly.

IIIIIIIIIIIIII

Crossing the Town Hall Square on his way home, Ari Thór bumped into Pálmi.

Pálmi nodded a greeting, apparently intending to continue on his way, but he suddenly turned and stopped.

'Thank you,' he said in a low voice, heavy with emotion, his eyes piercing behind his glasses. 'I heard about your . . . well, your theory about my mother's death. I'm inclined to believe it.'

'Did Tómas speak to you?'

'Yes, yesterday morning.'

'Karl will probably get away with it, in spite of everything.'

'That's of no consequence,' Pálmi said. 'Losing my mother was terrible. It happened so fast I didn't have a chance to say goodbye to her. It explains so much, if Karl did it. It explains how a woman who watched every penny died destitute, and how Karl could buy that jeep.'

'Tómas has been in touch with the man who sold it to him,

spoke to him yesterday. He remembered it well, how the lad arrived with cash and paid for it on the spot,' Ari Thór said, with a flutter of pride.

Pálmi nodded. 'You can exhume her if you need to, if it would help put him away,' he said in a dark voice.

'We'll see,' Ari Thór said gravely. 'I'll stop by this evening.'

||||||||||||

The Dramatic Society's opening night was always a big event and tickets had immediately sold out. Everyone wanted to see Pálmi's play, and everyone wanted to see the last performance with which Hrólfur had been involved, the one that could perhaps have cost him his life.

The Siglufjördur road had finally been cleared on Friday afternoon and Ari Thór felt as if a burden had been lifted from his shoulders, although the oppressively long nights and the nagging claustrophobia remained in the background. He still struggled to sleep, his thoughts wandering, but he was excited about the next day, eager to see Ugla on the opening night. Giving up on having any sort of real rest, he went down to the living room and fetched the book she had lent him, the masterpiece, *North of the Hills*. It seemed fitting to be dipping into Hrólfur's book as a mark of respect.

It was as if the book drew him into a magical world, both with its narrative and the exquisite prose. The bittersweet *Verses for Linda* were so much more than just love poems; he felt himself overwhelmed with emotion. Ari Thór was unable to put the book aside until he had finished it. For the first time in months, he slept peacefully.

43

SIGLUFJÖRDUR: SATURDAY, 24TH JANUARY 2009

The old theatre on Adalgata bustled with life. It had started to snow again, but this time the soft flakes fell gently to earth. Many of the guests had dressed in their best for the occasion. There was anticipation in the air, a definite excitement.

Ugla's starring role had been a triumph, and Ari Thór had been unable to take his eyes off her throughout the entire performance. Leifur had also been surprisingly good, considering that he had been an understudy, probably with limited rehearsal time. The play itself came as a surprise, much better than anything he had expected. It was a bittersweet love story, obviously set far away from Siglufjördur, about lovers who were never able to make their relationship known. Pálmi clearly had a talent.

There were three curtain calls for the cast and the final one received a standing ovation. Ugla gazed out into the auditorium under a roar of applause, her eyes fixed on one member of the audience: Ari Thór.

The reception following the performance was packed. Chairs were stacked against the walls to make space and senior pupils from the school circulated with canapés. Everyone made an effort to make the evening a success. Tonight, it mattered more than ever.

Ari Thór and Tómas talked to Pálmi, Rosa and Mads on the stage. Nína stood nearby, still on crutches and apparently waiting for an opportunity to join the conversation.

'We are travelling to Reykjavík in the morning,' said Rosa, the old lady, in English. 'We can finally go home. But it has been an unforgettable visit, and wonderful that we had a chance to see Pálmi's play performed.'

'It wasn't always easy to follow,' Mads said with a laugh. 'We might have to learn some Icelandic before our next visit.'

Ugla joined them and Ari Thór gave her a shy smile. He longed to be alone with her once the reception was over. Was he falling for her? He couldn't really bear cheating on Kristín, at least not more than he already had, so presumably he had to make up his mind. If he was going to give Ugla a chance, there was no option but to make a very uncomfortable call to Kristín.

Ugla introduced herself to the Danish guests and they continued the conversation in English.

Mads took her hand. 'Hello, my name is Mads. We are visiting from Denmark and have been staying with Pálmi.'

The old lady extended a hand. 'I'm Rosalinda, but call me Rosa. Everyone does . . .' she said, with a glance at Pálmi. 'Except your late father, Pálmi. He always called me Linda.'

44

SIGLUFJÖRDUR: SATURDAY, 24TH JANUARY 2009

Ari Thór started as he saw the pieces click into place. The break-in, the photograph, the umbrella, the child Hrólfur was rumoured to have fathered. He understood where Pálmi's talent had stemmed from; there was no doubt he had written a fine play.

It was suddenly all so clear: Hrólfur's will, and the reason he had retired so young with only one good book to his name.

'He called you Linda?' Ari Thór finally asked Rosa.

The old lady nodded.

'And maybe he wrote a poem for you?' Ari Thór suggested.

Rosa looked confused. 'No, no. He didn't. Not that I know of.'

Ari Thór looked at Pálmi, who appeared to have aged ten years in a matter of moments.

'Pálmi,' he said, switching to Icelandic. 'Who wrote the book, *North of the Hills*? You know who wrote it?'

It was clear that Pálmi would not deny anything. He didn't

have the same stamina that Karl had shown, the same strength of will. Instead, he seemed relieved that someone else had stumbled upon the truth at last.

He sighed and spoke in a low voice, in Icelandic. Rosa and Mads looked on in confusion, not understanding a word.

'Well, my father wrote it.'

Tómas and Ugla stared at Pálmi as if incapable of believing what they were hearing.

'Not Hrólfur?' Ari Thór asked.

'No . . .' All the energy appeared to have drained from Pálmi. 'Hrólfur. That bastard Hrólfur,' he said, raising his voice before dropping it again. 'He stole my father's book. My father was in Denmark, and Hrólfur sat over him on his deathbed. It was obvious that he had written the book for Rosa . . . Linda, as he called her, *Verses for Linda*. I had never been able to work out why Hrólfur had never written another book, considering what a talent he was supposed to be.'

'When did you figure this out?'

'The day before Hrólfur . . . the day before he died. I was talking to Rosa about the years in Denmark and she told me that my father had always called her Linda. She told me a little of their affair and there was so much that was reminiscent of Hrólfur's book. I connected what she had told me with the book, but still didn't immediately put two and two together. I knew that Hrólfur had spent time with my father before his death, sitting with him at the hospital, and then the suspicion started to grow in my mind and I asked myself if it could be that my father had written it.'

He paused and drew a deep breath before continuing.

'I needed to speak to Hrólfur as soon as possible, and the

first opportunity was that evening . . . I left to go home for dinner, like everyone else . . .'

'Taking the umbrella,' Ari Thór added.

'Yes, precisely, and I forgot it in all the fuss when I came back . . .'

'Nína tried to keep you out of trouble,' Ari Thór interrupted. 'She took the umbrella home as if it were her own, even though she had been at the theatre earlier in the day, before it started to rain. She probably thought that the umbrella would focus our attention on you. If we had known it was yours, it would have suggested that you had already returned from dinner. Then she broke into my place that night to steal my camera.'

'What? What on earth for?' Pálmi asked in amazement. Nína stood nearby, staring as if spellbound at Pálmi, and Ari Thór could see admiration towards Pálmi, even love, in her eyes.

'I took some pictures that evening, in the auditorium and in the lobby, and there's one picture that shows your umbrella hanging on a hook,' Ari Thór said. 'Nína broke her leg on the ice just outside my door when she was hurrying home after breaking into my house. I heard her moving about and almost caught her in the act. I heard someone scream in pain right before I passed out myself, having fallen in the darkness. The hospital confirmed that she had come to them that same night with a fractured bone in her leg . . . I showed Ugla pictures of the scene and she told me that was your spotted umbrella, which is fairly distinctive, plus she said you're one of the few people in Siglufjördur who uses an umbrella.' He looked first at Ugla and then at Nína. 'That's right, isn't it?'

Tómas glared but said nothing. Ari Thór knew that there were some harsh words due to come his way for having shown

Ugla pictures that were part of a case in which she was also under suspicion.

Nína came closer, hesitated, and her gaze rested on Pálmi.

'Yes. But I did it . . . for him,' she said firmly.

'You took the umbrella?' Pálmi demanded, clearly discomfited and more than a little angry. 'I wondered what had become of it.'

'I was going to give it to you tonight and tell you . . . tell you that I know the whole story. Pálmi, my love, it was going to be our secret,' she said.

'Our . . . ?' he asked in astonishment.

Ari Thór stepped in and directed his next question to Pálmi. 'So you went home to dinner and came back?'

'Yes, I had forgotten the script. Úlfur and Hrólfur had a few corrections and had already asked me to take it home at the dinner break to print out a final version. I was halfway home when I remembered. When I came back Hrólfur was on his own up in the gallery and Nína wasn't at the ticket desk.'

'I was down in the basement,' Nína said, interrupting him. 'I heard an argument upstairs. You had already gone when I came up, and I didn't notice that you had forgotten your umbrella until the police were here,' she said, clearly pleased that Pálmi realised what risks she had taken for his benefit.

'Did you confront Hrólfur with your suspicions?' Ari Thór asked Pálmi.

'Yes. I asked him straight out if he had stolen my father's book. He'd had a little too much to drink and just laughed. He said it couldn't really be called *stealing*, and that he had saved the book – given it life. He said that my father would never have been able to sell his book or make anything out of it. For some absurd reason he seemed to think that he had just as much right to it, because *he* was the one who put it on the map. You can imagine that I didn't accept his version without an argument. I called him a liar and a damned thief. I actually asked him if there was anything in the book that he had written.

'"No, your father did such a fine job," he said, with that horrible smug look on his face. "I didn't have to change a thing." He told me to calm down, told me that he had given me a chance at the Dramatic Society to right the wrong. "One favour deserves another," he said. My father had made him a novelist so he had made me a playwright.'

Pálmi fell silent, although his hands shook with fury.

Rosa and Mads listened in confusion to their host, who appeared to have lost all control of his temper.

'I asked if my father had requested that the book be published, and Hrólfur admitted that he had,' Pálmi continued. 'The old bastard. My father wanted the book published and asked specially that she . . .' – he pointed at Rosa, who appeared to understand nothing – '. . . that she should get a copy. Hrólfur betrayed everything, betrayed a dying man. He even admitted that he had made sure the translation rights were never sold to a Danish publisher, so that Linda, Rosalinda, would never read it and realise its true origins.'

Pálmi paused.

'I'm happy that it's out in the open now. I can tell her the truth and she can have an opportunity to read the book that my father wrote for her.'

He smiled at Rosalinda, who seemed puzzled that she had become the subject of conversation.

'So he must have decided it was fitting that you should

inherit the rights, a small way of making amends, finally,' Ari Thór said.

'That damned old bastard. As if that was going to change anything. He lived on another man's efforts all his life. My father dead and forgotten, and Hrólfur living like a king for seventy years. But . . . I never meant to kill him.'

'You pushed him?' The question was unnecessary.

'I jostled him, in the heat of the moment, and rushed out when I saw he was dead. That was when I forgot the umbrella. I had hung it up out of force of habit in the cloakroom when I came to fetch the script,' Pálmi said, and a sob escaped him. 'I had no intention of killing him. I've hardly had a night's sleep since. Thank God it's over.'

'I think you had best come down to the station, Pálmi,' Tómas said gently. 'We need to take a statement.'

'Hmm, yes, of course,' he said, obviously bewildered.

'One more thing,' Ari Thór said. 'The child Hrólfur was supposed to have fathered? Was that a lie?'

'Yes,' Pálmi replied, with a look of shame on his face. 'I'm so sorry. I was so shocked when I heard you were treating this as a murder investigation, I wanted to lead you astray. I regret it deeply.'

Ari Thór had no doubt that he did. 'And I walked straight into the trap.'

'I had Nína in mind when I told you the story,' he said, as if failing to remember that she was standing close by. 'Nobody ever knew who her father was.'

Nína started in surprise, as if her whole world was crashing in around her.

'Were you . . . were you trying to put the blame on me?' she asked in disbelief.

Pálmi looked at her with guilt on his face. Nína's eyes seemed to have gone blank, as if she had disappeared in her mind into another place.

'We ought to be going, Pálmi,' Tómas said.

||||||||||||||

The reception guests watched in amazement as the police sergeant escorted Pálmi out of the theatre.

Úlfur had heard enough of the conversation between Pálmi and the police to draw his own conclusions. He had suspected for some time that something was wrong, and had realised as he left Hrólfur and went home to dinner that Pálmi had not taken the script, despite discovering, upon his return to the theatre, that Pálmi had found time to correct it.

He had decided against asking Pálmi about it, and was even less inclined to mention anything to the police.

He felt an enormous sympathy for the man.

||||||||||||||

Pálmi looked back, his brow furrowed, as if the Siglufjördur mist and its devastating blizzards had enveloped him.

He was frightened, fearful of finding himself in prison. But that wasn't at the forefront of his mind.

His greatest desire was for the forgiveness of the little community at the edge of the northern ocean; more than anything, he wanted to be able to look in the eye the people he had known for so many years.

||||||||||||||

Ari Thór had been pleased with himself when he questioned Pálmi, proud of himself, even.

Then he saw Pálmi's face as he looked out over the auditorium for the last time, devastated.

It was supremely unjust. Pálmi was in the hands of the police while Karl was a free man.

For a moment, Ari Thór had found himself thinking that the world was fair.

Bloody stupidity. He knew well enough, from his own bitter experience, being orphaned as a child, that justice was nothing more than an illusion.

45

SIGLUFJÖRDUR: SATURDAY, 24TH JANUARY 2009

Karl was on his way out of town. He had a lift to Akureyri. He had taken a job with an old friend, intending to stay there for a while, before making any further decisions.

He hadn't taken very seriously Tómas's request not to leave town. He was hoping to get away without being prosecuted – he'd always been lucky on that score.

He left most of Linda's possessions behind in the flat, taking with him only things of value, not wanting to carry too much baggage – either physical or metaphorical. It was a bastard losing out on that ten million in insurance. That would have been handy to have.

He never really understood why Linda had stuck with him, even though he treated her so badly. Beat her up more than once, well, quite a few times. He had of course been charming at first, lured her in. Of course he'd never told her about his dark deeds in the past. He had the feeling that she had always been trying to save him. She was too kind for her own good. And he'd probably never see her again; the doctors said she wouldn't recover and he had no intention of going to Reykjavík for a final visit.

The news coverage on him in recent days hadn't been favourable, and he would probably have to leave the country sooner rather than later. It was clear that public opinion had already decided that he was guilty.

The car went through the tunnel and Karl didn't look back. He'd never see that ice-cold town again, if he could help it.

||||||||||||||

Leifur felt pleased with himself after the performance. The audience seemed to like him. And, to his surprise, he had even found himself enjoying the limelight. Perhaps he would now seek more time on stage rather than off for the next play. He had stepped out of his comfort zone and it had felt good. At the reception he had even walked up to Anna and asked her out. She had politely turned him down. But at least he had tried. And tomorrow he would go down to the police station and formally ask Tómas and his colleagues to look again into the hit-and-run that had killed his brother. Of course, deep down, he knew nothing would come out of it – too many years had passed. But he felt he needed some sort of closure, and then he could try, really try, to move on with his life.

||||||||||||||

Since the news had broken about Karl's alleged offences, Anna had been aware of her own lucky escape. She hadn't spoken to him since and had no intention of meeting him again. She hoped he had already left town. Thankfully their relationship hadn't become public knowledge. And hopefully it would remain a secret, although secrets had an awkward habit of coming to the surface in a small town like this. Until then, she was determined to focus on the job at the school and felt excited at the prospect. Surprisingly, that timid bloke, Leifur, had come on to her after the play – in his very shy way of course. Rather cute of him, she thought, but she had decided to keep clear of any sort of relationship, illicit or not, for the moment, and Leifur really lacked the dark and dangerous qualities that had drawn her to Karl . . .

46

REYKJAVÍK: SATURDAY, 24TH JANUARY 2009

Kristín had been trying to call Ari Thór for two days, and his phone was always unavailable.

She had been upset at his decision to leave her so suddenly, moving to the north with little notice, and even less discussion – the woman with whom he'd just agreed to share his life. She thought she had found the man she could love, possibly even the man with whom she would spend the rest of her life; and then he was gone, moved to Siglufjördur. She had been left alone in his flat for too long, with only books for company.

Kristín couldn't bring herself to go with him that first weekend; a tearful farewell and the long drive back south alone would have been too much to bear.

How could he just go without a backwards glance and leave her alone?

The same thoughts returned day and night, on some sort of demented loop, and she struggled to concentrate on her textbooks. It was the first time that she had allowed herself, even felt it was possible, to be distracted. She *had* to be in love. For the very first time.

It had taken her weeks to try to understand her own feeelings, to find her direction again. It had been increasingly painful to talk to him on the phone – a heartrending reminder of just how far away he was. She was reminded of the sweetness of his voice; reminded of the fact that she could not reach out and touch him, kiss him, feel the warmth of his arms around her.

Not long after Ari Thór left for Siglufjördur, Kristín's father was given notice at his job and shortly thereafter her mother was also made redundant. Every bit of stability she had was gone. More than anything, she wanted to call Ari Thór and cry down the phone. Her need for him had become greater than ever.

Then there was Christmas and he let her down again. He had *promised* to come to Reykjavík for the holiday. She had looked forward to it with childlike sincerity and joy, right up until the day he called and said he had to be on duty.

She had been speechless with disappointment, hanging up the phone after a cursory goodbye, and weeping, crying as she had not done since she was a child. Missing him had left her aching with something that hurt almost physically. She cursed her pride; her own inability to express herself, to right the situation. To be open about her love, her genuine need for him.

She bitterly regretted not calling him on Christmas Eve, but she had been so angry, with a fury and a feeling of loss that she could hardly control.

Little by little, she had regained her balance, and now was the time to set things right. She thought they had made progress, even if the calls had been few and far between. They both needed time, and Ari Thór should know that she was never one to show much emotion, and that sometimes she really was too busy to talk. But now she was taking a giant leap to try to salvage their relationship, their future. She had applied for a summer job at the hospital in Akureyri, close enough to commute to it from Siglufjördur. She had been offered the job, as well as the chance to do her final year of medical training there. She had to give her answer right away, more or less. She had tried to call Ari Thór on his mobile on Saturday, but it seemed to be turned off. So she made up her mind, took the offer, and rejected a similar offer from the National Hospital in Reykjavík; a place that had immediately been snapped up by someone else, so there was no turning back.

It was late on Saturday evening when her phone rang, a call from an unfamiliar mobile number. She answered and Ari Thór was on the line.

At last she could give him the good news.

EPILOGUE

SPRINGTIME

Tómas looked over the rising mist on the fjord; it was early morning and the town was still sleeping. The days were lengthening, reminding people that summer was almost here. For a place so cold and dark in the winter, Siglufjördur was so very bright and warm in summer, generally considerably warmer than Reykjavík and the southwest.

Karl had left town for good. Despite Tómas's best efforts, no charges would be filed against him. He expected him to continue doing harm elsewhere, but Tómas had succeeded in making at least Siglufjördur, his town, a safer place. Linda had passed away without ever regaining consciousness, so all hopes of charging Karl in relation to domestic abuse had more or less vanished.

Karl hadn't pursued any complaints against Ari Thór, so the boy had been lucky. Tómas liked him, he was smart, and though inclined to be temperamental and impulsive, his intentions were always good, which made all the difference. Ari Thór certainly didn't speak much about his private life, but Tómas couldn't avoid knowing that he had split up with his girlfriend in Reykjavík. Ari Thór seemed lonely and miserable following the breakup, but Tómas hoped that the brighter days of summer might cheer him up.

Tómas was fairly sure that Hlynur, not Ari Thór, had leaked all the information to the press. Hlynur actually seemed less and less focused on his work as the weeks passed. There was something troubling that young man, but Tómas wasn't sure what. He wasn't certain enough to confront Hlynur about the press leaks. Also, he was in a way glad that the information about Karl had been leaked, and that Anna and her relationship with Karl had not been. If Hlynur had been behind this, he had at least kept some sense of right and wrong.

Tómas stood still, watching the fjord and the mountains gradually coming to life as the sun rose in the sky and shone on the slopes, sparkling on the water. It was the start of a beautiful day. Tómas's wife had decided to move to Reykjavík to study. He wasn't going with her, not right away, at least. He wasn't ready to leave Siglufjörður just yet.

ACKNOWLEDGMENTS

I would like to thank the people of Siglufjördur for allowing me to use their wonderful town as the setting for this book, especially my late grandparents, Þ. Ragnar Jónasson and Guðrún Reykdal, who lived in Siglufjördur for most of their lives and would hopefully have enjoyed reading about the town in this unusual context. I would of course like to make it clear that the story is entirely fictional and none of the characters portrayed is based on any real person.

I was very lucky when Karen Sullivan and Quentin Bates conspired to bring *Snowblind* to the UK. One could not wish for a better or more hardworking publisher than Karen. Quentin has been a tireless advocate of my work in the UK, and it's difficult to imagine a translator better suited to the job than him, a renowned writer of the Iceland-set Inspector Gunnhildur crime fiction series.

Furthermore, I would like to thank my wonderful U.S.

publisher, Minotaur, and in particular my editor Marcia Markland, for now making the series available in the United States.

I would also like to thank my agents, Monica Gram at Leonhardt & Hoier in Denmark and David Headley at DHH Literary Agency in the UK, for bringing Ari Thór to an English speaking audience, as well as my Icelandic publisher, Pétur Már Ólafsson and my Icelandic editor, Bjarni Þorsteinsson, for their invaluable support in creating the Dark Iceland series.

Many others have, in one way or another, played an important part in the process of getting *Snowblind* to the UK, and I would like to mention one person in particular, my friend Bob Cornwell.

My parents, Jónas Ragnarsson and Katrín Guðjónsdóttir, also cannot be thanked enough for encouraging me to write from a young age and for reviewing every draft of every book or story I've ever written or translated.

Last but not least, I want to thank my wonderful family for their endless support and understanding – my wife, María, and my daughters, Kira and Natalía.

1. The author of *Snowblind*, Ragnar Jónasson, has translated fourteen Agatha Christie novels into Icelandic. If you're familiar with Agatha Christie, do you think her books have influenced *Snowblind*? How so?

2. Ari Thór decides to accept the job in Siglufjördur without first consulting his girlfriend, Kristín. What did that choice lead you to expect from him as a character, and in what ways did he conform to or flout those expectations later in the book?

3. Early on, Tómas warns Ari Thór that "nothing ever happens around here." Though this ultimately proves not to be the case, what does this statement tell you about Tómas's character?

4. How does the relationship between Tómas and Ari Thór evolve throughout the story?

5. How did each character's backstory contribute to your understanding of the Siglufjördur community? To your understanding of Hrólfur's death?

6. Who did you initially suspect had a hand in Hrólfur's death? Were any clues particularly misleading?

7. How do you feel about Hrólfur? In what ways did your opinion of him change as your knowledge of him deepened?

8. Throughout, there are italicized flashbacks to a woman under attack in her home. In what ways did these flashbacks contribute to your understanding of the main story? When did you begin to guess how the two plotlines might weave together?

9. Ari Thór informs the reader that "the Icelandic tradition of reading a new book on Christmas Eve, and into the early hours of the morning, had been important in his family's home." How are the arts (literature, theater, music) important in this novel? What does their centrality reveal about the characters?

10. "Jonassón's true gift is for describing the daunting beauty of the fierce setting, lashed by blinding snowstorms that smother the village in 'a thick, white darkness' that is strangely comforting," said *The New York Times Book Review*. Do you agree that the setting—which has also been called "claustrophobic" by reviewers—is somewhat comforting? If not, what was your reaction to the setting?

11. At the end of the novel, Ari Thór makes the statement, "It was supremely unjust," referencing that fact that a true murderer isn't charged, while an accidental death may make its way to trial. In what ways is this "unjust" ending a reflection of the themes throughout the book?

An exclusive extract from Ragnar Jónasson's Nightblind, *translated by Quentin Bates and published by Minotaur/St. Martin's Press.*

'. . . *In my house I'll have no truck with either suicide or smoking.*'

CHAPTER 1

Repugnant.

Yes, that's the word. There was something repugnant about that ancient, broken-down house. The walls were leaden and forbidding, especially in this blinding rain. Autumn felt more like a state of mind than a real season here. Winter had swiftly followed on the heels of summer in late September or early October and it was as if autumn had been lost somewhere on the road north. Herjólfur, Siglufjördur's police inspector, didn't particularly miss autumn, at least not the autumn he knew from Reykjavík, where he had been brought up. He had come to appreciate the summer in Siglufjördur, with its dazzlingly bright days. He enjoyed the winter as well, with its all-enveloping darkness that curled itself around you like a giant cat.

The house stood a little way from the entrance to the Strákar tunnel and as far as Herjólfur had been able to work out, it was years since anyone had lived in the place, set apart from the town itself by the shoreline. It looked as if it had simply been left there for nature's heavy hand to do as it wished with the place, and her handiwork had been brutal.

Herjólfur had a special interest in this abandoned building and it was something that worried him. He was rarely fearful, having trained himself to push uncomfortable feelings to one side, but this time he'd been unsuccessful, and he was far from happy. The patrol car was now parked by the side of the road and Herjólfur was hesitant to leave it. He shouldn't even have been on duty, but Ari Thór, the town's other police officer, was down with flu.

Herjólfur stood still for a moment, lashed by the bitter chill of the rain. His thoughts travelled to the warm living room at home. Moving up here had been something of a culture shock, but he and his wife had managed to make themselves comfortable, and their simple house had been gradually transformed into a home. Their daughter was at university in Reykjavík; their son had remained with his parents, living in the basement and attending college in nearby Ólafsfjördur.

He had a few days holiday coming up, assuming Ari Thór was fit to return to work. He had been planning to take his wife by surprise with a break in Reykjavík. He had booked flights from Akureyri and secured a couple of theatre tickets. This was the type of thing he tried to make a habit of, to take a rest from the day-to-day routine whenever the opportunity presented itself. Now, in the middle of the night, and while he was still on duty, he fixed his mind on the upcoming trip, as if using it as a lifeline to convince himself that everything would be fine when he entered the house.

They had been married for twenty-two years. She had become pregnant early in the relationship, and so they were married soon after. There hadn't been any hesitation or, indeed, choice. The decision wasn't anything to do with faith, but more with the traditions of decency to which he clung. He had been properly brought up – a stern believer in the importance of setting a good example. And they were in love, of course. He'd never have married a woman he didn't love. Then their daughter was born and became the apple of his eye. She was in her twenties now, studying psychology, even though he had tried to convince her to go in for law. That was a path that could have brought her to work with the police, connected in some way to the world of law and order; his world.

The boy had come three years later. Now he was nineteen, a stolid and hard-working lad in his last year at college. Maybe he'd be the one to go in for law, or just apply straight to the police college.

Herjólfur had done his best to make things easier for them. He had plenty of influence in the force and he'd happily pull strings on their behalf if they decided to choose that kind of future; he was also guiltily aware that he was often inclined to push a little too hard. But he was proud of his children and it was his dearest hope that they would feel the same about him. He knew that he had worked hard, had pulled himself and his family up to a comfortable position in a tough environment. There was no forgetting that the job came with its own set of pressures.

The family had emerged from the financial crash in a bad way, with practically every penny of their savings having gone up in smoke overnight. Those were tough days, with sleepless nights, his nerves on edge and an unremitting fear that cast a shadow over everything. Now, at long last, things seemed to have started to stabilise again; he had what appeared to be a decent position in this new place, and they were comfortable, even secure. Although neither of them had mentioned it, he knew that Ari Thór had applied for the inspector's post as well. Ari Thór had a close ally in Tómas, the former inspector at the Siglufjördur station, who had since moved to a new job in Reykjavík. Not that Herjólfur was without connections of his own, but Tómas's heartfelt praise of and support for Ari Thór hadn't boded well. And yet the post had gone to him and not to Ari Thór – a young man of whom Herjólfur still hadn't quite got the measure. Ari Thór had not proved to be particularly talkative and it wasn't easy to figure out what he was thinking. Herjólfur wasn't sure if there was a grudge there over the way things had turned out. They hadn't been working together for long. Ari Thór's son had been born at the end of the previous year, on Christmas Eve, and he had gone on to take four months' paternity leave plus a month's holiday. They weren't friends or even that friendly, but it was still early days.

Herjólfur's senses sharpened, and all thoughts of his colleague were pushed from his mind as he gradually approached the house. He had that feeling again. The feeling that something was very wrong.

If it came to it, he reckoned he could easily hold his own with one man; two would be too much for him now that age had put paid to the fitness of his earlier years. He shook his head, as if to clear away ungrounded suspicions. There was every chance the old place would be empty. He was surprised at discomfort.

There was no traffic. Few people found reason to travel to Siglufjördur at this time of year, least of all in the middle of the night and in such foul weather. The solstice was due on the weekend, and it would confirm what everyone already knew up here in the north – winter had arrived.

Herjólfur stopped in his tracks, suddenly aware of a beam of light – torchlight? – inside the old building. So there *was* someone there in the shadows, maybe more than one. Herjólfur was becoming increasingly dubious about this call-out and his nerves jangled.

Should he shout out and make himself known, or try unobtrusively to make his way up to the house and assess the situation?

He shook his head again and pulled himself together, striding forward almost angrily. *Don't be so soft. Don't be so damned soft!* He knew how to fight and the intruders were unlikely to be armed.

Or were they?

The dancing beam of light caught Herjólfur's attention again and this time it shone straight into his eyes. Startled, he stopped, more frightened than he dared admit even to himself, squinting into the blinding light.

'This is the police,' he called out, with as much authority as he could muster, the quaver in his voice belying his false bravado. The wind swept away much of the strength he'd put into his words, but they must have been heard inside, behind those gaping window frames.

'This is the police,' he repeated. 'Who's in there?'

The light was directed at him a second time and he had an overwhelming feeling that he needed to move, to find some kind of refuge. But he hesitated, all the time aware that he was acting against his own instincts. A police officer is the one with authority, he reminded himself. He shouldn't let himself be rattled, feel the need to hide.

He took a step forward, closer to the house, his footsteps cautious.

That was when he heard the shot, deafening and violent.

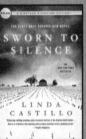

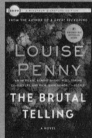
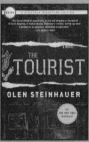

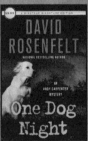